On A Silver Platter

Linda Morganstein

Quest Books

Port Arthur, Texas

ISBN 978-1-935053-51-4

First Printing 2011

9 8 7 6 5 4 3 2 1

Cover design by Donna Pawlowski

Published by:

Regal Crest Enterprises, LLC
4700 Highway 365, Suite A, PMB 210
Port Arthur, Texas 77642

Find us on the World Wide Web at
http://www.regalcrest.biz

Published in the United States of America

Acknowledgments

There are always so many people who help a book to come together. I would like to thank those generous Sonoma County residents who helped me with my research. I would also like to thank my readers, including Rrrose Carbinela, Chris Jimenez, Mary Jaeb, Meg Graham and Mary Ellen Kavanaugh. Diane Ferreira was instrumental in my procedural research, in addition to being a good friend. Thanks to Adam Gottfried for information on gamers. Mary Roth helped me with prison systems. Thanks to my editors and publisher. I learned about dog grooming and animals as friends from Susan Rouse. With much love, I say good-bye to my beloved dog, Sherman, who was the best.

For Melanie, who helps me to see the big picture

THE CAST AND CREW OF *ON A SILVER PLATTER*

Hollywood Cast:

Buddy Brubech
Best known for his role as Dr. Moody in a long-running television medical drama. After *Riverview Hospital's* cancellation, Buddy starred in a string of mediocre productions that never obliterated his famous doctor persona from the public mind.

Ken Sloan
Son of a stagehand and set dresser. Ken developed a passion for Shakespearean drama in high school and learned early to portray royalty. Best friend of Buddy. Husband of Shirley.

Shirley Sloan
Daughter of perfectionist stage actors in New York. Shirley fled the pressure to succeed her parents by going to Hollywood. Met Ken and Buddy at Penny Studios.

Salome D'Amico
Youngest daughter of famed director Freddy D'Amico and actress Mary D'Amico (born Maria). Girlfriend of Jerome Lasky.

Producers and Directors:

Jerome Lasky
Great-grandson of the Hollywood mogul, Poppa Weiss. Family still runs the famous movie studio founded by Poppa.

Marlon Sloan
Only son of Ken and Shirley Sloan. Jerome's best friend.

Chase Stuyvesant
Jerome's cousin. Daughter of Conrad, a conservative Republican Boeing engineer. Chase's mother is Judith, a failed actress who deserted Hollywood to marry Conrad.

Local Cast and Crew:

Alexis Pope
Self-defense instructor and amateur sleuth.

Paula Coleman
Former basketball star presently working in her hometown as a corrections officer. Moonlighting security guard and generous activist for local charitable causes.

Rickie Coleman
Paula's younger sister. Dog groomer and generous activist for local charitable causes.

Pete Szabo
Sonoma County sheriff's deputy. An extra, he plays a Sonoma County sheriff's deputy. Pete and his twin sister, Mary, are good friends of Alex's. Mary is a high-level public defender with Sonoma County.

Chapter One

ALEXIS POPE ADJUSTED the silk scarf hiding her face. She sucked in an energizing breath.

"Take five!"

"Action!" called the director.

Alex launched a roundhouse kick that would knock anyone's lights out. She twisted full circle and executed three lethal palm thrusts as fast as a camera clicking on auto-shoot. She thrashed through the liberated ninja warrior version of Salome's Dance of the Seven Veils as her gauzy costume flashed tantalizing glimpses of flesh. She was nailing the tricky kung fu moves thanks to years of martial arts training. At least *she* thought so. The crew and cast were smirking. So she wasn't Madonna. Let them smirk. She personally was feeling liberated, thank you, from a few tough years of grief.

"Cut!"

Jerome Lasky strutted up to her, his condescending look etched onto his pretty-boy face.

"Alexis."

Jerome's tone was as self-inflated as his expression. At five-ten, he was three inches taller than Alex. White teeth, unblemished skin, 4.0 grade point average. She could have taken him out with her roundhouse kick and he wouldn't have known what hit him.

"I prefer to be called Alex," she reminded him.

"Alex. Do you understand your motivations? You suspect you're performing for galactic aliens morphed into loved ones that suck your bodily fluids. Didn't you study my script?"

Alex squirmed like a kid, although the writer-director was nearly ten years her junior. A twenty-six year old ambulatory ego. She *had* studied the script, but she wasn't about to tell Jerome that his masterpiece was incomprehensible. Despite the conflicts with Jerome, she wanted this gig.

"I read the script," she said to Jerome.

"Again," she added.

"For at least the fourth time," she embellished.

The embellishment added passive-aggressive punch to her initial meekness. She hated adding that kind of below-the-belt jab. It reminded her of her mother. Or, at least the shadow mother she harbored in her unconscious mind.

"Let's take a break." Jerome waved to a young woman some

distance away. She wore a duplicate of Alex's costume. "Salome, can you come here?" he called across the room. As Salome approached, a young man broke from the crew and rushed up. His eyes were deer-caught-in-the-headlights wide. "We have three more scenes scheduled for today."

"Isn't that just too bad?" Jerome replied. "I won't have this film compromised, Marlon."

"We have a small budget and a tight schedule," Marlon squeaked.

"You have a small budget and a tight schedule. It goes with your small dick and tight ass. Dude. I made you line producer and I can fire you. My father's studio is funding the project anyway. Ponder that."

"Fire me?" Marlon was taller and skinnier than Jerome, with bad skin and a hollow chest. His Adam's apple bobbed as he spoke. "Don't fire me."

"Don't freak," Jerome said. "I'm letting off steam. You're my best friend. You should know I'm a pain in the ass." He turned to Alex, smirking. "I'll bet you'd enjoy popping me in the jaw, wouldn't you? You could probably take Marlon and me both out at once, couldn't you?"

"With my hands tied behind my back." Alex had no desire to take out either of them. They were a Mutt and Jeff pair of dominance-submission; they weren't real-world evil. Despite their youth, she saw the appreciative looks on the two boys' faces. Although she wasn't astoundingly beautiful, men and women alike tended to melt at her copper-colored hair and blue eyes. According to her cousin Jeffrey, she radiated something intangibly sexy. She preferred to keep this fact only marginally conscious in her own mind, except when it had its uses.

By this time, the lead actress had arrived. Salome D'Amico was Alex's height and roughly the same weight of 128 pounds. Salome *was* astoundingly beautiful, unrealistically beautiful, an archetypal Mediterranean princess with raven-black hair, olive skin and dark eyes. Unlike her boyfriend, Jerome, she had a genial, patient expression etched onto her face. They were two children of entertainment dynasties madly in love. Like Romeo and Juliet without the angst. It was touching, really. The boy featuring the girl in his cinematic masterpiece. Salome as Salome. Clever. Too bad the script sucked.

"Salome, can you go over your inner motivations with Alex?" Jerome asked.

Salome hooked her arm around Alex's waist and led her away, getting only a few yards before she tripped over a power cable, nearly sending them tumbling to the ground. Alex reacted quickly, keeping them both on their feet. They carefully proceeded through the set.

"I am such an unbelievable klutz," Salome moaned without much heartache. "You see why we need you. As good as a trained stunt woman."

"But cheaper. Jerome thinks I stink."

"He doesn't. He's just got this bug in him about how rebellious geniuses behave."

By this time, they were in the hallway leading to the restrooms at Old Vines, the restaurant where Alex's cousin Jeffrey was front-end manager and which was now serving as a location for the production of *On A Silver Platter*, the tale of alien invasion based roughly on the beheading of St. John the Baptist.

Salome winked at her. "We're supposed to be dissecting motivation. All my life, I've been surrounded by people hung up on their motivations. Not me. Even if I understood what the script was about, which I don't, I would stink at this discussion."

Alex liked Salome. Despite her transcendent beauty, the young actress had a down-to-earth personality and an apparent intrinsic tolerance of creative pomposity. "Then how do you pull off the acting?" she asked.

"By having the most talented father and mother on earth putting you in diaper ads before you could walk. I absorbed acting." Salome shrugged. "Don't hate Jerome. He's smart and kind, but he comes off spoiled. Everyone is telling him he's the next Quentin Tarantino." She nodded in the direction of the set. "Let's go get some real advice."

Salome led Alex to the cluster of performers bunched in a corner of the lovely wine country dining room of Old Vines. Jeffrey had worked there ever since an ugly series of incidents at a resort in Guerneville had gotten him and Alex fired two years before.

The actors were still smirking. It occurred to Alex that they might not be reacting to her or her kung fu routine. In the face of a confusing production, smirking might be the defense mechanism of choice, like the sick jokes of medical workers in an intensive care unit.

On the other side of the room, Jerome was conferring with the script supervisor. Salome turned so Jerome couldn't see her face. "We have three Hollywood icons here doing a favor to our fathers. Help Alex with her motivations."

Alex was mildly star-struck facing the celebrities, despite her prominent parents and a general disinclination for Hollywood adulation.

"Your mother is Arlene Pope," Ken Sloan said with admiration. "*Ask Arlene* is your mother's advice column."

Ken and Shirley Sloan were one of Hollywood's most respected and enduring couples. Like Paul Newman and Joanne Woodward, they were tremendously generous with their time and finances. Ken's large forehead was accentuated by a receding hairline. He was still very handsome at sixty-six, a gracefully aging king. His wife, Shirley, was short and slightly feral-looking. Her offbeat looks were balanced by a glow of matriarchal intelligence.

Alex nodded. Of course everyone gossiped. They all must know about her.

"I'm one of her biggest readers," Shirley added. "Her advice is so heart-warming, sane and solid."

Alex reflected on growing up with a mother whose advice was so heart-warming, sane and solid, yet the actual person was distant and distracted. Recently, her mother had begun to experience a sort of personal global warming, but that was another story.

"Your father is Arthur Pope, internationally renowned painter and sculptor," Buddy Brubech said with grave respect. The classically handsome star was idolized for his role as Dr. Moody on the long defunct television series, *Riverview Hospital*. Although it had been many years since the series ended, most people still thought of him as Dr. Moody. His square jaw promised honesty. His eyes hinted at a past kept hidden for the sake of his patients.

They were all looking at her with awe. As usual, she felt an archaic stab of underachievement. "I need to explore my motivations," she said.

Shirley Sloan placed a hand on Alex's shoulder. "Have you ever seen Oscar Wilde's version of *Salome*? In the next scene, go over the top."

Buddy Brubech took a step closer. Alex felt a magnetic pull. *This* was a man with charisma. "Have you felt that someone you loved wasn't the person you thought he was, but someone else, a secretly malevolent person who you'd never be able to expose?"

Alex shivered. "I don't know." If that little piece of exploration didn't hit home, what did? Throughout her marriage to her now deceased husband, she'd wondered with guilt about his secrets.

Buddy nodded. "Use your closet skeletons to push you." He pulled a gold pendant attached to a chain from beneath his costume. "Know what this is?"

Alex examined the symbol. "Chinese zodiac."

"It's the Year of the Rooster. A special person gave this to me. If all else fails, find a lucky charm." He kissed the charm and handed it to her. "In the meantime, borrow mine."

"TAKE SIX!"

"Action!"

Alex slithered on to the set, aware of the stares. Ken and Shirley Sloan sat regally at a lavish table center stage. They were her mother and stepfather, whose souls were now inhabited by visitors from a distant galaxy. Something like that, anyway.

For a moment, she almost panicked. She took the calming breath of *chi* that brought her back to center. She began to move and all of her fear vanished. She danced with abandon, channeling all her doubts and old wounds through a whirling pattern of ancient moves, both beautiful and lethal. She was aware of the placement of every object on the set; she saw where all the other actors stood or sat. But her true focus, achieved through the breath and relentless practice, was on the purity of her movement, the deep connection of her mind, body and spirit with the universal forces of nature. Bruce Lee was smiling down on her from his perch in kung fu heaven, or at least she hoped so.

"Cut," Jerome cried. "Wow. That was killer."

There was a moment of silence, then everyone in the room broke into a round of applause. Alex took a bow. Salome pumped her fist at Alex, grinning.

"Great," Buddy Brubech said. "You rocked."

"Definitely rocked," Ken Sloan added.

"Lovely and yet menacing," Shirley Sloan said. "I don't know what you were funneling, but I'd buy some, if you bottled it."

Alex beamed. "I must have burned a thousand calories. Is it time to eat?" She handed Buddy back his rooster talisman. "It worked like a charm."

"Ha ha," Buddy replied with good-natured tolerance at her lousy pun.

Jerome waved his hand in the direction of the patio. "Great grub from some local caterers. Go pig out." He turned to Marlon. "Not you. We have some business to discuss in private."

Marlon blanched. "What are you blaming on me now?"

"You are such a sissy," Jerome said to Marlon. He turned to Alex. "I changed my mind. Beat Marlon up. He's a wishy-washy Barbie doll compared to you." He glanced around at the disapproving looks of everyone in the group. "Jesus Christ. I didn't mean it. Get out of here before I make a total ass of myself."

In Alex's opinion, Jerome had already achieved that dubious goal.

Chapter Two

THE ACTORS AND crew sat on the sun-dappled terrace eating food catered by Maddie Rockwell, owner-chef of Old Vines and a protégé of the food goddess Alice Waters. There were whole-grain bagels topped with local goat cream cheese and Bodega Bay smoked salmon. Organic red grapes, marinated artichoke hearts, baked Gravenstein apples and late harvest baby carrots complemented the main dish. It was a glorious Sonoma County day in October. Alex felt alive in a way she hadn't for some time.

"Excuse me."

A woman in a security uniform came up to them. She was at least six-four, with pleasant but heavy features and a blond ponytail pulled tightly behind her head. The muscles of her shoulders and chest stretched the fabric of her starched beige uniform. She held out a napkin, clutched in a massive hand. "Could you sign this? My name is Paula."

Buddy took the napkin and signed it, and then handed it to the Sloans, who did the same, followed by Salome. Paula inspected Alex without extending the napkin. Alex, slightly miffed, held out her hand.

"Are you somebody?" Paula asked.

Alex dropped her hand. "Not really."

"Sign it," Buddy said. "Maybe you'll come to L.A. and become a star." He glanced at the tall woman with a puzzled frown "I know you," he said. "Who are you?"

"Besides a moonlighting security guard?" Paula smiled. "A corrections officer at the county jail."

"Before that?" Buddy persisted. "Who *were* you?"

"Twenty questions," Paula responded. "I never was much at word games."

Buddy grabbed an apple and threw it at Paula.

In a quick, graceful maneuver, Paula caught the fruit and tossed it back at Buddy. It landed squarely in his lap, right on his private parts. He glanced down, looked up and grinned. "Good shot."

Paula shrugged modestly. "Two points with no defense to speak of."

"What's your full name?" Buddy asked.

"Paula Coleman."

"*The* Paula Coleman. I'm a huge women's basketball fan. I

followed your career at Stanford. You went to Spain to play in the European league. What are you doing here? You're a legend, Paula Coleman."

"I grew up here." Paula frowned. "It's a long story."

Alex studied Paula's face. She understood the invisible veil that had suddenly shrouded the officer's expression. It was how she felt when people asked too many questions about her rocky past. As if sensing their commonalities, Paula turned to Alex. "I recognize you now, too."

Alex blanched. Paula's expression signaled the association of Alex and numerous questionable deaths featured in the media. Not to mention the involvement of numerous Sonoma County police and judiciary, all colleagues of Paula's, no doubt.

Paula kept silent. She held out the autographed napkin. "Sign it for me?"

Just then Marlon came rushing up to the table, still looking like an endangered species of wildlife. "Can you stay overtime?" he blurted out to Paula. "We're going to go past six."

Paula shrugged. "I have tomorrow off from the jail."

Ken reached over and squeezed his son's hand. "Marlon, calm down. These are the kinds of headaches we have on location. We dragged you onto too many sets for you to be so uptight."

"It's his nature," Shirley reminded her husband. Although Marlon was standing right next to her, Shirley turned the conversation into third person, as though Marlon was not there. "Marlon is thin-skinned. A dreamer. I don't know what possessed him to get into production. You need elephant hide."

So the nervous line producer was Ken and Shirley's son. Now that she knew this, Alex recognized his features in theirs. Poor Marlon had gotten the worst of each set of genes.

A general sense of embarrassment settled over the table, broken by Buddy. He groaned. "I'm getting too old for sixteen hour days."

"Get used to the rat race, my friend," Ken Sloan said. "You're going to be busting your butt on a new TV series."

Buddy turned to Alex. "I just had a pilot accepted by CBS. Keep this under your hat." He turned to Paula. "You, too." He smiled broadly. "A new medical show featuring me as Dr. Billy Mercy, an older version of a Dr. Moody type. Only this time I'll be playing a veterinarian. The producer is Serge Wilson. The show is cutting edge, witty and cool."

Alex thought she saw palpable relief on the faces of everyone at the table. Although she didn't follow Hollywood gossip much, she knew Buddy had been through some rough times. Poor guy. He seemed well intentioned. She hoped the new show resurrected his career.

Alex watched as a curious look appeared on Paula's face. A young woman in jeans and a t-shirt came up, accompanied by one of the crew.

"Rickie?" Paula asked.

The young woman flashed a lovely smile. The best words to describe her were adorable, a pixie in modern dress. "Don't arrest me, sis. I was invited." She turned to the actors. "*PAWS TO GO.* Where are the paws?"

"This is my sister," Paula said. "Rickie Coleman."

They made a very peculiar sibling pair. Paula was the Clydesdale to Rickie's Shetland pony. Rickie had to be a good foot shorter than her sister. She wore her black hair in an elfin cut. A small gold nose ring pierced her left nostril. She looked sixteen, but was of course older. Late twenties?

"I'm a local dog groomer," Rickie said. "My mobile grooming van is outside."

Salome leaped from the table. "It's for Norman." She glanced at her watch. "Jerome is arguing with the crew. That'll take at least forty-five minutes." She turned to Alex. "Come and meet my baby."

"Give the puppy an extra kiss from me," Buddy said.

"I will, Uncle Buddy," Salome said. She led Alex and Rickie across the dining room. "Buddy isn't really my uncle," she explained. "He's been a part of our family, though, for as long as I can remember. He used to date my aunt a long time ago. It's all very complicated. I suspect I don't know half of it."

"Uncomplicated human relationships are impossible," Rickie the dog groomer commented. "I prefer animals. They operate from their core emotions."

They walked out the patio door and into the parking lot behind the restaurant. In a far corner, a young woman sat under a tree beside a portable dog crate. She jumped up and opened the cage. A small white dog burst out and streaked to Salome, leaping with joy. Salome stooped and let him lick her face.

"I love Westies," Rickie Coleman said. She turned to Alex. "West Highland terriers. Great breed. Are you a dog person?"

Alex shrugged. "I have a cat named Henry."

Rickie beamed at her. "I love cats, too."

Salome patted her dog. "He's very good with groomers. He's been with me everywhere. He's very sophisticated. Uncle Buddy gave me Janet Leigh, my first dog. She died a couple of years ago. Norman is her son."

Rickie bent down and held out an open palm. "Hi, Norman."

Norman ran up to her without hesitation, wagging his tail.

Rickie took the leash. "I think we'll be getting along just fine."

"You're great," Salome gushed. "He loves you already and he's very intuitive."

BY 7 P.M., EVERYONE was getting grouchy and fatigued, but Jerome demanded they do a fourth take on a scene even more incomprehensible than most. Marlon was in tears. Salome knocked over an electrical stand, infuriating a technician who could barely refrain from shouting at her.

As they were about to shoot, a commotion at the front entrance of the restaurant brought everything to a halt. A skinny young man burst into the room. The kid had an unhinged look on his face. He searched the room. Alex adopted a defensive posture. She didn't want to do anything rash, but this seemed serious. The invader's search ended quickly. His eyes lit upon Buddy. Buddy backed up, with a horrified expression. Alex glanced around again. Where was Paula?

"Buddy? Buddy?" the boy shouted. As he got closer, Alex realized he was older than he first appeared, not a teenager, but more likely in his late twenties. He was attractive in a sweet, nerdy way, with pale skin and apologetic eyes. His long hair dangled in his face like a teen pop idol.

Buddy held out his hands in a defensive posture. Everyone froze.

"Just tell the truth. She won't bother you anymore. Don't lie anymore, Buddy." The intruder approached Buddy, who continued to back up with a frightened look. "It's Chip to the rescue," the guy announced to no one in particular.

Alex did a careful assessment of the situation. No apparent weapon. She wasn't more than ten feet from the perpetrator. She sighed, her adrenalin rising. Teaching self-defense and defending in real life were not the same. Never mind the galactic space invaders and the artsy kung fu. She was fast and she knew what to do, that's what mattered. The real-life moves were simpler, more brutal and not pretty. She closed in quickly.

Chip was facing away from her, staring at Buddy. She executed a kick to the back of Chip's knee, followed by an arm lock, which sent him to the ground, face first. Alex held his arm behind his back and positioned her knee near his neck, ready to break his upper spine if necessary.

"Ow, ow," Chip cried.

"What the heck?" Paula came out of the hallway leading to the restrooms, took in the situation and walked professionally through the room, at a brisk but non-panicky pace. She approached Alex and Chip, stopped a few feet away and looked the situation over. Her calm had a defusing affect. She sighed and removed the gun from the holster on her belt. "Let him up," she said.

"I just want him to tell the truth," Chip said. "She'll forgive him." He stood and held up his arms. "I'm not going to hurt anyone."

Paula glanced quizzically at Buddy, who had rearranged his face into an inscrutable mask. "Do you know this person?"

"No," Buddy said.

Alex took pride in reading inscrutable masks. Buddy was lying.

"You're trespassing, dude," Paula said.

"Chip," the invader said.

"Chip what?"

"Chip Welch."

"Chip," Paula said patiently and kindly. "You can't come charging into a place like this, shouting crazy things."

"I didn't mean anything," Chip said. "I want to help him."

Alex didn't like the new look on Chip's face. It had turned crafty and falsely petulant.

"Let him go," Buddy said. "I can tell if it's serious."

"Hey, things like this happen all the time," Jerome piped up. "Fans going overboard."

"This is pretty overboard," Paula said.

"It's harmless," Buddy insisted. "No arrests."

Paula turned to Chip Welch with a menacing expression. "I don't want to ever see you in this vicinity again."

Chip nodded, eyes directed at the floor. Just before he turned to leave, he glared venomously at Buddy. A chill ran down Alex's spine.

Chapter Three

THE NEXT MORNING, Alex pulled into the restaurant parking lot experiencing a lingering headache. She'd dreamed of aliens all night. As the dreams persisted, practically everyone she ever knew was under suspicion of harboring space invaders in their brains. Well, as her advice columnist mother would suggest, Alex did have a few trust issues. Not that she would stand for maternal suggestions. Alex had made a pact with her mother many years before. No unsolicited advice, no free analysis. In any case, it didn't take a guru to interpret the nightmares.

If anything, she was even more excited to be arriving on the set. To use one of her mother's favorite words, Alex needed catharsis. What could be better than unmasking alien attacks? She'd read over the script once again just before sleep — which didn't help with the bad dreams, of course — and decided to forget comprehending its meaning. She would consult with Buddy about motivations. He knew his stuff.

She climbed from her Lexus and waved at Salome's assistant, who was setting up the pet encampment, including a large, luxurious crate under a sun umbrella for Norman. He looked very handsome with his new haircut and strutted on his tethered leash.

Paula's sister Rickie had done a bang-up grooming job on Norman. Rickie herself was pretty adorable. She wondered if Rickie was available for dating. No, she wasn't going to get involved right now. She was still too suspicious. Looking for aliens everywhere. Who knew what awful inner secrets Rickie harbored? *Nice*, Alex thought. What a heartening view of humanity. She laughed to herself. What a great date they could have, she and Rickie, ranting about the cerebral faults of people versus innocent animals. When she thought about it, she trusted her cat Henry more than most people.

The set was bustling, as usual. Members of the crew adjusted light stands and microphones. Another few hauled props, including a large silver platter that would hold the head of Buddy's character, Jimmy John Baptist. Jimmy John was the invasion leader who would eventually be destroyed in the only way possible, by chopping off his head.

Buddy walked up to her. Alex gasped. He cradled a severed head in his arms. It was an amazing reproduction of Buddy's real head, complete with his compassionate Dr. Moody expression, except that the neck was splayed open, revealing a wriggly mass of bloody arteries and veins.

"Isn't this great?" Buddy said. "Look at my face."

"Dead ringer," she replied.

Buddy laughed. "That's good. *Dead ringer*. I love a woman who puns. You have many talents. Very attractive."

Alex shrugged modestly. She didn't get much heat from the flirtatious remark. Buddy seemed more brotherly than predatory.

"Jerome created this masterpiece." Buddy shook the head so that its lips quivered.

"I know his painting mentor, Max Hirshberg," she said. "He thinks Jerome is extremely gifted and thinks Jerome should stick to painting and sculpture."

"You know *Max Hirshberg*? Almost as famous an artist as your father."

"He's my cousin Jeffrey's partner."

"Business or romantic partner?"

Alex hesitated.

Buddy laughed. "Believe me. You don't have to worry about my judgments of sexuality."

"Romantic. They've been together awhile."

"Congratulations to them. If you've followed anything about me in the gossip columns, you know I haven't been known for longevity in my relationships."

"I don't follow Hollywood gossip much." Alex did know about Buddy, however. You'd have to live in a cave not to have heard *something*. She knew he'd been in and out of treatments for alcohol and drugs, not to mention flings with younger women and a string of mediocre movies and failed television pilots.

Buddy smiled. "That's changed. I've found someone to spend the rest of my life with."

"That's fine to say!" Alex replied, startling the both of them. She felt her face redden. "I'm sorry." She'd lost too many people recently to swallow foolish beliefs about spending a lifetime with anyone.

Buddy inspected her expression. She watched as he took in something in her look that told him it wasn't wise to pursue this topic of conversation. He winked at her. "You read the scenes for today, of course."

Alex grimaced. "I tried."

"If you want to go over motivations, I'm available."

"Thank you."

A young woman in coveralls rushed up. "I was looking for that head." She glared at Buddy.

"I'm sorry, Emily." Buddy looked at the prop girl teasingly. "I was using my severed prop to delve into the deeper emotions of my character."

Emily rolled her eyes. Before she could reach for the head, Buddy's expression changed. Emily turned to follow Buddy's gaze and her mouth dropped open. Alex turned to see what had caused the stir. A tall woman wearing expensive jeans and a linen blazer entered the dining room. Although everyone continued preparations, there was a distinct change in the atmosphere, like the barometric drop just before a storm. The woman surveyed the room. She frowned, apparently not seeing what she wanted. Then she turned in their direction.

Alex watched the newcomer's approach. She prided herself on her ability to interpret body language. This was an easy read. The woman moved with economy, as though she was metering out her energy with habitual efficiency. She was a person with an executive's soul. Alex felt a certain reactionary jolt, the kind she reserved for authority figures. She'd always had a slight problem with authority.

As soon as the woman was within a few feet of them, Buddy held up the severed head by the hair, so that his own face and the fake face leered at her.

"Hello, what brings you up here?" the fake face said.

Emily, the prop girl, burst out laughing. "That's awesome."

Buddy smiled modestly. "I learned ventriloquism for a lousy movie I made in the late eighties. Probably the second most incomprehensible movie I ever made." He paused, with a significant look on his face, leaving unspoken what the most incomprehensible movie was.

"Hello, Emily," the woman said to the prop girl. "Nice to see you." She turned to Alex and inspected her gauzy costume.

Despite the draconian vibes, the woman's short curly hair and athletic glow highlighted her attractiveness. She looked like she ate lots of fruits and vegetables.

"This is Chase Stuyvesant," Buddy said. "Executive producer on this film. Usually big shots stay at the studio. Every so often they come on location to check up on things." He paused. "And this is Alexis Pope, who likes to be called Alex. As you can see, she's Salome's stunt double."

"I know most of the stunt women in Hollywood," Chase said.

"She's local," Buddy explained. "She came with the set location. She's very good."

Alex did not like the doubtful look on Chase's face. The producer had a stick up her butt, as Alex's cousin Jeffrey would say. She accepted Chase's hand. Chase had a firm handshake.

They were interrupted by the arrival of Jerome and Marlon. It was hard to tell who looked more upset.

"You made it, I see," Jerome said with forced restraint. "I wasn't all that happy with the shortness of the advance warning, if you want to know the truth."

"Good to see you, Jerome." Chase smiled wearily. She actually sounded like she liked Jerome. "The studio just wants to make sure we're all on the same page."

"My father wants to make sure we're on the same page. Someone tattled to my father and he sent you up here." Jerome turned to Alex. "Chase is a rising executive at my dad's studio. Usually, she specializes in our gay-themed stuff. But she also happens to be my cousin and my baby-sitter."

Chase smiled at Alex. "I'm the bad guy."

"You said it, not me," Jerome said. "Who ratted on me?"

"Why would someone have to rat?" Chase asked.

Jerome glanced around the room with suspicion. "It wasn't you," he said to Marlon, who jumped at the words. "You're supposed to be in charge of local production. You wouldn't want them to think you've been a wimp."

"Nobody's accusing anybody of anything," Chase said patiently. "We just want to be sure the film you're making is the film you envisioned."

There was a moment of silence. Everyone, Alex was convinced, was trying to imagine Jerome's vision except Jerome.

"My cousin Chase is the female version of the proverbial knight in shining armor," Jerome said to Alex. "She saved me from blowing my bar mitzvah even though she wasn't into religion. So, I respect her and her budgetary obsessions." He clapped his hands. "Time is Money!"

"*Time is Money! Time is Money!*" crowed Buddy's dummy head.

"Ventriloquism, very nice," Jerome said. "That gives me an idea for a major rewrite. Ventriloquist aliens."

A look of panic passed on Buddy's face. The real face. Marlon gulped, activating his Adam's apple. Chase blinked, doing what appeared to be inner financial calculations.

"I was *kidding*," Jerome crowed, grinning.

Chapter Four

ALEX WAS CROSSING the set on her way to her first scene of the day, when someone called.

"Alex!"

"I thought I saw your truck outside," Alex said. "Boy, do you look stunning."

If Pete Szabo blushed, it was impossible to tell. He was made up and gleaming, obscuring his already lovely complexion with a slightly deeper tan. His wholesome, slightly Slavic features had been elevated to movie star status. He wore his sheriff's uniform. "I'm an extra," he explained. "I'm playing a Sonoma County sheriff."

"I can see that," she replied.

Pete Szabo was the male half of the Szabo fraternal twins. The brother was a sheriff's deputy and the sister was a leading public defender with the D.A.'s office. Both had become close friends with Alex since she'd moved up to the wine country, despite a messy start to their relationship.

Pete looked puzzled. "I think I'm supposed to capture an alien disguised as a kindergarten teacher, but I'm not sure."

"Don't worry about it. Nobody is quite sure."

Someone gave an appreciative whistle. Paula Coleman approached with a lascivious look on her face. "What a stud. Look at you with the make-up."

"If you'd have said that to me in high school, I would have died on the spot," Pete said. "Actually, if you'd said anything to me in high school, I would have died." He nodded at Alex. "Paula is the best basketball player ever to come out of Sonoma County. You know each other, then?"

"We met on the set," Paula said. "How about you two?"

"Friends for a few years," Alex said.

"I asked her to marry me, but she refused," Pete said.

"Pete!" Alex exclaimed.

"I was joking," he replied. He turned to Paula. "I have this tendency to fall for unavailable women. Married, gay, disinterested. Whatever. Like Alex. Like you, in high school."

"I see." Paula glanced around with a conspiratorial look, apparently choosing not to delve into Pete's fixations. "They sent up an executive to get Jerome on track. I heard she's one of the few people he might listen to."

"How'd you hear that?" Alex asked.

Paula shrugged. "People like to confide in uniformed women. We seem beyond pettiness and subterfuge."

"You are," Pete said, eyes bright with awe. "I'd trust you with my life."

Paula took in the gooey adoration with practiced modesty. She acted like a winner. What was she doing back in Sonoma County with a lackluster job as a corrections officer?

WITH CHASE ON the scene, a change came over the set. Jerome's bloated creative lollygagging vanished. Although Chase kept a quiet distance from the proceedings, her executive aura beamed out, instilling a sense of thoughtful economy on everyone.

On the first take of the scene she was in that day, Alex still wasn't sure what any of it was about, even after Jerome had explained it. She took her mark, aware of Chase's serious stare.

"Take one!"

"Action," called Jerome.

Alex's alien stepfather, played by Ken Sloan, burst into the dining room, wielding a ridiculous alien death-ray device. Alex threw her arms in the air, projecting a sense of betrayal. Ken waved his silly weapon at her. She knocked the weapon from his arms, sending it across the room. He punched at her and she countered with a graceful series of blows using both hands and feet, ultimately sending him fleeing from the set. In the script, Alex was to stand momentarily in a victory stance. Instead, in a burst of spontaneity, she performed a victory dance. She channeled joy laced with anger and sadness, ending with a twirl of impassioned closure.

"Cut!"

As Jerome approached her, her heart fluttered.

"Where the hell did that come from?" Jerome asked.

"I don't know what came over me."

"It was great!" He pumped his fist in the air. "Listen, people. The first scene in this whole shoot was done in one take. Due to Alex."

The cast and crew looked truly pleased and relieved.

The rest of the day's scenes went nearly as well. They were finished for the day at 5:15 p.m. A miracle.

Just as they were wrapping up, Chase came up to Alex. "Are you coming to the dailies?"

"I don't think so," Alex replied. She studied Chase's expression. It was hard to tell how she felt about Alex's performance. Unlike the rest of the cast and crew, however, Chase did not look deeply impressed.

"I think it would help you to watch what you did today," Chase said, frowning.

"You didn't like my interpretation, did you?" Alex asked. She didn't want to care what Chase thought, but she did.

"A very wise mentor once told me, never use terms such as 'liked it,' or 'hated it,' if you're trying to teach solid creative skills. Talk about what worked or didn't work," Chase said.

"It sounds like the same thing," Alex replied.

Chase smiled at her. "It isn't."

"I don't get it." Alex resented having to ask for an explanation from a woman who seemed short on creative skills and heavy on budgetary supremacy. Her authority complex was most definitely raising its ugly head.

"You were raised by parents who expected you to be perfect," Chase said. "It's written all over you. I know who you think I am, but you're wrong."

Alex's lips tightened. She felt like her inner life was being invaded. This time by an uptight accountant who thought she was an amateur psychologist. Who needed galactic invaders? Earth had enough soul-suckers disguised as do-gooders.

"I'm sorry," Chase interjected. "I was overstepping my bounds."

"Forget it." Alex turned to leave. "Looking forward to seeing you at the dailies," she called over her shoulder. How was that for giving a nice mixed message?

ALEX WAS ALMOST to her Lexus in the parking lot, when Salome came rushing up with Norman tugging at his leash. Norman barked at her, wagging his tail. Alex bent down and pet his head. "He remembers me."

"Of course. I told you, he's very intuitive and intelligent."

"What does he think about the fate of this movie?"

"I'm afraid to ask." Salome grinned half-heartedly. "Bad sign, huh?" She glanced over her shoulder. "Can you keep a secret?"

Alex suspected she was getting involved in something that wasn't her business and could lead to unpleasant consequences. "I'm not sure if I can."

Salome giggled. "Don't try and wiggle out of this. I dare you to hear me out."

"What is it?" Alex asked. She hated being dared.

"I'm the one who tattled about the problems on the set." Salome's eyes grew teary. "I love Jerome. I know he's difficult, but he can be put on the right track. God, I sound like a D'Amico.

Daddy got in touch with Murray Lasky, Jerome's father. Murray sent Chase. Please don't tell *anyone* I did this."

"Okay." Alex hesitated. "Why are you telling me?"

"Look at us!" Salome laughed with genuine delight. "We're *doubles*! We're stuck with each other and we have evil aliens to conquer."

THERE WAS A subtle melancholy in the room that evening as the filmmakers and cast watched the dailies. The performances were good, but the scenes were a mess. Alex had been informed that the complexities of judging the isolated scenes, without music or editing, was challenging to even the most knowledgeable attendees. But something wasn't right. At the end of the last scene, Jerome stood up abruptly. "They look great," he announced. He turned to Marlon. "They looked great, didn't they?"

Marlon glanced at his parents. "Yeah. They looked great."

Jerome looked around the room. "What is with you people? Oh, damn. Forget it. I know this is what Tarantino had to go through. Cassavetes, in the old days. Fellini." He faced Salome. "Your father, at least in his early days."

The room was quiet.

Jerome yanked one of his Keds off his feet and clutched it in his hand. He glanced around wildly and began banging it on a nearby table. Then, with a Russian accent, he shouted: "My will is iron! I am your leader!"

The room remained quiet. Then, in unison, everyone burst into laughter while Jerome wrapped up his Khrushchev bit and returned the Ked to his foot. He pointed at Chase. "Let's go. We'll have a beer and discuss all the things I know are swimming in that executive head of yours." He waved to the room. "The rest of you go get some sleep."

ALEX WAS NEARLY to her Lexus when she heard someone behind her. She whipped around, arms shielding her body, hands and feet ready to attack.

"Whoa," said Salome.

"Habit," Alex said.

"I wouldn't want to meet you in a dark alley."

"Cliché!" Alex cried.

Salome looked offended.

Alex grinned. "It's a game my cousin Jeffrey and I invented when we were teens. We called ourselves the cliché police. I only play it with people I like a lot."

Salome returned the grin. "Then I'm pleased as punch."

"I thought you might like being on the bandwagon."

Salome took Alex's arm. "Seriously, we're in this together. I told Chase that."

Alex stiffened. "What do you mean?"

"She thinks you don't have enough polish. She was rumbling about bringing up someone she knows from L.A. I told her I want *you*."

"She said I did okay. On the set, after the take. She said it was good."

"She didn't want to hurt you. She's a perfectionist."

"What a hypocrite." The stick-up-her-butt executive was like her parents, or at least the parents she remembered as a child. Nothing would ever be good enough. Alex knew how to shut out her parents emotionally and she had learned how to do the same with phonies like Chase. Too bad. She'd thought that Chase was kind of cool. A powerhouse with style and blunt honesty. So much for that estimation of character.

"Never mind," Salome said soothingly. "What are you doing Saturday night?"

"Nothing."

"There's a *really* big charity event happening. Rickie told me about it. Will you come?"

Alex hesitated. She'd planned on staying at home, feeling sorry for herself.

Salome took her arm and squeezed. "They've prepared an evening of surprises." She turned to go, then stopped. "Please come. You'll be sorry you missed it."

ALEX HAD PARKED at a distant spot in the lot. She was almost to her car when two shadowy figures came around from a parked Winnebago. Instincts ignited once again, she tensed with anticipatory fight, then sighed with relief. "You scared me."

Buddy and Marlon trooped up, wearing silly grins. "We were checking out Maddie Rockwell's organic gardens. Marlon loves plants," Buddy said.

Alex thought the pair looked like they were hiding something. She didn't care what they were up to. She was tired of investigating inner motivations.

Chapter Five

SATURDAY'S CHARITY GALA took place at Spreckels Performing Arts Center in Rohnert Park. Alex's stomach fluttered as she pulled into the south parking lot. Spreckels had been a key location in a nasty case she'd dealt with last year.

She entered into the center courtyard, an expansive stone patio dominated by a cement lake spouting water from fountains lit by submerged lights. Following the placards, she stepped into the lobby and reception area. It was a lovely space, a curved room with one wall constructed almost entirely of glass.

She was late, with no excuse other than avoidance. Ushers hustled the stragglers into the Nellie W. Codding Theatre. On the stage, eight people, including Paula Coleman and her sister Rickie, sat at a dais on either side of a podium.

A stocky man closest to the podium stood and waited for the crowd to settle. It was a relatively large theatre, seating over five hundred. This evening, it was full. After waiting for the applause to subside, the speaker pointed to a huge screen hanging above the stage. An elderly woman in a hospital bed cuddled a dachshund wearing a bow tie.

"Welcome to the annual Pet Angels fundraiser. Most of you know me as Sonoma County Supervisor Fred Daley. Tonight I'm here as one of the area's most enthusiastic fans of this wonderful organization and its director, Paula Coleman. Also attending is the project manager and Paula's sister, Rickie Coleman."

The crowd broke out in devoted applause. The sisters responded with humble looks of gratitude. Alex's stomach relaxed as she absorbed the warm enthusiasm.

"Paula and I lived next door to one another. Starting in grade school, she beat the pants off me and all the other boys in pick-up basketball games. She was always a star. She was always as generous as she was talented. Tonight, in addition to asking all you to contribute generously to Pet Angels, I'd like you to celebrate with me the first Sonoma County Heroine Award, created with women like Paula in mind, to be awarded to her in honor of her service in our community." He reached below the podium and pulled out a golden statue of an angel in flight.

Paula stood to the cheers of the crowd and took the podium. She waved the statue in the air. "I'll accept this, but only if you all agree to double what you intended to pledge tonight."

"Go, number twelve!" a man from the crowd cried.

"None of this would be possible without the person who does most of the work. My sister Rickie."

Rickie blushed and waved from her seat on the dais.

"Together we've managed to get our staff of volunteers, both two- and four-legged, into more and more nursing homes, hospice centers, and units for terminally ill." As she spoke, pictures flashed across the large screen. Sick kids and frail elders clutching dogs and cats. Even Alex, who considered herself a cynic in recovery, grew teary-eyed.

There was a rustle in the audience. A straggly man and woman pushed an emaciated bald boy in a wheelchair onto the stage. Paula acted out surprise. She handed the father the microphone. *Was that look of surprise rehearsed? How much of this was staged?* Alex scolded herself for the cynical questions.

"We were meth addicts," the man said. "We almost lost our son, first to neglect, then to leukemia. I tried to knock off a convenience store and got stuck in the county jail during trial, where I met Officer Paula. She grabbed me by the balls and turned my life around." The man grimaced at his own use of profanity.

No one in the audience minded. They were too enthralled.

"When my son got sicker, Paula came through. All I can say is give all you can. This lady is a real angel."

The audience cheered. "Twelve, twelve, twelve!"

As the family exited, Paula held up her hand. "We've got a very special surprise for you." She pointed to the left side of the stage.

A gasp went through the crowd. Buddy Brubech entered. He wore his Dr. Moody expression. "Hello, Sonoma County."

"Hello, Buddy!" the crowd chanted back.

Buddy gestured at Paula. "I have the pleasure of working with Paula on the set of a movie we're filming locally. She is truly a heroine."

More applause. Buddy grinned. "I would like to introduce my own heroine. My wife." A spotlight swept the crowd and illuminated a statuesque blond woman in her early fifties. "Felicity Strauss, veterinarian. Many of you know her as the author of *Animals Are People, Too.* She has been an impassioned supporter of animal rights all her life."

Wild applause.

"Before Felicity, I was lost. Now I'm found. One of the greatest gifts I've gotten is a new understanding of how humans must support our animal companions. This isn't an option. It's a necessity. The animals return our love a hundredfold." Tears rolled down Buddy's cheeks. The eight people seated at the dais rose for a standing ovation, joined by the audience.

Buddy bowed. "And watch my new show, coming out next fall on CBS. Many of you remember me as Dr. Moody. Watch what would have become of him if he'd been a vet. I guarantee you won't be disappointed."

At least Buddy's blatant plug for his new show left Alex's cynical side with a shred of evidence for intractable selfishness in human nature. Nevertheless, the night was dominated by hope and humanity's better inclinations.

By the time she entered the reception area, hearing the mellow sounds of Less is More, a popular local band, she couldn't help but feel high on the future, a welcome change from the last few years. She had just picked up a drink at the cash bar when Salome came up. Salome took her elbow and led her to a corner of the room. They surveyed the large crowd, who were merrily drinking and dancing. "My parents couldn't make it," Salome said. "But all their friends are here. I want to introduce you to my brothers at some point."

Alex studied the dewy look on Salome's face. People got off on her skills and tough attitude. It was the woman warrior thing. Alex was used to crushes. If they only knew what roiled below the surface. Still, she couldn't help feeling a pleasurable tingle at this gaze from Salome. It was like the young Elizabeth Taylor mooning over you. They watched as Chase Stuyvesant emerged from the crowd.

"There's the Iron Maiden," Alex said. "What a stiff."

Salome grinned. "She's not so bad. She has her hidden sides. Remember? She's my boyfriend's cousin. I know some private stuff."

"Secret hobbies?" Alex asked, not sure she wanted an answer. The less she knew about Chase, the better.

Salome sighed. "I wish I didn't know all the dirt on people. I get tired of all the intrigue and nowadays you can't do anything without getting exposed on the Internet."

"So it seems," Alex said uneasily.

"I have a secret," Salome said.

Alex's heart thumped. She didn't want to have any ugliness to tarnish Salome. Salome should stay on a nice, safe pedestal.

Salome laughed. "It's not that horrible. Just something I can't tell most people."

"What is it?" Alex asked.

"I *hate* being an actress." Salome averted her gaze. "I should do what I want in life, but there's a family pressure so deep I can't fight it. I might die."

Alex was pretty sure Salome was exaggerating with the drama

of youth. At least she hoped so.

"Do you know what I dream of?" Salome asked.

"What do you dream of?"

"I've always wanted to be a dog groomer. It's like Cinderella dreaming of being the cleaning girl."

Alex laughed. "Like the princess kissing the prince and he turns into a frog."

"That's it," Salome replied with delight.

"Did you know in the original Grimm version of the fairy tale, the princess throws the frog against a wall?" Alex asked.

"No way."

"Way." Alex shrugged. "My parents hated sanitized versions of classic tales. They exposed me to the uncensored archaic versions along with crushing exposés of Santa Claus and the tooth fairy."

Salome grinned ruefully. "I only got the modernized versions. My parents idolized Disney. They couldn't help worshipping him, even though they knew all about his conservative politics. You should see what the tooth fairy left under *my* pillow."

Not too far away, Jerome Lasky was standing in a group, holding a bottle of beer and expounding on a passionate topic. Salome glanced over at him with fondness. "Jerome grew up the same way. He's my Prince Charming."

"I guess the prince turning into frog wouldn't go over so hot with Jerome, would it?" Alex commented. "Not to mention getting thrown against a wall."

"You underestimate him, Alex. Look at his movie. Despite his background, he's not afraid of ugliness and evil."

"How about downward mobility?" Alex asked.

Salome frowned. "You're right. He wants a Hollywood princess. Me becoming a dog groomer would be like being the nanny or the landscaper."

Alex pointed to the crowd. "Speaking of having an image, here comes Buddy and his treasured wife."

Salome waved at Buddy. His face lit up. He took Felicity Strauss's arm and they approached looking happy and relaxed. Before he and Felicity could get to them, a couple of fans corralled them.

"He seems very happy with her," Alex commented.

"She's the real thing," Salome said. "Devoted to animals. Generous to everyone. They're staying at my father's winery. I've gotten to spend some time with her."

"That's right. Your father makes wine now."

"Started after I finished high school. He bought a failing winery on twenty acres in Kenwood. My parents spend as much time as they can up here, when they're not making films. There are a couple of cottages. One of them is Buddy's retreat." Salome hesitated. "Buddy is very sensitive. Our family estates have always been a place he can feel protected."

By this time, Buddy and Felicity had broken free.

"Uncle Buddy," Salome said.

"My darling Salome," Buddy crooned. He turned to Felicity. "I changed her diapers. She's my godchild."

"You've mentioned that a few times," Felicity said, but her tone was warmly teasing. Felicity turned to Alex and held out a hand.

"You're Alex Pope. Buddy told me all about you." Her handshake was firm, her voice oratorical. Felicity Strauss radiated confidence, the kind of woman who was born to speak at rallies and invoke social change.

"Buddy taught me about motivations," Alex said.

Felicity nodded. "He's generous that way."

"I wasn't always so generous," Buddy said.

"We don't worry about the past, do we?" Felicity asked.

"We use the past to move into the future. Our judgments of others are a projection of our own lessons." Buddy looked dreamily at Felicity. "How many points, sweetie?"

Felicity smiled seductively. "Four points. Two for each truism."

Buddy winked. "I like to collect as many points as I can with my mentor here. I love to redeem them."

The sexual innuendoes would have been embarrassing, if the bliss wasn't so cute.

"Speaking of negative projections," Buddy said, looking over Alex's shoulder. "Look who's arrived."

"Hello," said Chase Stuyvesant.

There was a silence. From the look on Chase's face, it appeared that she was used to ambivalent reactions to her presence. "What a great event," she said.

Everyone nodded. Feet shuffled.

"Time to mingle," Salome said lightly.

"Same for us," Felicity added, taking Buddy's arm.

Some friends. Now Alex was stuck with Chase.

"I hear you teach self-defense," Chase said. To her credit, she looked interested.

"I teach a combination of exercise and self-defense. It's more about empowerment and strength on all levels."

"That's great," Chase replied enthusiastically. "I would have loved to come to a class. But I'm hoping to wrap production immediately."

Alex shuffled in place. She wanted to get away without

seeming rude. She watched as Chase's eyes drifted around the room.

"Look at the people on the dance floor," Chase said. "I love it. Grandmothers dancing with gay guys in leather."

"That's Sonoma County," Alex replied.

"Would you like to dance?"

Alex's mouth dropped open. "Dance?" she blurted out. "With *me?*"

"It wasn't a come-on. I'm happily in a relationship. I thought it would be nice."

"Dance?" Alex repeated. She knew she was going to have one of her more regrettable outbursts. "Why would you want to dance with me? You think I'm a klutz."

Chase frowned. "Who told you that?" She held up a hand. "Never mind. Don't tell me."

"It's true, though," Alex persisted. "You knocked my performance."

A troubled look came over Chase's face. "I made some comments about your stunt work, that's true."

"If you have things to say, say them to my face," Alex said.

It was as though Chase had become wrapped in a cocoon of protective invisible filament. "I'm sorry," she said stiffly. She started to walk away.

No," Alex said impulsively. "Let's dance." She took the startled Chase's hand and led her to the dance floor. "I'm warning you, I'm not Madonna."

"I know Madonna."

"Really?"

"Alex, I don't lie, except to myself at times."

"You lied to me about liking my performance."

"I did like your performance. I expressed some critical doubts behind your back, but it doesn't mean I didn't like your work."

"Why behind my back?"

"I was confused. Chalk it up to neurotic negativity. Can we just dance?"

Less is More wailed a slow song about love. Alex wasn't much of a butch, but she took the lead, holding Chase in a close squeeze. She could feel the warmth rising from Chase's middle. By the end of the song, she felt Chase's hand pressed against the small of her back. Alex responded, moving closer still.

Chase pulled away abruptly. "No more of this. I told you, I'm in a relationship. What were you trying to prove?"

"What makes you think I was trying to prove something? I wasn't." Alex felt a pang of guilt. Maybe she was trying to make a point. But she wasn't about to admit it.

"I'm off target again," Chase said. "I am really giving the wrong impression."

Alex shrugged. "Don't worry about it."

"This sounds stupid, but I'm not a bad person."

Alex was still feeling the heat of the dance. She felt angry, agitated and aroused. All she needed was to bottle up some of this concoction of confused emotions and she'd never have to worry about inner motivations again.

Chapter Six

ON MONDAY MORNING, Alex arrived on the set to find Jerome in a huddle with Chase and the primary actors. They turned in unison as she approached.

"Buddy didn't contact you over the weekend, did he?" Jerome asked.

"He's not here?" Alex asked. He was always the first actor to arrive.

"I just called Felicity," Jerome replied. "She left yesterday. She said he was in the bungalow at the D'Amico winery when she took off. She hired a limousine to take her to the airport. She wanted Buddy to relax. She knew how important it was for him to get plenty of rest." Jerome frowned. "She wanted to make sure he didn't have any meltdowns from exhaustion or stress."

Alex felt a sense of loyalty for Buddy. He really seemed like he'd conquered some demons. If she could have, she would have willed him into the room.

"This has happened before," Ken said. "He always turns up."

"He'll be here," Shirley added firmly.

"I just sent one of the drivers to the cottage." Chase glanced at her watch. She sounded cool and calculating, as though Buddy's disappearance was merely an annoying and expensive budget problem. "I suggest we start with scene seventy-two."

"The show must go on," Salome piped up. She grinned at the cliché.

"After all, there's no business like show business," Alex replied.

Salome groaned appreciatively. The rest of the group looked at them like they were slightly deranged.

"I guess we see eye to eye on this particular peccadillo," Chase said. "We'll get this movie done, come hell or high water."

Alex knew she looked surprised at Chase's comments.

"I'd like to play your cliché game," Chase said. "I like clichés."

Alex winced. "My cousin Jeffrey and I were once the only members of the cliché police. A little while back I let a woman who just happened to be from Hollywood into our squadron. That didn't turn out so well. Salome is the only other person I've invited since."

"I hope you have a change of heart," Chase said. "Give me the benefit of the doubt and invite me into the club."

"You're putting me between a rock and a hard place," Alex said. "You puzzle me. You run hot and cold."

Chase winked at her. "That's just the tip of the iceberg."

JUST BEFORE THE cameras rolled, Jerome announced that scene seventy-two would be shot in its entirety with one camera. He had just reviewed Antonioni's seven-minute scene in *The Passenger*. The continuous take would heighten the mood of panic and existential fright.

Marlon squeaked, a nonverbal and cowardly protest. He glanced at Chase, who shrugged but didn't interfere. Apparently she was going to allow Jerome a little length on his leash to express himself.

The actors took their places. Alex took a deep breath. She would be in the entire scene now as Salome.

"Take one."

"Action!" called Jerome.

Alex started slowly with two evasive moves against an invisible alien. She imagined using the invader's energy as a tool to wield against him. The more evil the opponent, the stronger her power of good prevailed. It was a universal law. She lost herself in the movements. The long take was wonderful, an eternity of possibilities. This time, no one would cut her off. She felt free, as pure in her beginner's mind as in the ancient *katas* she'd done in isolated meadows shielded from others' judgments and, more importantly, shielded temporarily from her own demons. Ken and Shirley watched from their dinner table. They looked mesmerized.

Alex chose a hard-soft series, combining twirling ax kicks with a sequence of roundhouse kicks, followed by a rapid one-two-three series of fist blows to the face, gut, and groin. With a burst of joy, she rolled across the floor and leapt to her feet, then jumped in the air for a sidekick, followed by two elbow strikes. She was feeling the strain of the long set of motions, but she finished with a prolonged, lightening fast combination of hand jabs and low kicks. She ended in a pose of tranquil power.

The dance was complete. This time, she held her position in a silent moment of prayer. She felt captured in the moment. Her heart pounded in anticipation as one of the local actors dressed as a waiter entered the set, struggling with a large silver platter. The weight of the phony head was inconsequential. The young actor's pretenses were a showy interpretation of the real weight of a severed head. Seven pounds. The weight of a bowling ball. The actor was doing a great job.

"Is this the special dish I requested?" Shirley said with regal pomposity. Shirley turned to her husband expectantly.

"It has very little salt," Ken replied. His eyes bugged out from a valiant attempt to not burst out laughing.

Alex's instructions were to finish her dance and stay on the set, ready to react. Jerome would not replace her with Salome. He wanted the entire scene complete, from the dance to the reaction to the platter. Alex couldn't believe she was being required to *act*.

"You can't mess up," he'd promised her. "You have the veil on. Just throw up your arms and faint." He'd placed a confiding hand on her arm. "Salome doesn't feel comfortable crashing to the floor. She needs you."

Alex's heart was beating too fast. She was terrified that she might *really* faint when she needed to *act*.

The local guy advanced towards her, breathing heavily. When he reached her, he bent down on one knee, with the platter balanced on his beefy thigh. He placed his hand on the silver handle of the dome that covered the platter. He lifted the dome with self-importance.

There was a high-pitched scream that seemed to come from a great distance. Later, she was told it came from her lips. That was after she awoke from fainting. There were probably many screams after that, but she didn't hear them. She'd remember a quiet nightmare and a sight that would never ever go away.

On the exposed plate was Buddy Brubech's severed head. The image would remain scarred in her brain forever. His eyes were open. There was almost no blood. The tissue and tubes that snaked from his neck were neatly tucked to fit on the platter. Most startling of all, he looked defiant yet peaceful. He was smiling valiantly. At least she thought so. Good God, who knew? That's how she wanted him to be at the end. Lionhearted.

Chapter Seven

BY THE TIME Alex awoke from her faint, Chase had called 911. Alex, despite her horror, let a portion of her mind appreciate Chase's capable response to the emergency. She prided herself on heroic braveries, but this time she'd flopped in the face of the gruesome sight.

"Don't touch anything," Chase warned. She backed everyone away from the head, but had them all stay in the room. "I told the dispatcher there was a medical emergency, not a death. If the local journalists are listening to the scanners, they might not pick up on this immediately. We want to avoid the press as long as possible. This is going to be a huge mess."

Alex understood what it was like to be hounded and harassed by the media vultures. She appreciated Chase's delaying tactic. In less than a couple of minutes, she heard sirens. Two Healdsburg police officers rushed into the room. Chase led them to Buddy's head. The younger of the two, a skinny kid who looked like he was a Boy Scout, turned green. His sergeant, a pot-bellied man with a pleasant face, transformed his expression into an experienced mask, but his eyes signaled repugnance.

"Where's the body?" the sergeant asked Chase.

"We don't know."

"We have a crime scene here," he said to the younger officer.

"No kidding," the kid replied. He turned red. "Sorry. Really sorry."

"Officer Freeman is a rookie," the older officer explained. He turned to young Freeman. "What's the procedure?" he asked sternly.

"Dispatcher sent us as first responders," Freeman said. "Dispatcher transferred the call to RedCom, where the 911 caller explained that there was a medical emergency, then fire and EMTs were dispatched."

"Okay," the sergeant said gruffly.

Just then the fire trucks and paramedics arrived. Two of the paramedics were young muscular men. The third was a short, plump woman in her mid-forties. The young ones struggled with looks of disgust. The veteran woman wore a subtle smile. It was an acknowledgment of the utter ridiculousness of it all.

In dreadful fact, there was no body to treat. No heart to revive. There wasn't even much blood. The head had obviously been drained elsewhere. Alex's stomach roiled violently. She was very aware of the routine that would follow. It wasn't so very long ago that she'd been in a similar situation, inhabiting a murder scene.

Everyone was hustled to one corner of the room, a sizable group of crew and cast members. Crime scene investigators took pictures and gathered physical evidence. When the coroner's unit arrived, one of the team, a weathered-looking woman with sad eyes, reached down and tenderly lifted the head, inserted it into a bag and carried it away. Alex felt a wave of dizziness. Not just from that awful sight, but from the latest arrival.

A young guy in a suit came in, accompanied by Detectives Harroway and Green, Sonoma County's crack homicide investigators. In unison, Harroway and Green surveyed the situation. In unison, their eyes landed on Alex. They were quite a team. Occupational twins, they operated as a unit. Alex watched as they glanced at one another after noticing her. She could hardly blame them. She'd probably just broken a record for one individual showing up on the most murder scenes in Sonoma County. Not a reputation she was proud of. What the frequency did, however, was make her an expert on the rest of the excruciating day.

Everyone would wait interminably, not allowed to mingle or discuss. They'd be imprisoned in their own thoughts, watching the flurry of activity, under the watchful gaze of the cops, who looked like they were fighting a certain amount of awestruck celebrity gazing.

"Alexis Pope?"

Alex stood and followed an officer down a hallway.

The homicide detectives had set up camp in Maddie Rockwell's private office. The office was utilitarian and nondescript. No matter. Harroway and Green had taken it over. They were industrial-strength squatters, infused with the power of their mission, to fight crime and find the truth. Alex appreciated their vibe, but unfortunately she had that admitted problem with authority. That's what came of having bohemian celebrity parents who'd written checks to the Black Panthers.

"Have a seat, Alex," Clarissa Harroway said. She looked like a fresh-faced farm girl, with pink cheeks and curly hair pulled into a partly successful bun. The first time they'd met, Clarissa had appeared untroubled. Now she looked subtly guilty—and she should. Clarissa had stolen Alex's good friend Mary Szabo's girlfriend away last year. Alex was not in a forgiving mood.

"Clarissa," she intoned, infusing the word with the weight of damnation. She was rewarded with a wince from the detective. "How's life treating you?" she asked. "Anything new besides home-wrecking?" Even she didn't like the tone of her own voice.

People in glass houses, an inner voice admonished.

"Let's get down to the business at hand," Detective Rob Green said gruffly. "Leave her alone."

Alex couldn't help liking Green. He was a loyal man in his fifties, with leathery tanned skin and a grey crew cut. The last time she'd been questioned by him and his partner, he'd possessed a growing roll of fat around the middle. Now he looked svelte.

"You look fabulous," she said to Green.

Green couldn't help smiling. "Weight Watchers and fitness boot camp. Thought about taking your class, but your fitness center is too expensive. And we have too much police business in common." He allowed himself a shudder. "This might be the ugliest one yet."

Alex felt a creeping sense of anxiety. She'd managed a pretty good sense of emotional numbness up until now. Clarissa, the traitor, spoke with a remarkable tone of compassion, given Alex's obvious incriminatory vibes.

"Horrible. I'm sure you're feeling terrible," Clarissa said sympathetically. "I was told the head was *presented* to you."

"Stop with the tactics." Alex turned to Green. "Don't do the good-cop/bad-cop routine with me. What are you two doing here anyway? Isn't this Healdsburg business?"

Clarissa and Green glanced at one another. Alex watched their silent dialogue. Really, they were like platonic husband and wife. She knew Green had a real wife, together twenty years, and four children. And Clarissa had Kim. The rumor mill had it that they were still together. Green nodded at Clarissa with the go-ahead to chat. It's in their plan now, Alex understood. Break the ice.

"Healdsburg police's homicide detective just retired," Clarissa said. "They've got someone in training. That woman is on vacation. So we came in."

"Besides, this is obviously going to be a high-profile case," Alex said.

"No shit," Green said. "Pardon my French."

"So, they're bringing in Sonoma's finest," Alex said.

"Watch the compliments," Green growled. "Makes you look suspicious."

The two women looked at him in surprise. He shrugged. "A little humor." He looked at his watch. "Ladies, let's get on with this. Others are waiting."

Alex filled them in on her role in the movie.

"So, you got to know the cast and crew pretty well?" asked Green.

"I guess so." Alex hesitated. "You want to know if any of them seemed to have a motive?"

Green smiled. "You ask the questions and answer them."

"Isn't that what you were going to ask?"

"So answer," Clarissa said.

From what she could tell, everyone adored Buddy. Despite his rocky past, he seemed so intent on reform and generosity of spirit. "No," she replied. "No one."

Green took a photo from a folder and held it out to her. "What about this individual?"

She nodded. "Him. I knew it. The stalker. A nut case. I knew it. It was him, wasn't it?"

The detectives adopted their mask faces. That sealed it for Alex. It was that nutty young guy with the pop idol hair. Chip Welch. She studied the arrest photo. "You caught him already?"

"Tell us what you know about him," Clarissa said.

Alex described the incident on the set when Chip burst in, including Buddy's odd reaction. She felt a stab of guilt at the decision to let Chip go, then quickly pushed it away. Hadn't she learned anything about the whims of tragedy? It was useless looking back with remorse. "Buddy said to ignore the whole incident." She stabbed an accusatory finger at the detectives. "You guys, you owe me. You know how I am. A hostile witness. And yet I always cooperate. Tell me. Did Chip confess?"

Clarissa stood. "C'mon, Alex. You know the routine. Wait a few hours. The whole thing'll blow up in the press. Let us do our jobs. Don't nag about the formalities. There's a reason for them."

"Formalities?" Alex said. "Try and respect formalities in your private life the way you do here."

"Can it," Green threw out, looking fiercely protective of his philandering partner. "You're one to talk." He looked immediately regretful at his unprofessional outburst.

Alex smiled at him. "Good point." She let the deputy lead her away, awash in an appreciation of the contradictory complexities of the humanity club. *People in glass houses*, no kidding.

Chapter Eight

TUESDAY MORNING, HARROWAY and Green called on her at home. Alex lounged on the shaded brick patio outside her rental unit. Her landlady, Sandy Knight, now lived with Mary Szabo, Sonoma County sheriff's deputy Pete's twin sister. After Clarissa Harroway had stolen Mary's previous girlfriend, Kim, from her, Mary had taken up with Sandy Knight. It was all a part of the lesbian merry-go-round sitting next to the philandering baby boomers fun house in the Sonoma County Relationship Carnival.

Sandy's funky Eden was a fenced acre with a gate that opened onto Patterson Road. The buildings were set back past a large dandelion-infested lawn that Sandy insisted go ecologically brown in the summers. With Sandy shacked up with Mary, the main house was occupied by a tofu-eating couple who worked at the local Whole Foods a few miles south in downtown Sebastopol. Wheatie and Kallinda maintained Sandy's organic grounds and played their musical instruments on the bench beside the Buddha statue in the meditation garden next to the arbor that attached to the house.

Alex's little nest was an addition built behind the main structure. It consisted of an eating-living area and a sleeping nook, all furnished with garage sale bargains. The amount spent on everything would barely have covered the cost of the Italian leather sectional in the den of Alex's former mansion in the East Bay. She had given up her mansion. After her husband's death, she'd fled up to Sonoma County at the urging of Jeffrey.

Ten minutes after she agreed to see them, the detectives pulled up the driveway. Alex had Green's industrial strength coffee and Clarissa's peppermint tea prepared for them. She smiled at their appreciative looks. "See? I'm cooperative."

"You're a saint." Green took a gulp from the mug and sighed. "Harroway is still nagging me about my caffeine intake."

"His blood pressure is barely under control," Clarissa said.

"One thirty-nine over eighty-five," Green retorted.

In unison, like the long-term partners they were, the detectives turned to Alex. Alex spoke before they could question her.

"I really thought I told you everything this time," she said.

Clarissa held out an evidence photo. "Recognize this?"

Alex's heart thumped. "Where did you find it?"

"No answering questions with questions today," Green said. He wore his all-business look.

"The Year of the Rooster," Alex said. "Buddy's Chinese zodiac charm. So much for good fortune."

The detectives glanced at one another. Green drained his mug. As they stood to leave, Alex called to Clarissa, "You didn't touch your tea. It wasn't poisoned."

Clarissa frowned.

"That was a joke," Alex said. She knew it wasn't funny. "I'd tell you to say hello to Kim from me, but she hates me."

Clarissa's face struggled. Green shook his head at Clarissa, but she couldn't resist the bait. "She's changed. She doesn't hate you. Alex, people change. You've changed. I've heard a little about you through the rumor mill."

Alex blushed. She wasn't sure she wanted to know the rumors. Before she had any temptations to ask, Green interrupted.

"We gotta go," he said. "You ladies can work out your relationship issues some other time."

LATER THAT DAY, she understood the reason for the detectives' visit. On the five o'clock Bay Area news, a super-coiffed news droid announced that a stalker named Chip Welch had been charged with the murder of Buddy Brubech. Police were being circumspect on the details, but reliable sources revealed that Chip had not only confessed to the crime, but physical evidence linked him with Buddy, including questionable blood stains and possibly incriminating items.

The rooster pendant, of course.

Alex had cancelled her classes at Namaste Fitness for the week. Everyone at Sebastopol's premier gym and wellness center loved her Cardio Kick-Boxing With A Self-Defense Twist, but she was grateful for the excuse to take a break. The class was getting tiresome. She still loved seeing women empowered by her techniques, but she needed something else in her life. The stint on the movie set had shown her that. Her cell phone rang.

"It's Chase. Can I come over?"

"I thought everyone went back to L.A."

"Except me."

Chase must have been hovering in the neighborhood. She arrived in roughly six minutes. She climbed from her rented Highlander holding a brown bag which she held out to Alex as she reached the patio.

"What's this?"

"Open it."

Alex recognized the label on the bottle. Erica Strong Vineyards was a winery for wine snobs like her cousin Jeffrey and her deceased husband, Stacy. Was this some kind of extravagant bribe? She hated to be so suspicious, but Chase wore the expression of a woman with hidden agendas. Before she could issue a dubious thank you, the tofu-couple who rented the main house, Wheatie and Kallinda, appeared with instruments in hand.

"We were going to play," Wheatie said. He was barefoot, as was Kallinda. He wore woven hemp shorts and was bare-chested. Kallinda wore a hemp skirt and a matching halter-top. They were a sweet, slightly plump couple that didn't raise their voices.

Chase took in the situation. She grinned at Alex, who couldn't help grinning back. The whole thing was so New Age California.

"We'd love it," Alex said to the couple. She looked at her watch. It was noon. "Is it too early to have a glass of this lovely wine?"

"Don't think so, we've got a lot going on," Chase said. "Join us?" she asked Wheatie and Kallinda.

"We don't drink alcohol," Kallinda replied. "But we're non-judgmental about people who do."

Alex went to her kitchen and returned with two glasses. Wheatie and Kallinda began a Bach sonata, Wheatie on the mandolin and Kallinda on flute. Alex shivered. It was a very weird coincidence.

"Is something wrong?" Chase asked. "It's beautiful."

It was a Bach sonata Alex's father, Arthur, used to play in his studio when he sculpted. *Prelude BMV 999.* Alex remembered watching him chip at a block of black marble, oblivious to her presence. She was mesmerized and terrified by his sculptures. In the night, she had nightmares that the works were eviscerated body parts. Her mother was usually in their renovated farmhouse, working on her advice column. Alex remembered a haunting yet delicious loneliness in her early years. She was shut out by emotionally absent parents and yet free.

"The sonata reminds me of something," Alex said. "Too complicated to explain." She had no sooner poured two moderate portions of the shockingly expensive cabernet than Henry and six barn cats came sashaying down the driveway. The spayed orange tom, Rocky, gripped a field mouse in his mouth. It was still alive, twitching helplessly.

Chase jumped up from her chair. "Yuck!"

Kallinda rested her flute on her lap. "They're unable to be vegetarians." She emitted a sigh expressing a mild frustration with the carnivorous side of Mother Nature.

Alex scooped up her beloved pet and shushed the other cats up the driveway towards the barn. "Henry lives in the house with me."

"I'm more of a dog person," Chase replied, reaching out to stroke Henry's silky black fur. "Cats are a little too independent for me. My partner and I don't have pets right now." A troubled look passed over her face. "Not a good time in our life for added responsibility."

Henry purred. Since his rescue from a troubled situation and subsequent adoption by Alex, he'd settled quite nicely into his pampered role in her life. Wheatie and Kallinda resumed their serenade. Henry pranced in the gardens, chasing butterflies, as the dappled sunlight filtered through the vines climbing the arbor on the patio.

"Are you wondering why I'm still here?" Chase asked.

"Yes I am."

Chase leaned forward in her chair. "I'm staying for the arraignment. I have an obligation to represent the studio. It looks better if I stay."

"I see," Alex said.

Chase smiled. "That doesn't explain the wine."

"Not really."

Chase sniffed the air. "I love the smell of eucalyptus."

They both took a moment to breathe in the pungent breeze. Like many of Sonoma County's transplants, eucalyptus was an immigrant that had come to define the sensuous landscape with its overpowering scent, a cross of turpentine and the pleasant aroma of botanical gin. Alex felt an ecological sadness enhanced by personal shadows. "The trees are dying. Some eucalyptus pest. I'm trying to be better about cynicism. Sandy Knight, my landlady and friend, insists you can be an optimist and ecologically aware, but she's a goddess."

"You're not so bad yourself," Chase responded.

Alex decided to direct the conversation in another direction. "Is the movie ruined?"

"No," Chase said, sitting up stiffly, resuming her professional demeanor. "That's why I came." She flinched.

This woman was like a four-year-old Alex once saw on a video whose face was smeared with chocolate. *Did you eat the chocolate? No*, the little girl replied. *Are you sure you didn't eat the chocolate?* Oh, no, said the little girl, completely confident in her deception as the camera recorded her guilt. Chase had about as much ability to hide her conflicts. It was endearing, really. Still, this was the woman who criticized Alex behind her back.

Chase glanced at Wheatie and Kallinda. "I don't want the wood nymphs to hear this."

"They're not interested."

"You'd be surprised. People aren't always what they seem."

"Obviously."

"Don't patronize me," Chase shot back. "I had a hard enough time coming here."

Alex must have looked startled.

"I'm sorry." Chase wiped her brow. "I feel so much pressure."

Alex couldn't help a sympathetic tug. "I cut you off."

"There was a note," Chase said. "I got it Monday afternoon. I reported it to the detectives."

Alex shivered. "Buddy?"

"You have to swear to keep this under your hat for now."

"I won't tell a soul," Alex said. "Two clichés."

Before Chase could reply, a loud howl pierced the air.

"Henry!" Alex said.

Henry came flying down the stone path, crying piteously. Alex picked him up. One of his eyes was swelling. Alex had never been much into the nurse-mother skill set. She could take out a swaggering bully, but she couldn't stand seeing helpless children with scraped knees, much less her injured pet yowling in pain.

Kallinda rushed over. "He's got a foxtail in his eye." She gently pulled at Henry's lid. He squirmed violently. "These are really hard to take out. I'd call the vet."

Alex fumbled with her cell phone, hands shaking. She jabbered at the receptionist. Kallinda handed Henry to Chase. "Keep him calm, I'll go get the pet transporter."

With Henry placed in the cage, Alex glanced around wildly. She knew she wasn't acting rationally, but she couldn't stand Henry's pain. By now, Wheatie and all six barn cats were hovering in the driveway. "We can take you," Wheatie offered. "We're supposed to be at the Whole Foods in an hour, but we can call in for emergency sick time."

"I'll take her," Chase said.

"You don't have to do that," Alex replied.

"I insist," Chase said. She held up her hand to quell any more protests. "Let me prove I'm a nice person."

Chapter Nine

THE SINGLE WORLD Holistic Pet Care Center shared a strip mall location in Cotati with a tattoo parlor, a Thai restaurant, a Birkenstock outlet and Rickie Coleman's grooming shop. In fact, Rickie had suggested the vet to Alex, who'd been shopping for a new one.

The concerned receptionist whose name tag read Brittany rushed over to Henry. "We can take him right back." The young woman glanced at Alex's ashen face. "Are you all right?"

Chase took Alex's arm. "I'll take care of her." She led Alex to a comforting plaid couch. Chase got her settled and plumped down beside her. She glanced at the handwoven rugs and the third world artifacts mounted on the walls. Every square inch of the reception room was plastered with animal-themed artistry. "Do you want some steeped roots?" she asked with a poker face, gesturing at the tea urn.

Alex emitted a relieved burst of laughter. "I wish we'd brought the wine." She glanced over at a male and female couple with matching gray ponytails. The aging hippies wore matching faded Guatemalan tunics. They scowled at her.

"Alex!" Rickie Coleman entered, lugging a large birdcage. A small elderly woman followed behind. "Is everything all right?"

"It's Henry. Foxtail in his eye." Alex's voice shook.

Rickie nodded sympathetically. "It's scary. But they're pretty easy to remove by a good vet. And Sally is the best."

"The best," echoed the elderly woman. "I wouldn't bring Shiva anywhere else."

Shiva, on cue, squawked in her cage.

"What a beautiful bird," Chase commented. "It's a cockatiel, isn't it?"

"This is Esther, my neighbor," Rickie said. "She lives on a former chicken ranch about a half mile from me. This is one of her three cockatiels."

"I need help with the cage," Esther said. "Rickie's a good girl."

"It's no trouble," Rickie replied.

"Yes it is," Esther said sharply. "You do it anyway." She apparently had no problem expressing her opinions. "You do a lot that's troublesome."

Rickie appeared to be troubled herself. Her pixie elf delight seemed weighted under a dark cloud.

"This is Alexis Pope and Chase Stuyvesant. Alex lives here and Chase is the producer from Hollywood I told you about," Rickie said.

"Nice to meet you, Esther," Chase said.

"Granny," Esther answered. "Everyone calls me Granny." She smiled wickedly. "I'm detoxifying the stigma of ageist labels."

Alex detected a Polish accent. One of her father's art buddies had come from Poland. He'd had the same accent and a similar biting wit. Granny was diminutive in size, but not stature. Her smallness was more like a version of compression, sediment squeezed into diamond. Her white hair was cut in a fashionable bob and she wore trendy tinted glasses. Through the tint, her eyes radiated intelligence. She looked to be seventy.

"Eighty-four," Granny said.

Alex blinked.

"I saw you assessing me," Granny said. "I'm eighty-four."

"Is your bird sick?" Alex asked.

Before Granny could reply, the young receptionist Brittany returned. "Henry will be fine. We got the foxtail out. He's resting. We want to keep an eye on him for a little while."

She smiled at Rickie and Granny. "Is my favorite bird here for her check-up?"

Shiva squawked at Brittany with warm recognition.

"She likes to take trips," Granny said. "Even better than she likes television. Except for the San Francisco Giants on the sports channel." She smiled indulgently. "I have three birds that love baseball, so I'm outnumbered."

Brittany shrugged with zen fortitude. "We're a little backed up. A couple of medical emergencies from the pound. Shiva will have to wait."

"I'll wait with you," Rickie said to Granny.

"Your shop," Granny protested. "You have to groom the animals."

"I cancelled my appointments," Rickie replied. "You can't lug this cage." She brought the cage over to the couch adjacent to Alex and Chase. Granny joined them. There was a momentary respite from conversation.

"Our Lab has incurable cancer," the female of the pony-tailed couple announced.

"I'm so sorry," Rickie said. She took a card from a pocket. "I do grief counseling. Sliding scale. Please call me."

The couple both grew teary-eyed. Granny slipped her hand into Rickie's. "You can trust her," Granny said with fondness.

"I saw you on *Bay Area Today*," the pony-tailed woman said to Rickie. "You rescue and rehabilitate abused animals."

Rickie shrugged modestly.

"Animal abusers should be tortured," the man of the couple burst out. "An eye for an eye. Put the researchers in a cage and rub toxic cosmetics on them."

There was a silence. No one apparently was going to challenge the man's Old Testament doctrines. Brittany emerged from the back, leading a limping yellow Lab with scabby skin and a soulful expression. The dog caught sight of her teary-eyed owners and wagged her tail bravely. "Take her home," Brittany said gently. "Keep her comfortable in her last days."

"I left our checkbook at our house," the woman said. She turned red. "Our account is a little low this month."

"Pay when you can," said Brittany.

Alex noticed a sign demanding payment at the time of services. The couple and their sick dog shuffled out without paying. The receptionist settled behind her desk. "It won't be much longer," she said to Alex. "I'm sorry, we're so backed up. We'll release Henry as soon as we can."

"It's no problem," Alex replied. What else could she say here in Compassion Land? She glanced at Chase. "Mind waiting?"

"I have time on my hands," Chase said, giving her the private cliché look. "Besides, what goes around comes around. All things being equal, good things come to those who help others."

Alex grinned. "When push comes to shove, we both see eye to eye."

"Point is," Chase replied, "Time heals all wounds."

"Does it?" Alex stopped grinning. "I don't want to play anymore."

"What's the matter?" Chase said. "I was honored that you let me into the cliché police."

"It isn't you," Alex hesitated. "I'm not sure time heals all wounds."

"Cliché aside, I think it does," Chase replied.

"Really? Maybe your head is in the clouds."

Chase frowned. "You don't know me. Don't judge a book by its cover."

They both looked up and realized that Rickie, Granny and Brittany were eavesdropping. The door chime rang. A couple rolled a Bugaboo baby stroller into the room, trailed by a Tibetan terrier on a leather leash. "We're late," said the harried-looking father. He didn't sound terribly apologetic, more annoyed that the world was interfering with his agenda. He glanced around. "Do we have to wait long? The baby is fussing." The infant wore a Lauren polo shirt and looked like a miniature disgruntled CEO of a Fortune 500 company.

The yuppie family replaced the hippie couple on the second couch. The entire time of their entry, the baby's mother had been attached to her iPhone. Finally, she looked up with delight. "I'm following Buddy Brubech's murder on CNN dot com." She shivered. "The killer won't tell them where the body is."

Brittany pointed to her computer monitor. "I've been watching too. What a horrible, gruesome thing. It's such a shame. He was turning his life around. Marrying Felicity Strauss. She's a deity in the animal-rights community. Buddy was becoming one of our most important spokespersons. He could have become more influential than Doris Day."

"He was a *putz*," Granny Wolinski exclaimed. She glanced around the room at the perplexed expressions resulting from her Yiddish displeasure. "No comparison with Doris Day. Who cares who killed him?" She smiled with unapologetic wickedness.

Rickie sighed with exaggerated equanimity. "Granny holds humanity to very high standards."

"As well it should be," Granny replied.

"High standards make room for a lot of disappointment," Alex offered. Why was she getting into the debate? She had the vague recollection of a Flannery O'Connor story that took place in a doctor's waiting room. She thought she remembered the protagonist eventually wallowing in a pigpen and hallucinating about staircases to heaven. She ought to know better than to enter into debates about humanity in clinics. Her reverie was broken by a light touch on her elbow.

"Here's Henry," Chase said.

ALEX CLIMBED FROM Chase's Highlander, balancing Henry and his transporter on her right hip.

"Let me help," Chase offered.

"I've got it."

They hadn't talked much on the drive back. Henry was dozing and there'd been just too much conversation and activity for one day.

"Listen." Chase leaned across the divider towards the passenger side. "Want to go to the arraignment with me?"

Alex hesitated. "I'm not sure I could handle going."

Chase looked puzzled.

"I've been through too many arraignments in the last few years. I hate courtrooms. I hated them even when I was married to a lawyer."

Now it was Chase's turn to hesitate.

Alex nodded. "I was married. To a man."

"Divorced?"

"No, he's dead."

"I see," Chase said carefully. "Don't get me wrong. I just got vibes."

"I am interested in women, if that's what you're getting at. Frankly, I'm not sure where I'm at with relationships, women or men."

"You can be whatever you want to be." Chase frowned. "My mother is a wonderful woman, but she cultivates ambiguity. It drives my father crazy and he adores her. He's got the mind and soul of an engineer while my mother comes from the Lasky Hollywood dynasty. Jerome's mother and my mother are sisters. You remind me of my mother. I'm sorry. It's a weird thing to say."

Alex wasn't sure if she felt complimented or insulted. "Then it's a good thing you're not interested in me." She started to close the car door. Before it was completely shut, she said: "I don't know how I feel about you. I'll go with you to the arraignment."

How was that for another nice mixed message?

Chapter Ten

ON THE MORNING of the arraignment, Alex guided her Lexus through the hills that rose above Dry Creek Valley. Alex's heart beat faster as she approached the grounds of the majestic Marlowe Manor, not in reaction to the aesthetics of the lovely resort, but to past associations with another lovely resort that had led to disaster. She still thought of the Overlook Lodge in Guerneville with a mixture of fondness and horror.

Marlowe Manor had been renovated from private residence to an upscale resort hotel consisting of a main building and a scattering of fanciful cottages. Nestled on private grounds in a secluded hilltop meadow, the original fairy-tale indulgence of a local financier blended old world charm and trendy touches to create a facade of timeless escape. Alex knew, however, that facades like the Overlook Lodge or Marlowe Manor could hide terrible secrets.

The original dwelling was an enormous multi-colored Victorian mansion surrounded by lush gardens. Supercilious attendants directed her to a ridiculously whimsical cottage at the edge of the property. As Alex drove up to the cottage entry, Chase opened the door and rushed to the car, looking sheepish. "It's extravagant."

"You don't have to explain."

"Just for the record, my uncle, Jerome's father, is a good friend of the owner. We got a great deal. I'm watching the budget, like I'm supposed to. As to old-boy favors, that's a fact of life. I choose my battles. Besides, I'm too weak to fight perks like this."

Alex shrugged. "I once lived a life completely built on perks, including a mansion that was a wedding gift from my in-laws, so don't fret about nepotism. Two peas in a pod. Don't cliché me back, I'm not feeling so great."

"Flu?"

"Nerves."

"Want to talk about it?"

"Not really."

Chase didn't persist, so they drove in silence south on 101, exiting on Steele Lane in Santa Rosa. The parking lots of the Sonoma County Hall of Justice were packed. They wound up parking a good hike away from all the action. Alex felt a cold sweat as she climbed from the Lexus. Her skin tone was chalky. She felt faint. Would she ever learn? What cliché would Jeffrey have spouted about this situation? Easy. *Jumping out of the frying pan into the fire.*

Chase interrupted her reverie. "Drink this." She pulled a bottle of greenish sludge from her designer leather sack.

Alex accepted the frightening concoction reluctantly. "Yuck."

"It's wheat grass, beets, carrots and six more super-foods. My lovely partner turned me on to it. I drink *two* bottles on really stressful days."

"This is desperation." Alex belted down the entire container in several large gulps. The elixir cascaded through her bloodstream. She felt a surge of energized equanimity. Maybe a placebo effect, but who cared? She needed all the equilibrium she could muster, however it was induced. "Look at the spectacle."

The entire landscape leading to the courtrooms was packed with spectators and an army of international media, both legitimate press sporting electronically enhanced vans and sophisticated broadcast weaponry and paparazzi sporting enhanced hormones. "Time to face the music," she said. "Pay the piper."

"Run the gauntlet."

"No bowing before the storm."

"No throwing in the towel," Chase added. "We'll plough through. Damn the torpedoes, full speed ahead."

"Enough," Alex warned. "Nothing worse than overdoing the clichés."

"Sure there is. Giving in to terror."

"A woman after my own heart. We both march to the same beat."

"Alex, you told me to stop."

"Okay, okay."

In cosmic unity, the entire crowd turned in their direction.

"*Chase Stuyvesant!*" News of the arrival spread like a rushing wave through the throng.

"Meld into the crowd," Chase whispered. "I'll handle this."

"I'll come with you," Alex offered.

"No way."

"You shouldn't have to do this alone," Alex said.

"Just how many untimely deaths have you been associated with in the last few years in this region?" Chase countered. "*TMZ* is here. It's the worst trash show ever."

"Point taken."

There wasn't much time. Laticia Stone from *TMZ* led the pack, racing towards them. Alex ran to the sidelines, close enough to still observe the brouhaha. Chase marched right up to the surging mass of reporters who shouted questions at her.

For a few minutes, Chase answered calmly, revealing nothing that wasn't already known. Alex's admiration grew. Chase's composure was worthy of any self-defense heroine Alex had ever studied with, even the mighty Sarge, Alex's self-defense mentor. Too bad Chase spoke behind people's backs. Otherwise, she was very interesting as a person.

Just when it seemed that Chase was going to try and escape, she pulled out a piece of paper. "I received this letter from Buddy just after his death," she announced. "This is a copy. The police have the original." She read:

Dear Chase:

I have done things in the past that have resulted in the attraction of enemies. There is the slight possibility that one of them will act on their hatred. There is no reason for everyone else to suffer. If anything happens to me, I beg you to make sure that the movie is finished.

Best, Buddy

Alex gasped. Wasn't the letter police evidence? What about the homicide investigation? Would the authorities go ballistic? What was Chase thinking? Was the whole thing a set-up arranged by the authorities?

Chase looked out at the crowd. The questions flew again. Chase held up her hand. "*On A Silver Platter* will be completed, as requested by Buddy. I have nothing else to tell you. Excuse me, I have to go."

Chase pushed away from the press and struggled through the doors of the hall, glancing back at Alex with a warrior's determination. Alex took a deep breath. She channeled her own warrior spirit and plunged ahead. If anyone recognized her, they weren't yet convinced of her newsworthiness, thank God. Still vibrating from the elixir and a healthy case of déjà vu, Alex made her way through the metal detectors and took the escalator to the second floor. The hallways were filled with humanity in the throes of crisis. Lawyers, families, accused and accusers huddled in animated clumps outside the courtrooms, mustering up rationales.

Judge Eileen Morse presided over Courtroom 3, the brightly lit arena for in-custody felony cases. Judge Morse was probably over seventy by now, but her demeanor was just as acute as when Alex first reluctantly attended a local felony arraignment. When order was called, Judge Morse glanced out at the crowd with a severe expression. There would be no messing around. Chip Welch was a number on the docket, just like the rest.

Nevertheless, when Chip's name was called, a murmur rose from the packed room. Even Alex took a deep breath as the alleged murderer shuffled in, led by a corrections officer. Chip wasn't bad looking, if you liked a certain super-sensitive boy singer type. He was talking to himself.

"*She made me do it,*" Chase whispered to Alex. They were in the third to last row. The room smelled moldy. It was an outdated building. On top of everything else, they were probably breathing toxic spores spewing from the ventilation ducts.

"You read lips?"

"A deaf aunt taught me. That's what he's saying. Over and over. *She made me do it.*"

Chip gibbered, seemingly oblivious to the proceedings.

"Young man," Judge Morse said patiently. "Can you afford a private attorney? Speak up."

Chip shook his head.

"Yes or no," the judge prodded.

"No," he replied. He avoided eye contact with the judge, but stopped mumbling.

"The court will appoint Mary Szabo," Judge Morse said.

Alex wasn't surprised. Pete's twin sister was by now a high-ranking star in the D.A.'s department, usually assigned the high-profile cases and this one was a doozy. Alex felt the inner surge of excitement. It was if she'd just swallowed a *really* big bottle of elixir. Crisis addiction elixir, main ingredients meddling and ignoring danger, with a sprinkling of interference with the law.

Mary and Chip Welch spent a brief moment in consultation, but this was as usual mostly formality. Mary entered a not guilty plea. Chip's bail hearing was set and most of the crowd fled, including Alex and Chase.

IT WAS A spectacular day. Sonoma County in its finest moments of Indian summer boasted a cloudless sky and a fresh breeze. The oak-studded golden hills in the distance past the city reinforced the county's lovely rural roots. The hills looked velvety soft, which was not true, a fact that Alex learned on her first hike in a county park above Petaluma Hill Road. The charming dried grass was scratchy, full of stickers and snakes. The adorable scrub oaks harbored ticks waiting for the scent of warm blood. So much for quixotic visions of nature, she thought. It worked, but from a distance.

As they were almost at the curb, someone called, "Alex!"

Alex turned to see Paula Coleman headed their way, accompanied by a vibrant-looking woman with a healthy stride. Although the other woman didn't nearly approach Paula's height, she was at least six feet tall.

"Look at those two," Chase commented under her breath. She hummed a few bars of *The Ride of the Valkyries*.

"No kidding." These were two individuals Alex wasn't convinced she could take out with her roundhouse kick.

Paula was in uniform. The other woman wore a beautiful grape-colored silk shirt, faded jeans and a pair of Red Wing boots. Her shoulder-length hair was parted in the middle, like a folksinger. She had a very compelling look, a combination of rustic and cosmopolitan style. Just like Sonoma County, with its teasing ambiguities of sophistication and hick charm.

"We saw you in the courtroom," Paula said. "Erica wanted to meet you. She and I go back a long ways. We played ball together all through middle school and high school."

Erica smiled seductively at Alex.

"This is Erica Strong," Paula said. "Erica, this is Alex Pope and Chase Stuyvesant. They're involved in the movie." Paula shivered. "Jeez, hate to have introductions happening in these circumstances."

Erica held out a hand and gave Chase and Alex each a firm handshake. Her palm was callused.

"Erica Strong Vineyards?" Chase said. "That's one of my favorite wineries."

"Yes," Erica admitted. "I won't lie. I'm proud of my production." She turned to Alex. "Paula has told me all about you."

Alex blushed. "Oh no."

Erica laughed. "It was all very complimentary. I hear you have the moves of a super-heroine. I had a crush on Wonder Woman for years as a little girl."

Alex didn't think it was the time to mention her past Wonder Woman shenanigans. However, anyone with a passion for Wonder Woman was okay in her book.

"What an ugly business," Erica said, shivering.

"I still kind of blame myself for not arresting Chip," Paula said. "But at least they got him."

"Did he actually do it? He must have. He confessed *and* they have evidence," Alex said.

Paula grimaced. "I really shouldn't discuss it. Professional ethics and all."

Alex noticed Erica was staring at her.

"Have you been to my winery?" Erica removed a business card from a jean pocket. "Give me a call. We have a wonderful tasting room. I'll give you a personal tasting." Then, as if realizing she was being rude, she turned to Chase. "And you, as well."

"Thanks, but I'll be back in L.A." Chase smiled tightly.

"Too bad," Erica said with blatant lack of regret. "Next time you come up here." She smiled at Alex. "I hope to see you again *very* soon."

After they'd climbed into the car, Chase glanced at her watch. "Eleven-thirty. I'm starving. The power drink wore off. Brunch?"

In response, Alex's stomach rumbled. "I can't go out in public. Too many busybodies."

"I'm leaving this evening." Chase looked at her expectantly.

Alex didn't reply. She honestly didn't know how she felt about Chase or the whole situation. If this was good-bye, why didn't they just say so and have that be that? Chase seemed to be good at reading her mind.

"Closure," Chase prompted.

"I've never been real good at that," Alex replied.

"Well, to contradict myself, I have a feeling we're not done with one another. Can we make peace?"

Alex shrugged. Chase was sensible. Annoyingly so.

"Come back to my cottage," Chase said. "We can have a bite to eat in my room. Can't get more private than that."

Chapter Eleven

CHASE STEPPED AWAY from the doorway of her cottage at Marlowe Manor and waved at the room. "Take a look."

Alex burst out laughing. "Bordello crossed with Buddhist temple."

Chase grinned. "Check out the Jacuzzi. Picture Tony Curtis taking a dip with Kirk Douglas."

"Chase, I'm not from Hollywood. I don't get all the references."

"*Spartacus.* Kubrick's 1960 Roman Empire opus with gay allusions. I'm the go-to girl for anything gay or bisexual in L.A. I know my stuff."

Alex slumped into a white couch that enveloped her like a heavenly cloud. "I didn't bring a swimsuit." She shrugged. "I guess we don't need one. They didn't wear suits in Rome. They still don't."

Chase stiffened. "I invited you for brunch."

Alex sat up. "I was kidding."

"It doesn't matter."

Any more awkward conversation on the topic was interrupted by a knock on the door. A dignified waiter wheeled in a cart laden with dome-covered platters, a bottle of champagne immersed in an ice bucket and a tray of chocolates in plastic wrapping. He smiled at them. "I personally arranged this for you ladies. Happy Honeymoon."

"It's lovely," Chase said, handing him a large denomination bill. When he left, she sniffed. "This smells fabulous. I took the liberty of ordering."

"For our honeymoon?"

"I had to tell them something to get the romantic adventure discount. I told you, I watch the budget."

Chase's cell phone rang. She frowned at Alex. "I have to take this." She flipped open the phone. "Are you all right?" She listened, a visible sense of relief growing on her face. "No, it's okay. I'm having a honeymoon brunch with Alex Pope. Thanks, we will. No, it's really okay. I'm just glad you're fine. Love you, too. Bye." Chase disconnected and shuddered. "My lovely partner is on a three-day fast. I'd rather be clogged up, to be frank about it."

"I agree."

"See? We agree on something."

"What's her name?"

Chase blinked rapidly. "Can we settle down first?"

Alex took a seat at the linen-covered table. She waved at the dinnerware. "Nice. Domed platters. Who knows what we'll uncover. Chicken heads?"

Chase emitted a yelp of reluctant, shocked laughter. "That's sick."

Alex shrugged. "My cousin Jeffrey is helping me to conquer cynicism with absurdity awareness." Nevertheless, she gingerly lifted a dome with a hint of trepidation, then sighed. A mound of sourdough French toast dusted in powdered sugar and speckled with plump raspberries filled the room with an ambrosial scent. She opened the sparkling wine and poured two glasses of En Tirage 1992 Russian River Valley Recently Disgorged Extra Brut. "Long fancy name," she commented. She waved her hand at Chase's attempt at an explanation of the wine's genesis. "I don't need to know." She held up the glass. "To us. Happy Honeymoon."

After they had sipped, Alex asked, "Does she work on films, too?"

"Wendy used to be an actress. That's how we met." Chase hesitated. "Wendy Swann?"

Alex blinked. "The one with multiple sclerosis?" Alex remembered the heartbreaking press coverage a few years back. It was one of those stories that tore at your gut. Especially since Wendy was both public about her illness and generous in her support of others with multiple sclerosis. Alex recalled that Wendy had also come out as a lesbian around that time. She visualized a hazy picture of Wendy and another woman in the newspapers. It was Chase, she realized. "How is she?"

"She's still Wendy. Beautiful and funny and creative. Last year wasn't so good. Her intestines quit on her. She almost had to get them removed, but the doctors did something and the pipes are working again. She's had some flare-ups, but a new designer protein drug seems to be helping. Now she's working on an entirely new project."

Unexpectedly, a tear ran down Alex's cheek.

Chase sat up stiffly. "She hates being felt sorry for."

"I wasn't. I was just touched by your feelings for her."

"She's my reason for living. Now, how's that for a cliché?"

"You told her about the honeymoon brunch."

"I tell her everything. Among other things, she probably rivals your cousin Jeffrey in advanced absurd humor."

Alex pointed to the French toast. "I really am very hungry."

They piled food onto their plates and ate ravenously, until Alex pushed away her plate. "No more."

"No kidding. I'm stuffed," Chase said.

"Same here." She smiled at Chase. "I apologize."

"For what?"

"I don't know. Everything," Alex said.

"Could you be more specific?"

Alex reddened. "First, for thinking you hated me. After that, for thinking that you were attracted to me. I guess I was wrong on both counts."

It was Chase's turn to redden. "I didn't tell you about Wendy to get your sympathy."

"Doesn't matter. I wish you could stay longer."

Chase stood up. "A person could get used to this whacky county."

"I know. I never thought I'd stay here."

"Still, I have to go home." Chase held out her hand to shake.

Alex stood and went over to Chase. She put her arms around her. The producer stiffened. "It's okay," she whispered. Slowly, she felt Chase's arms encircling her. She had the oddest thought. *Don't leave me.* She quickly pushed it away and Chase with it. They parted with a few conversational inanities, none of which Alex could recall.

AS SHE DROVE down the driveway leaving the Marlowe Manor, Alex's cell rang.

"It's Paula Coleman."

"Hi, Paula. What's up?"

"What are you doing Saturday night?"

"Feeling sorry for myself."

"Excuse me?"

"Never mind. I'm free."

"Erica's brother John is my boss. His wife is in Europe for the month. Saturday is a charity event for injured war vets. Erica and I would like to invite you to make a foursome. You'll be my date and Erica will be her brother's."

"Very non-traditional."

"It's cool. Keep the gossips confused."

"Why would there be gossips?" Alex asked.

There was a distinct moment of hesitation before Paula spoke. When she did, she sounded guarded. "People just like to talk. It's a small county full of people with, I'm sorry to say, dirty minds. John and I are good buddies. People like to get the wrong impression about things like that. I *hate* the backwoods tongue wagging."

How about tongues of adrenalized news anchors on national television wagging about your husband's death? How about the same tongues wagging just because a person happened to be involved in a few homicides or so? Alex knew from experience about tongue wagging. "I understand," she said.

"I knew you would," Paula said warmly. "That's what I told Erica. She's very impressed with you. If you come with us, you can get to know her, too." There was a pause. "She's single. And not crazy. A real catch for someone. You know what I mean."

Alex knew only too well what she meant. "Sounds good," she said with casual tone. She disconnected and immediately pushed a number on her speed-dial. "Jeffrey, get over here!"

When her cousin screeched up the driveway, panic etched on his face, she realized how unthinking she'd been. Poor Jeffrey. He'd been racing into her homes too many times for terrible reasons.

"I need a fashion consultation."

Jeffrey's mouth fell open. "I almost had a heart attack." But his natural curiosity and good humor quickly obliterated any anger. "You always need a fashion consultant. But you won't listen. We have the three safe wardrobe items of increasing propriety that we established for you. We assumed that was it for the long term. I'd given up hope on refreshing your couture."

"I'm going to a benefit on Saturday. I'd like something different."

Jeffrey squinted at her. She knew her cousin could read her like a book. From their earliest days together, they'd been each other's allies. It was due to Jeffrey that she was in Sonoma County at all. Her cousin and his boyfriend, Max, were her closest and most trusted friends.

"Spit it out," he demanded.

"Do you know Erica Strong?"

An ecstatic and worshipful expression came over Jeffrey's face. "A wine goddess."

"According to informed sources, she's not loony. And she's sort of attractive."

"Sort of?"

"She might be *too* perfect."

"Alex, let's skip over the commitment phobia and get to the point."

"I think I'm going on a blind date with her."

Jeffrey swooned. "Get in the car, we're going to Ann Taylor."

"No," she cried in mock horror. "Not Ann Taylor. Can't we go to Macy's?"

Jeffrey came over and held out his arms. When she rose, he engulfed her in a gripping hug. "I want you to be happy," he whispered in her ear.

Alex rested her head on his shoulder. "I know," she whispered back. Then she whispered the words so hard to speak. "I love you, Jeffrey."

"I love you, too, honey."

"I want to wear t-shirts to everything."

"I still love you."

"With vests. I might really be a dyke."

"You can be anything you want."

"I'm attached to being confused."

"There are worse addictions. Look at me, for example. I've managed to conquer my addiction to abusive men." Jeffrey pulled away. "Enough. Let's shop. But we *will not* go to Macy's."

Chapter Twelve

ON SATURDAY NIGHT, as she walked across the patio outside her place, Alex was greeted by a lascivious whistle. It was Wheatie, of all people. She glanced down at herself. She did look pretty hot. A silky, revealing aquamarine blouse that accentuated her eyes. Black silk pants. New turquoise earrings and a necklace hand-crafted in Sante Fe. After a long debate, mostly Jeffrey talking to himself, they'd given up on Ann Taylor and chosen the more funky and expressive Chico's.

"Wheatie, I'm surprised at you," she said.

"He's a man," Kallinda said.

"I used to play football," Wheatie offered. "I was the strongest boy in the tenth grade. I learned all the chauvinist stuff in the locker rooms. Then I stopped growing. I'm a reformed sexist grunt-head. I don't care, you look great."

"As long as we're confessing, I was varsity captain of the cheerleading squad," Kallinda said. "I hope the outfit works," she added.

ERICA STRONG VINEYARDS was located west of Sebastopol, not more than five miles from Patterson Road. Alex felt jittery as she pulled into the crowded parking lot. She'd arranged to meet Paula, Erica and Erica's brother at the event, but Paula had made clear that Erica was not officially hosting. She was socializing.

Erica's vineyard was as rural and chic as she was. The main structure appeared to be a converted farmhouse, expanded with a huge additional wing of stone and glass. Beyond that were the winemaking facilities, a cluster of hulking utilitarian steel-sided buildings. The vineyards stretched across rolling hills in undulating rows.

Alex approached the veranda. Her new friend was waiting.

"Welcome," Erica Strong said warmly.

Alex burst into an uncontrollable laugh.

Erica looked puzzled.

"It's your outfit. Oh, jeez. I don't mean it's your outfit. Well, yes I do."

Alex had officially made a total idiot of herself. Now she could continue her burbling and complete the process. "You're wearing a t-shirt. And a vest."

Erica glanced down at her outfit. To her credit, she broke out into a self-effacing grin. "It's a unique hand-crafted t-shirt and vest," she offered. "They were very expensive."

"They're great," Alex sputtered. "You, too."

Before Alex could die a humiliated death right on the spot, Paula Coleman came up, accompanied by an athletic-looking grey-haired man. Both were in uniform. "We're representing the department," Paula explained. "Wow, you look fabulous. Alex, this is Captain John Strong, my boss."

"Nice to meet you," Alex said. She was aware that the captain was trying not to look lecherous. Erica was making no attempt to hide her lascivious reaction to Alex's makeover. She really ought to go shopping more often.

"I am the luckiest man. I have three of the most beautiful women in the county as my companions," John said.

"John, don't be chauvinist," Erica admonished.

John shrugged. "Don't be the controlling little sister."

There was a short pause of suppressed tension. Paula interrupted. "I think it's time to go to our table."

They were seated at a large roundtable for eight, forming a circle that included a judge and his wife; another judge and her husband; and, a husband and wife team of prominent realtors. During the appetizers and main course, John rambled about his wife's current trip to Madagascar. This was followed by a litany of boring tales of unadventurous travels in foreign countries, peppered with complaints about inconvenient cultural practices. Alex was happy. This was exactly what she needed. A boring evening among nice, boring people.

Halfway through dessert, during one of the judge's blow-by-blow descriptions of a gastric incident in Cancun, Erica lifted a subtle eyebrow of mockery. Alex responded with a nod of disdain. Then the memories hit her like a sack of bricks. All the law firm parties and endless charity galas she'd attended with Stacy as a dutiful lawyer's wife. The mind-numbing conversations. They'd exchanged subtle looks, then gone home, broken out a bottle of wine and made fun of the bores followed by hot, superior-minded sex. She'd never felt right about it, but she'd never tried to analyze any of it too deeply, either. Until Stacy died. In the course of her grief, to avoid thoughts of Stacy's charisma, she'd focused on their sins together. Mockery, snobbery, self-delusion.

Now Erica. The last thing she wanted was a female version of Stacy.

The evening droned on through a series of mind-numbing speeches, while Alex wrestled with internal conflicts. She tried not to meet Erica's gaze and, when she did, was rewarded with a puzzled look from the wine-maker. Time was beginning to stretch out, like cosmic taffy. She was afraid to look at her watch. The hands might have stopped moving.

At 11 p.m., eternity was interrupted by a sheriff's deputy rushing up to their table. He whispered something to Paula and Captain John. They both jumped up.

"Emergency," Captain John said, looking disturbed.

"Oh, no," Erica said.

"Not personal," John said, but Alex thought he looked unusually anxious for a work-related incident. Paula, too, was pale and grim-looking.

"We have to go," John said. He turned to his sister. "Sorry."

Erica shrugged. "Law enforcement. I'll stick to wine-making."

The activities were almost over, in any case. The catering staff cleared the last of the dessert dishes and coffee cups from the table while the guests stretched their arms and struggled to their feet, fighting the effects of rich food and glorious wine. As the party broke up, Erica pulled Alex aside.

"Can I walk you to your car?" Erica asked. "It was not the most exciting evening in the world. I thought we could work up a little scintillating chat before we parted ways." She smiled apologetically. "I'm a lot more interesting than I appeared tonight. That's my act for the more conservative straight people occasions. It's for charity."

"I'm very tired. I can barely stumble out." Alex fled before Erica could say anything else. She ran for her life, chased by demons of karmic relationships. *Damn.* She really didn't want to spend the rest of her life running away from sex life reruns.

It was around midnight when she'd settled into a set of decidedly unfashionable lounging clothes. A faded t-shirt from Habitat for Humanity and a pair of cut-off sweat pants. Something had occurred important enough to pull John Strong and Paula away. Maybe big enough to make the news. Taking a chance, Alex turned on CNN.

It was big enough. Way big enough.

Chip Welch was dead.

As the "breaking news" banner flashed across the screen, the excited news droid announced that Buddy Brubech's alleged killer had been found in his cell at the Sonoma County jail, writhing in agony on the cement floor. He'd died on the way to the hospital. Despite police attempts to hold back information, initial reports indicated poisoning.

The phone rang. The call was from L.A.

"Chase?"

"How do you like them bananas? Sorry to be calling so late,

but I suspected you'd be up." A pause. "Are you alone?"

"Of course I am," Alex said, then realized her solitariness was perhaps not such a done deal. She changed the subject back to the killing. "What a mess. Someone killed Chip. Why?"

"He was in solitary under suicide watch. Someone had to make an effort. Are you all right?"

"Yes."

There was a pause on other end. Alex waited.

"How was your date?" Chase asked.

"Okay. She's attractive."

Another silence. Then, "Well, good. Erica sounds promising."

Alex felt an urge to confide her doubts about Erica to Chase, but something held her back.

"I called to ask about something important, besides the Chip mess. You don't have to answer immediately," Chase said.

"What?"

"We'd like you to come down. For an added scene. We need you. I hate to say this, but the studio is aware of how the Chip Welch publicity will trigger one hot movie opening. Suddenly, we're on the fast track."

Alex's heart leaped at the request. But she felt a perverse desire to play hard to get. "Can I think about it?"

"I wish I could say take your time, but we need you to make up your mind quickly."

"Give me until the morning, I'll call you back."

Why the hesitation? Alex knew she wanted to see everyone again. She wanted the rush of being on a movie set. The ambivalence was due to one complication. Chase.

Chapter Thirteen

THE FOLLOWING WEEKEND, Alex rolled her carry-on to the sidewalk outside baggage claims at LAX. The air reeked of diesel fumes and smoggy particulates. Chase swerved her red Mazda Miata convertible to the curb and waved, a delighted expression on her face. Alex waved back, surprised at how pleased she was to see the producer. She tossed her suitcase into the miserable little excuse of a back seat and squeezed her torso into the low-slung bucket front seat.

"You look great," Chase said. A horn blared behind them. Insistent bursts of hostility demanding their spot. Chase raised her arm into the air and flashed a peace sign. "Nice outfit."

"Erica Strong turned me on to this local artist-designer. She creates masterpiece t-shirts. I love them."

"The fabric is out of sight. Hemp?"

"Save the planet."

Chase gunned the engine, jerking them out of the terminal area and onto a crowded lane heading to the freeway. "You like her? Erica Strong, I mean."

"We had one awkward date. Anyway, I can't wait to meet Wendy."

"She can't wait to meet you."

They cruised north on CA-1. Chase guided the roadster with calm authority on the manic roads. Los Angeles was a city on amphetamines. Drivers gunned their engines, horns blared. The air was tinged with smog and smelled industrial.

Alex grinned at Chase. "Somehow I didn't imagine you'd own this kind of car."

"What did you expect? A Subaru?"

"I'm putting my foot in my mouth, as usual. Let's change the subject."

Chase nodded. "What about the shenanigans in your neck of the woods? How about Chip Welch? Well, at least his death closes one chapter."

Alex sighed. "Apparently, there were rumors among the prison population that Chip was a child molester besides being a stalker and murderer. That he raped little girls."

Chase shivered. "Even I know that child molesters earn a quick trip to hell in the prison system. Pretty clever, getting to him through his digestive system. Poisoning. Hard trail to follow. A lot of people probably had access to his meal."

"The whole investigation is a mess anyway. They haven't found Buddy's body yet." The intensive search for headless Buddy would continue. However, everyone would be spared the ugliness of a murder trial.

Once in Santa Monica, Chase took the Lincoln Boulevard exit and continued north. On Arizona Street, she turned east. She smiled. "I have a feeling my house is going to surprise you as much as the car," she said.

The wrought iron gate swung open. In the paved courtyard, a stone spring bubbled. The yard was a mass of flowers, bushes and vines. "We used to take care of it ourselves, but Wendy can't now and I'm too busy. We have a crew of cute lesbian helpers. The estate is inherited. You don't just buy places like this anymore unless you own a country laden with oil wells or invent a microchip."

The house was moderate by mansion standards. Its appeal was vintage California, a Mediterranean style fantasy with towers, turrets, multi-paned windows and creamy stucco walls. Alex inhaled appreciatively. "This is lovely."

"No kidding. Paradise. Climb out."

When they crossed the entryway into the Spanish-tiled vestibule, Wendy zipped over on a motorized wheelchair. Alex felt a sudden jolt of recognition. She had never been a *Lena: Amazon Queen* groupie, but some of her self-defense students had worshipped Lena, whose ranch girl looks and spunky grin had contrasted with her exotic alternate world Amazon persona.

"The venerable Alexis Pope," Wendy said. Her speech was slurred and her head drooped slightly. Her gaze was intense yet amused. She still radiated grit and humor. "Chase had a lot to say about you."

"I hope some of it was good."

"Let Alex get past the front door, honey," Chase piped up. "We can harass her over cocktails."

AFTER SHE HAD freshened up, Alex met up with Chase and Wendy on a screened porch set up with an elaborate appetizer buffet. Wendy openly scrutinized her as she entered. "Chase was right. You're a foxy lady. Have some *insalata caprese*. The heirloom tomatoes and purple basil are from our garden. The mozzarella is made in Malibu."

"Do you want anything?" Chase asked Wendy.

"Too much of an ordeal to eat. I'll wait until dinner. I'm not hungry, anyway." She grimaced at Alex. "I have to watch dysphagia, swallowing problems. Besides, I'm not burning the calories I used to." Wendy looked pointedly at Alex. "I used to eat like a horse. But I was extremely active in my *Lena* days."

Alex loaded a plate with the *insalata*, some sliced salami and a hunk of baguette. "Thanks for letting me stay."

"Hotels are for strangers," Wendy said. "This is your home. You have your own entrance and we'll give you the code for the gate."

"Thank you," Alex said with heartfelt gratitude. She was touched by the effort her new friends were making. She accepted a glass of red wine from Chase. She grinned, noticing the label on the bottle. "Erica Strong Vineyards 2008 Syrah."

Chase smiled ruefully. "I couldn't help myself."

"Chase is a little jealous concerning you and Erica Strong, I think," Wendy said.

Chase reddened. "Wendy!"

Wendy shrugged. "Ignore us. Old married couple behavior. Inappropriate teasing."

A young woman with green-tinged hair stood at the doorway leading from the main house. "Dinner in an hour?"

"I hope you like steak," Wendy said to Alex. "I was raised on a cattle ranch in North Dakota. My childhood was all about beef, rodeo, 4-H and the Nebraska Cornhuskers. I learned to shoot and fish. I was a Dairy Princess. We are not vegetarians."

"I'll eat anything." Alex held out her wine glass for Chase to refill.

A Johnny Cash song rang out from a cell phone lying on a tray attached to Wendy's wheelchair. "Excuse me, it's rude, but it might be important news about my latest venture." She flipped open her phone and read the text message. Her expression darkened. She snapped the phone shut. "It's nothing," she said.

Alex glanced back and forth at the two women. The text message *was* something, but apparently it wasn't going to be discussed. "Your latest venture?" she asked. "Chase mentioned you were starting a new project."

Wendy's face lit up. "I've always wanted to do this, even when I was acting. I never thought..." Her voice trailed off for a moment. "Fate and all that. My body is erratic at best, but my mind is still an explosion of ideas. Chase, show her the promo materials."

Chase left the room and returned with an armful of flyers and posters.

"My goodness," Alex commented. She flipped through a sales catalogue of salacious garments and kinky accessories. Her cheeks flushed.

"How do you like the garter belts?" Wendy asked.

"It goes well with the whip and the stilettos," Alex replied.

"Hot and racy outfits for women designed by women. Leather and fur and black lace," Wendy said.

Alex remembered Lena's woman warrior ensembles. These duds, however, made Lena look like a Catholic schoolgirl.

"Yes," Wendy said, as if reading Alex's mind. "Some of the designs are based on my warrior stuff, but way more outrageous."

"It's cutting edge outrageous," Chase added. "Lena meets Victoria's Secret, then another leap into sexual ambiguity and challenges to the status quo."

"You sound like a marketing maniac," Wendy said. "I love it." She sighed. "Lena was a hot chick, wasn't she? I still have fan websites. They're still debating my sexuality — my character's sexuality I mean. I go to sci-fi conventions and mega-malls and fantasy bookstores. Wheelchair and all. Good education for people. I'm still Lena. I'm still Wendy. Only now with MS."

Wendy gestured at a large poster. "My new line is premiering Tuesday night. We've been preparing for months. LenaWear will be a fashion sensation. You can stay after your reshoots and be my guest at the show. It's going to be spectacular."

"I'll have to check my schedule." Alex knew she had very little on her schedule these days. The last thing on earth she could imagine enjoying, however, was a fashion show. An exuberant cousin Jeffrey voice materialized in her brain, crowing with euphoric delight. Besides, she *was* trying to be more open-minded and less cynical.

"The theme is women warriors and goddesses," Wendy said passionately. "Cross that with a defiance of boring conventionality and restrictive women's roles as good girls. Supergirl as an S&M lesbian. Why not? It's all play."

"How about Wonder Woman?" Alex asked.

"Don't get Wendy started on Wonder Woman," Chase chimed in.

"Lynda Carter is my spiritual godmother," Wendy said. "She's invited to the fashion show."

"No way," Alex said. Her heart thumped.

"You mentioned Wonder Woman up in Sonoma," Chase said, taking in Alex's reaction.

"She was my secret savior. I had a secret room next to my bedroom as a teenager. Posters, comics, you name it. An outfit." Alex smiled proudly. "It's a major collectors' item."

"You're perfect," Wendy exclaimed. "Can you get the outfit?"

Alex blinked.

"Be in my show," Wendy said.

"Do what?" Alex stuttered.

"You'll come in as Diana Prince, do that whirl she did on the show and transform into Wonder Woman. I'll alert my special effects dude. Oh, this is great. I hope we can pull it off."

"Wendy," Chase said, looking nervous and apologetic. "You're overwhelming her."

"It's okay," Alex said. She was wrestling with competing sub-personalities, the show-off and the recluse. The inner Jeffrey voice was doing cartwheels. Alex Pope in a fashion show. Unreal.

"This is so amazing," Wendy said. "No pressure, but I was looking for something more dramatic to open the show. If Lynda Carter shows up, I'll have her adopt you."

Chase sighed. "Wendy is the most stubborn woman on earth."

"It will keep me alive," Wendy replied.

"I *know*, honey," Chase said.

Wendy looked pointedly again at Alex. "Don't make me pull the guilt card."

"Okay," Alex blurted out. "I'll have to make a phone call."

"MOM? ARLENE?"

"Honey, it's been some time since I asked you to call me Mom. Calling me Mom and Arlene simultaneously is a sign you're conflicted about our growing attachment as mother and daughter. It sounds like a comic strip character. *Momarlene*."

Alex was in a guest bedroom after dinner, ear attached to her cell phone. When she was nine, her parents had asked Alex to call them Arthur and Arlene. She'd done this for her childhood and most of her adult life until her parents announced a leap into the world of popular culture and everyday intimacy. They were cooking and doing yoga and trying to watch the Yankees, although baseball wasn't going over so well. Most unsettling, they were becoming overtly affectionate.

"Let's make a deal," Alex said. "Let me call you Arlene, then we can say *I love you* right to each other."

Arlene sighed. "Negotiations with my grown child. What do I expect? It's human nature to resist change, especially in your aging parents. I know this. I'm an iconic advice columnist."

"Who only recently started to apply the advice to her own life."

"Don't berate me, Alex."

"Truce? I do love you."

"I know. Same here."

"I need a favor," Alex said.

"What would that be?" Arlene asked.

"I need my Wonder Woman outfit shipped to Los Angeles immediately."

"The last time you wore that costume, you were almost killed. You made me promise to hide it."

"I'm going to headline a fashion show for a new line of women's wear. A favor for a friend." It might be best to avoid a description of the new label.

"This wouldn't be that new sexy LenaWear, would it?"

"Mom, how do you know about that?"

"Now it's Mom?"

"Okay, so I'm conflicted. How do you know about LenaWear?"

"I work for a magazine that caters to women at the height of their careers and accomplishments. They get younger every year and I'm probably going to get booted out any time now for a younger version of myself. How could I not know about LenaWear?"

"Lynda Carter might be at the show."

A sigh. "I was jealous of her, you know."

Alex's stomach lurched. The last thing she wanted to debate was ancient history maternal jealousy. It was too complicated how the past and present lived in one reality, like insoluble pebbles in a rushing stream. "Will you send it?"

"Of course."

"Overnight shipping arriving on a Sunday, it'll cost a fortune. I'll send you the money."

"Of course you won't. No money."

Alex cleared her throat. "Is everything else okay with you and Pop?"

Arlene laughed. "He's quite taken with being called Pop. We're preparing for the Dutchess County Fair in August."

"What? Let me guess. Pop is doing landscapes on velvet and you're giving psychic readings."

"Passive-aggressive humor, Alex."

"Sorry."

"Actually, your father is entering a pie-baking contest and I'm exhibiting a prize chicken."

Alex had to practically gag to prevent an acerbic comment. "Chicken?" she squeaked.

"I told you, honey. I think you're unconsciously forgetting details of our lives that contradict your image of us. I'm raising a few backyard chickens. Egg layers. Some unusual breeds, but I don't suppose you want to listen to a lecture on chickens."

"Baby steps," Alex replied. "Maybe next time."

"I'll email you some pictures of my girls." Arlene chuckled. "Honey, I appreciate you. I know this is hard, how we've changed."

"Good night, *Momarlene*."

Chapter Fourteen

ALEX WOKE UP early the next morning. The girl with the green-tinged hair, whose name was Joelle, brought her breakfast in the sunroom. Fresh fruit, blueberry muffins, scrambled eggs and coffee. Light streamed through the glass. In the abundant gardens, a cute lesbian caretaker raked leaves with broad, graceful swipes. Add a few animated songbirds, butterflies and a Randy Newman soundtrack and it could have been a Pixar movie.

"Chase had to go to the studio for an emergency meeting," Joelle informed her. "She won't be home until late."

"She works hard," Alex said.

"Too hard." Joelle shook her head with fond consternation. "She's a cool lady, but she needs a chill pill."

"I noticed." Alex glanced around. "Wendy?"

"Meditating upstairs until the rehearsal." Joelle waved out the window at one of the gardeners, who blew a kiss in her direction. "That's Rory. My wife."

"She looks nice."

"She's awesome," Joelle replied with youthful enthusiasm. "More cantaloupe?"

"Full." Alex patted her stomach. She'd woken up hungry and had consumed most of the breakfast.

"Have plans for the morning?" Joelle asked. "There's a rental car with GPS navigation outside for you to use."

"I was thinking of going to a gallery called Nomad. My father's good friend owns it. He asked me to stop by if I had time."

"Your father's an artist?"

"I guess you could say so." She decided to avoid discussion of her father's stature in the art world.

"Are you an artist?"

"No." Alex hesitated. "I teach classes. Cardio-kickboxing with a self-defense twist."

"Way cool. It's like the rage around here." Joelle, who looked to be about twenty, smiled appreciatively, casually studying Alex's physique. "I thought you worked out."

Alex shrugged modestly. "I try." She reflected on the sexy intimations emanating from Joelle. It might be best to put even innocent flirtations on hold during this visit. Why complicate matters?

"I'm preparing a late dinner for after the rehearsal," Joelle said. "What would you like?"

"Tater tot hot dish?"

Joelle laughed. "You betcha. I'll have to get the Campbell's cream of mushroom soup. How did you know I was from Minnesota?"

"The accent. I have friends. I was kidding about the casserole."

"We call it hot dish in Minnesota." Joelle's expression was indicating deep flirtation. "I'll make you any kind of hot dish you want."

"I was kidding," Alex said. "Anything is fine."

Alex didn't go to any galleries. She went to the ocean. She walked along the promenade, from Santa Monica to Venice and back, reveling in the energy of the roller bladers, bikers and strollers. She and Stacy had taken a trip to Santa Monica in the first year of their marriage. They'd stayed in a luxury suite at Shutters on the Beach. Nothing but the best, Stacy always insisted. Alex was already in the habit of protesting the extravagance after a single year of matrimony, as her existence rigidified into living luxuriously and making fun of the indulgence.

She walked to the end of the Santa Monica pier and inhaled the fishy smell of the ocean, feeling deliciously lonely and simultaneously cleansed of pretensions. Back at the tacky concessions area, she bought a chili cheese dog and ate the dripping mess under the watchful eyes of a gang of intent sea gulls while speakers blared eighties pop music.

Something was different in her inner world lately. It felt a bit like falling in love, only she had no one to feel it for.

EARLY THAT AFTERNOON, with considerable expense, Alex's costume arrived via overnight courier. Alex and Wendy were transported to the fashion show rehearsal by a burly, tattooed woman with the unlikely name of Taffy, in a van outfitted for wheelchair accessibility. The guard at the gates of Paramount Studios directed them to the New York City back lot. Taffy helped Wendy from the van and into her wheelchair with genial strength.

The lot was a re-creation of landmark locations in Manhattan. Alex felt a surge of nostalgia for her former East Coast life, as she scanned Times Square, Rockefeller Plaza and Central Park, or at least their fabricated mock-ups, attractions with no substance behind their painted facades.

"Is this fantastic or what? They filmed *Batman Returns* here. This was Gotham City," Taffy said.

"Taffy is an under-employed film historian with a doctorate from UCLA," Wendy informed Alex. "If you have any movie trivia questions, ask her."

They were greeted by one of the coordinators, an effeminate man who looked like he could be named Taffy, but was called Rocky. With the event scheduled for Tuesday night, Rocky was panicking regarding the last-minute change in the show opener — in the form of Alex as Wonder Woman. They proceeded to the dressing room, with Rocky expounding on the headaches Alex was causing. He continued his commentary until Alex slipped into her outfit and stepped out to be inspected.

"Oh my lord," Rocky commented. "She's fabulous. She looks like Lynda Carter's daughter."

"I told you," Wendy said.

Several of the models, skinny women with strange hair, also stopped to stare.

"Look at those biceps," one of them said.

Alex flexed both impressive biceps, adopting a feminized Charles Atlas pose. A round of catcalls and whistles ensued.

The appreciation fest was interrupted by an imposing middle-aged man in carpenter pants and suspenders, who looked like a Rocky, but was named Leslie. He was introduced as the special-effects master. "It's a good thing I'm a genius," he announced, taking in Alex and her antics. "I'll make this work. She's worth it."

The rehearsal went blessedly well, despite outbursts and stagy tantrums, all apparently routine in the fashion show environment. Alex had never seen more cowhide, fur, whips and stiletto heels in one place. Overt public sexuality was draining. She was exhausted by the time things wrapped up.

Although Wendy held up through most of it, her speech slurred badly and her body trembled as things wound down. She, however, had remained the calmest throughout and was just as composed when Taffy guided her into the van.

Back home, they were greeted by green-haired Joelle, who led them to a late supper in the dining room. Chase, she informed them, had arrived an hour earlier and gone to bed.

"Her secret is sleep," Wendy said. "If she sleeps six hours, she feels she can do anything. Whatever works." She shrugged at Alex. "MS is a doozie as far as knowing what your body needs. I had the relapsing kind for a lot of years. I had little spells, they would go away. Didn't matter. Now I've moved into the progressive form and that's a bummer. Take some of that mushroom pâté, it's Joelle's specialty."

Joelle helped Wendy to eat some of the pâté on a piece of soft bread. "Taffy said you didn't eat during the rehearsals. That's not good," she admonished Wendy.

Wendy looked repentant. "I used to get away with that. I'm

pretty good at staying in the moment, except at these opening prep things. Then I insist on trying to be my old self. Not smart. The progressive type MS is a devil, tempting a person to say, 'So what?'" She smiled philosophically. "But that's pretty much temptation in a nutshell, isn't it?"

"No kidding." Alex helped herself to another round of mushroom pâté on a pita cracker. It really was outstanding. She didn't adore rosemary, but it was perfect in this pâté.

"I just pray I don't have the most aggressive version of this damned disease. It's not pretty. But it's rare." Wendy's cell phone chimed. "Can you look?" she asked Joelle.

Joelle checked the phone. Her face blanched. "Oh shit."

"It's happening again," Wendy said.

"You got one yesterday," Alex said. "When we were on the porch."

They both glanced at Alex with disturbed expressions.

"Show her," Wendy said to Joelle.

Joelle handed the Nokia to Alex.

UR a bad gurlll. Always a sick gurlll in your spirit and bad ways. U will go to hell. And your accomplices, too. You do bad things, you did bad things in the past. UR a very bad gurll. Watch out.

The text message was from a free Hotmail account. Hard to trace.

"I've changed all my accounts and it was fine after Chip Welch died," Wendy said. "I thought it was over. I thought the monster was eliminated."

"Have you reported this to the police?"

"No police. No publicity." Wendy shivered.

Alex's trusty and annoying instinct bells went off. In addition to the blatant ugliness of the message itself, there was the odd timing of the warning and Alex's arrival in L.A.

"Nothing comes of it," Wendy said. She didn't look convinced and neither did Joelle, who was stirring gazpacho with studied obliviousness.

Chapter Fifteen

EARLY MONDAY MORNING, Taffy drove Alex to the set for her reshoots of *On A Silver Platter*. Wendy had suffered a setback in the night and was spending the day in bed, managing final plans for the fashion opening via conference calls. Taffy pulled up to the front door in a vintage limousine, jumped out of the car and held the back door open for Alex.

"Oh, come on." Alex climbed into the front passenger seat, ignoring the open back door.

Taffy slammed the door shut. "If I got the chance to be a diva, no way I'd pass it up." She swooned, wiped at her furrowed brow and did a Gloria Swanson sashay to the driver's seat, an interesting and impressive sight, given her tattooed arms and overall truck driver bulk. "I'm ready for my scene, Mister DeMille," she enunciated with proud and weary grandeur, then glanced expectantly at Alex.

Alex grinned. "Even I know *Sunset Boulevard*."

"But did you *love* it? I *love* it. Maybe more than *Citizen Kane*, but less than *Wizard of Oz*."

"Taffy, I don't come close to you on the movies passion meter."

"It's a thing," Taffy admitted. "How do you like the jalopy? It's on lease for the fashion show opening. A 1960 Rolls Royce Phantom V, such a sweet thing. Take a whiff. What do you smell?"

"Soft, buttered cow hide," Alex said. "Wood polish. Privilege." Alex swooned. "Take me to the set, my darling Taffy," she enunciated with jaded majesty.

"Now you're in the spirit," Taffy said enthusiastically.

"That's kind of scary," Alex replied.

Taffy took the indirect route to Griffith Park, avoiding the freeways, navigating city streets, conducting a monologue on the history of Los Angeles and the film industry. Alex pretended to listen, but she was mentally reviewing the script notes Chase had given her the previous day. She was confused. Was that surprising? Why would Jerome's opus have grown coherent, even in the re-filming? Her preoccupations were interrupted as they entered Griffith Park, passing the Greek Theatre and climbing the winding route upwards through the enormous, hilly sanctuary.

By now, Taffy was enraptured. She recited a litany of movies shot in the park, ending with a triumphant: "*Rebel Without A Cause*. Oh my God, I feel like a part of the *Bible*, this is so iconic."

Alex's heart thumped, but not from movie worship or biblical passion. As they pulled into the parking lot, she could see the crew setting up in the front of the towering observatory. No one acknowledged her at first. This was a crew of locals who didn't know who she was. Leave it to Taffy to take charge. "Jill," Taffy called to a pompous-looking woman wearing a many-pocketed work vest, "This is Alex Pope, Salome's double. This is Jill Cranston, the new stunts coordinator."

The stern-looking woman glared at Alex. "The one they dragged all the way from Sonoma?"

"She's the one."

Jill squinted off into the distance with barely suppressed annoyance. "We have a lot of trained stunt women here in town."

So much for warm receptions. Jill directed them to a group of trailers in the parking lot.

The first friendly greeting came from Norman, who barked and wagged his tail ferociously as soon as he caught sight of Alex. Salome's terrier was tethered outside one of the trailers, in the company of his attendant. The barking brought Salome outside. She flew down the rickety stairs and threw herself into Alex's arms. Jerome followed on her heels. He smiled stiffly, watching the embrace. Alex glanced at him with obvious amusement, although she tried to suppress it.

"Screw you." Jerome tugged at his costume. He resembled a Star Trek groupie with unusually bad taste. "This is what I get for buckling under pressure." He gestured to another trailer. "Costume and make-up for you. Get going. We have the Observatory for one day and a lot of strings were pulled to get it."

After he'd marched away, Salome hugged her again with even more enthusiasm. "I'm so glad to see you." Her usual serenity seemed shaken. "I'm having nightmares about Buddy. At least that awful creep who killed him is gone. Now maybe things can go back to normal."

Alex didn't think it was wise to reveal the latest emails to Wendy. Not to mention her latest musings on the existence of normal. She hooked her arm into Salome's. "Let's get dressed."

Alex allowed the wardrobe woman to fuss over her, feeling a rise in anticipation. A pang of grief ran though her, too. She was imagining how Buddy would have instructed her to get through the confusions of the upcoming scene. Poor Buddy. He had not only been wiped off the face of the earth, but he'd been written out of the final scenes of the script as well, according to the latest pages.

Once she emerged in costume, Alex spied the Sloans lingering by an observation platform. It was a relatively smog free day and the whole of Los Angeles spread out before them. All three Sloans were staring at the venerable Hollywood sign perched on a distant hill.

Shirley and Ken walked up, with Marlon lagging behind. "We're so glad you could make it," Shirley said, hugging her. Ken took his turn, with a great bear hug. By now, Marlon had shuffled up. He gave her a surly, amiable tap on the shoulder. "Hi, lady."

Ken waved at the panoramic landscape. "See the Hollywood sign? A young actress threw herself off the 'H' in 1932."

"That's a promising welcome," Alex said.

Ken smirked. "Inappropriate gallows humor."

Before they could go on, Jerome arrived, red-faced. "I don't have much patience today. I don't want to get in trouble with my anger, so let's just go." He marched away stiffly.

"Touchy little whippersnapper," Ken remarked with studied calm. "Unusually bad costume."

Shirley lowered her voice to a deep, melodramatic stage whisper. "Bug up his butt. Chase Stuyvesant did some rewriting. Have your read your script pages?"

Alex nodded. No words were necessary. The new stuff sucked like the old stuff had.

"Come on, people," Jerome roared from the set. "Marlon, get these people organized. Where's your mind, man?"

Ken turned to his son. "I thought you were going to stand up to him."

Marlon gulped, Adam's apple bobbing. "Yeah. I will." He took off like a puppy, tail between his legs.

"I think we raised him too passively," Ken commented.

"Jerome is intimidating," Shirley said. "They'll work it out."

When the cast was lined up, Jerome shook the script pages at them. "I am now a renegade alien who has decided to side with the humans after the death of the revered leader. Buddy's character has been killed prematurely and I'm the new focal point. I fall in love with Salome and save the earth people." He glanced around at the crestfallen faces at the mention of Buddy. "On with the show and all that bullshit. Buddy wanted it that way."

At the mention of Buddy, Marlon emitted a strangled gulp. Jerome glared at him. "Don't wimp out on me, dude. You *have* to direct this scene. I can't act and direct at the same time." He gestured at Alex. "You got a fighting dance in mind?"

"I have." In fact, she'd spent half the night obsessing over it.

"Then, let's do it."

The cast took their places. Marlon conferred with the director of photography and the camera people. He came back to the actors, looking terrified. "It's a long take with two cameras, everything in motion, no stopping."

From his place on the set, Jerome grimaced pessimistically. "Do it, Marlon."

Everyone stepped up to his or her marks. Alex's heart thumped. *Use your fear to channel strength.* Unbidden, the image of Buddy's defiant leer frozen on his severed head leaped into her imagination. *Use it. Use it.*

"Take one."

"Action!" Marlon called.

Alex twirled and leaped, kicked and chopped. She went over the top for Buddy, while Ken and Shirley watched against the backdrop of the Observatory, the domed access to the heavens. She was thinking about Buddy and feeling his loss. When Jerome entered, holding a hatchet, she was truly horrified. He really did look peculiar and deranged. Despite her veil, she projected her revulsion through her body language. She cowered, but the cowering was a ploy, a defensive preparation, like the coiling of a tight spring before it unleashes.

Jerome crossed the set, doing something like a Quasimodo limp. As he approached Ken and Shirley, they cringed, at first with studied fear, like the professionals they were. Jerome mugged ferocious valor. He snarled and grunted.

Ken Sloan fell apart. "Hah, hah, hah!" The venerable, disciplined icon doubled over, laughing uncontrollably.

Jerome halted, ax above his head.

"Cut!" Marlon said.

"I'm humiliated," Ken said. "I don't know what came over me." He wiped his brow. "I think it was the next moment." He bent over a low wall and pulled out two severed heads. Someone in the crowd gasped. Alex's stomach lurched. The heads of the king and queen of the aliens were too much like Buddy's head on that terrible day. It was too terrible and too funny. Not to Jerome.

"I can't believe this. Get ready for take two."

"Action," Marlon called, after they had set up again.

Although his lips were blue and his eyes bugged out with effort, Ken maintained a royal dignity as Jerome squiggled over.

This time Shirley snorted, choked, then broke out laughing until tears ran down her face.

"Unbelievable," Jerome raged.

Ken and Shirley looked just as shocked as Jerome. If possible, Marlon looked even more stunned. He was twitching. "Let's try again," he said.

"Take three!"

Marlon surged forward as Alex danced. In an act of supreme clumsiness, he knocked over one of the camerapersons, who yelped in dismay, clutching his camera protectively away from the ground.

"Hah, hah, hah!" Ken and Shirley laughed in hysterical unison.

Marlon looked like he might have a stroke. Jerome marched up to him and thrust his nose nearly into Marlon's mouth, like a sadistic drill sergeant confronting a quivering recruit who'd peed in his pants. "Loser. Pussy. You're fired. I can't take you anymore. Get out of my sight."

"Wait a minute," Ken said gruffly.

"Keep out of this," Jerome said.

"He's not at fault," Shirley persisted. "We are."

Jerome backed up, still clinging to his hatchet. He waved Salome away as she approached him. "Keep out of this, Salome."

"I'm sorry," Marlon squealed. "Out of respect for Buddy, let's move on and make the movie."

"Respect?" Jerome laughed. "Is that how you felt about Buddy? Was Buddy in your pants? If he wasn't, you wanted him to be. You *are* a pussy."

Marlon blinked, backing up as though he'd been slapped.

"How mean," Shirley said with quiet anger. She glanced at her son with concern.

Marlon continued to back up. He tripped over an electrical cord and fell backwards, landing on his ass. He scrambled up, dusting at his pants. "That's it. I quit." He turned and scurried away.

Chapter Sixteen

EVERYONE SERVED THEMSELVES from the food tables at lunchtime, but there was little conversation. Halfway through the desultory lunch, Chase arrived.

"Naturally," Jerome said, watching her approach. "My cousin the watchdog has been summoned."

Alex felt warmth mingled with defiance. Really, Chase sparked more conflicting feelings than anyone Alex could recall in recent times. Maybe ever.

When she arrived at their table, Chase took in the expectant faces. "Hello, everyone."

"Just in the neighborhood?" Jerome asked.

"Of course not," Chase answered.

Jerome glanced around the set. "I wonder who the tattletale was this time. Probably lame-assed Marlon as he drove down the hill like a pussy on wheels." He glared at Ken and Shirley, who refused to respond.

Chase handed out a stack of script sheets. "I rewrote your rewrites of my rewrites."

"Screw you," Jerome said.

Chase waited while everyone scanned the sheets. "I'd like to have the scene shot this way in an hour."

"Who the fuck will be directing?" Jerome's face lit up. "You do it."

Chase's jaw dropped. "No."

"You went to film school."

"Just to learn the business."

"I saw that short you did for Professor Newsome."

"Oh, no!" Chase cried. "How on earth did you get hold of that?"

"Your mother found a DVD." He turned to Alex. "My aunt, Chase's mother, thinks Chase is brilliant and repressed. She thinks Chase is too much like her father. She thinks Chase needs to express her creative potential. She thinks Chase is a goddamned Lina Wertmuller."

"Enough," Chase said, looking mortified.

"Her master's project was a documentary about sexuality in insects."

Chase reddened. "It was a fluke."

Jerome turned to Salome. "You saw it."

"It was great," Salome said. "I learned to admire the cockroach."

"Oh my God, did you show it to everyone on the planet?" Chase said to Jerome.

Jerome grinned. "At least I didn't put it on YouTube." He rustled the new script sheets. "Okay, let's go over this." He pointed to a chair. "Ms. Wertmuller, what's your vision?"

ALEX WAS RETURNING from the portable toilets when Chase approached her.

"Ready for your big moment?" Chase asked.

"More than before," Alex said. She hesitated. "You made some interesting changes."

Chase blushed. "Desperation. Emergency triage."

"I agree with your mother. Be creative and free."

Chase's blush deepened. "I told you. You remind me of my mother."

"I remember. That's why I said it."

"My father is a giant among men. My mother loves his stability, even while she complains that he's boring. If he's boring, I'm proud to be boring."

"You're not boring," Alex said. Her heart was beating unnecessarily quickly.

"We'd better get going," Chase said. "I hate holding anything up."

"Of course you do," Alex said.

Chase stared at her. "No complications, okay?"

"I wasn't..."

"Never mind." Chase marched away.

WHILE THE CAST waited, Chase spent a good half hour conferring with the director of photography, the lighting crew and the set people. Even from a distance, they all looked like prisoners released on parole. Chase looked regal and exhilarated.

"She's a good-looking gal when she's not so grim," Ken commented.

"I like her vibes," Shirley said. "I intuit her basic goodness."

Ken laughed. "My wife is getting more like Shirley MacLaine every day. Kooky."

"I'm probably not supposed to say this," Salome added. "Jerome pretends to hate Chase, but he's actually crazy about her."

After what seemed like an eternity, they were ready to shoot.

"Action," Chase called.

Alex as Salome danced before the tribunal. This time, when Jerome entered with his hatchet, doing his Quasimodo send-up, he exuded a sympathetic pathos. Alex grieved, she grew angry and defiant, then she acknowledged her love for the renegade alien who had given up all for her. She was infused with cosmic transcendence and hope. When he chopped off the heads of his former comrades, she dropped to the ground, sobbing.

"Cut," Chase called. She approached Alex.

"Are you all right?" Chase asked, bending down on one knee.

"Did I ruin the take?" Alex asked. "It was at the end, you could edit it out."

"It was lovely," Chase said. "The end needed your improvisational closure. Lesson learned. I shouldn't try to control everything. That's why Jerome will eventually be a genius director. He's spontaneous."

"Or you," Alex said with conviction. "You could be just as good."

Chase shrugged. "This was the exception. I prefer my creative wildness in my associates and close ones." She stood and held out a hand.

Alex accepted Chase's help although she was more than capable of getting off the ground in a flying leap. She was aware of the rest of the cast watching. Who cared? Let them gossip. Classic case of actor getting hooked on director. Transference, her mother would say.

Nevertheless, Alex felt mildly guilty that night when they'd joined Wendy for a late supper. She and Chase recounted the day, omitting any flirtation. When they were almost finished, Alex's cell rang.

"Sorry, I need to take this. It's my house sitter. Something may be wrong."

Alex went out into the hall. When she returned, Chase and Wendy looked at her expectantly. "Do you remember Paula Coleman?" she asked.

"The security guard who used to be a hot shot basketball star," Chase said. "Seems secretive. Hiding something. Too nice."

"My housemates Wheatie and Kallinda went out of town. There was no one to watch my cat Henry. Paula volunteered. Insisted, actually. I think she's got a Good Samaritan complex."

Alex took her seat. "She was curious about how things were going. I guess she feels like a part of the project. She asked a lot of questions."

"Doesn't seem like she has much of a life, compared to her previous celebrity," Chase commented.

"It's a trap," Wendy added. "I had to climb down the celebrity ladder myself after Lena. I still crave admiration and glory. It's in my blood. With all the crap that happened to me, I had to find another way. Something may give Paula a kick in the pants." She turned to Alex. "You understand being kicked in the pants."

"On many levels and in too many circumstances." Alex stood. "Think I'll go to bed. Long day."

As she left the room, she was aware of a dense and complicated vibe. From Wendy and Chase? Or was it her own inner demons? Didn't matter. She was leaving very shortly. The weird vibes could die a natural death back home in Sonoma.

She was climbing the stairs when her cell rang again. "Hi, Salome, what's up?"

"You evasive thing! I heard about your guest appearance at the LenaWear show."

"That's top secret."

"Top secrets in Hollywood are created in order to be leaked. I can't wait to see you. You're my heroine, anyway."

Alex sighed. "I suppose the whole world is coming."

"Practically. Wendy is majorly respected. Everyone is pulling for her. I myself might have to purchase a leather thong or two. Say, listen."

"Yes?"

"I just started getting some horrible emails."

"Oh, no."

"They mention Buddy. It's strange, because his stalker is dead."

"Why would you be getting emails about Buddy?"

The line remained silent for a moment. "I told you. He was like part of the family."

"Then, what's the connection? And why are you telling me this? Why aren't you going to the police?"

"They mention you, too, Alex. I thought you might want some time to check it out."

All of this did not make for a restful sleep. Alex tossed and turned, dreaming her usual nightmares about falling.

Chapter Seventeen

AMERICA WAS EAGER to adore LenaWear. Wendy's fashion line shamelessly invoked a popular television show that had achieved cult status in syndication. The designs embodied sadomasochism infused with ambiguous sexuality, with enough laundering to get a tantalizing C-minus on the Puritanism report card.

Not everyone agreed, however. Outside the gates of Paramount Studio, protesters shouted indignities at the arriving guests. Evangelical right-wingers and anti-pornography feminists, bonded in outrage over public displays of overt and kinky eroticism, waved threatening placards. Their presence only boosted media coverage and publicity buzz.

Just before the arched entry, Taffy squealed on the brakes as a scarecrow-like woman with wild straw hair lurched in front of the leased Rolls. A security guard dragged her away, but not before she had managed to rap on the hood of the limo with a wooden cross. Alex and Chase sat in the back seat, unable to hear the woman's words, but observing her twisted mouth spewing at them. Wendy had gone to the studio many hours before, leaving them to make a grand entry.

"What's she saying?" Alex asked, remembering Chase could read lips.

"Not worth repeating," Chase replied. "Too ugly."

They pulled up to the red carpet to more ranting, this time wildly enthusiastic. Alex took a deep breath and climbed from the back seat, allowing Taffy to take her elbow. She was disguised as Diane Prince. According to the master plan, Alex would arrive in character. Chase led her up the carpet to curious stares and shouted questions. She stayed mysteriously silent, as she was hustled to the green room. In what seemed like an eternity, she waited for her entry to open the show. She meditated. She invoked cheesy silent pep talks.

Fifteen minutes before entry, she was called to backstage. Leslie, the special effects dude, reviewed the magic he would perform and, sensing her near panic, gave her an actual cheesy pep talk filled with the platitudes of a seasoned vet. She wasn't really listening to the words, but was calmed by his soothing voice. She remembered her black belt test. In one portion of the grueling two-day event, she'd been blindfolded and attacked by three men from the dojo. She could do this.

Alex came through the curtains to a burst of wild applause. The lights were blinding. She couldn't see the audience clearly, but she felt the currents. Her heart thudded as she reviewed her transformation. She was ready. The universe was ready.

She twirled as the audience screamed; smoke rose from vents and the escapable binds of her Diana Prince disguise released. She was Wonder Woman, twirling her lasso, invulnerable to the frailties of mortals, willing to defy any who questioned that immortality. Her being glowed. She *was* Wonder Woman.

Alex strutted the runway, in her glory, feeling like she was everything she ever wanted to be. The audience admiration was frenzied and self-serving, but she didn't care. *Talk about live for the moment.* She was having one of those precious peak experiences her mother was so passionate about extolling. She had always wanted to be a heroine. For this brief moment, she was superhuman, above all the nitpicking and insecurities of real life. She left the spotlight reluctantly, still aware of the catcalls and handclapping at her back.

The rest of the show was a daze for her. The models with strange hair floated in and out of the staging area to the delight of the crowd, primed by Alex's lead-in. Backstage, Wendy wheeled through the chaos, shouting directions. The mood was drunkenly euphoric yet controlled, like an ancient harvest ritual. The show ended with a great cry for Alex. She came out to a standing ovation, nearly sending her over the top, her heart was so full.

The reception did nothing to dampen Alex's rapture. The New York back lot was a mythic city of dark promise, complete with shadowy lighting, an orgiastic array of foods, haunting tunes and an eerie décor. From the moment she arrived, admirers surrounded her. Ordinarily, she would have been at least marginally jaded and uncomfortable with the absurdity of it all. Tonight, she was enthralled. She waved at Chase, who raced up to her through the crowd.

"Great job," Chase said.

"I was good, wasn't I?" Alex glanced around the room, trying not to gawk at the icons of female empowerment (the pro-sex ones) mingling with fans. She spotted Martina Navratilova and Susie Bright. "Oh my God," she breathed out. "Oprah Winfrey is here."

"I thought you weren't a Hollywood groupie," Chase said, smiling.

"I'm having a moment."

She felt a tap on her shoulder. From habit, she turned quickly, adopting a defensive stance.

"Wow, you are a superhero," someone said.

Alex gasped. It was *Lynda Carter*. The real and gorgeous Lynda

Carter. Alex swooned.

"You are great," Lynda said.

Alex mumbled something like a protest combined with thank you, but the end result was an incomprehensible burble. Cameras flashed, people pushed closer. Her head began to spin.

Wendy wheeled up, accompanied by Taffy. "I see you two have met," she said.

"She looks more sexy than I did in that get-up," Lynda said. "You're not an actress, I heard. You should be."

"I couldn't," Alex sputtered. "Not talented enough."

Lynda winked at Chase and Wendy. "An innocent." She glanced at her watch. "Need to leave. I'm signing cardboard tiaras in Pasadena."

Out of nowhere, a shriek pierced the air.

The scarecrow protester with the straw hair raced up, waving a bottle filled with blood. She scrambled to Lynda Carter, intent on dousing her. Alex didn't have to calculate for long. From years of training, she leaped in front of Lynda, snatched the woman's wrist and applied a pressure point pinch. The bottle fell to the floor at the woman's feet, splotching the entire group's legs with droplets of animal blood of some sort.

"You should all be ashamed of the images of women you promote," the woman cried. "You're worse than men. You're collaborators of the worst kind." As the security guards dragged her away, she continued her rant. "Women haters! Capitalistic misogynists!"

"I get this all the time," Lynda Carter said, looking blasé. She glanced across the room. "Gotta go, kids. Pasadena beckons."

Alex and Chase watched her leave.

"That's funny," Alex said. "That kook was anti-porn. I could have sworn she was one of the evangelicals. The wooden cross threw me."

"That's because you can't read lips," Chase said.

"No big deal. Some people will claim it was a publicity stunt anyway," Wendy added.

"Was it?"

Wendy smiled slyly. "Let's enjoy the party."

Without much more negative fanfare, the celebration continued. At around midnight, Wendy wheeled up to Alex and Chase. "I'm exhausted. Been running on adrenalin up until just now."

"Let's all go home in the van together," Chase suggested. "We'll have someone deal with the limo."

They had just pulled in the driveway, when Wendy's cell phone alerted her to a text message. "Oh, no," she said.

"Not more?" Chase asked.

Wendy's face was ashen. "Worse. This is really bad."

"What?" Chase asked.

Wendy shook her head. "Let's go inside."

When they had settled in the living room, Wendy held out her phone to Alex.

"Ugly. Scary." Alex shivered.

U R very bad girls, all three of you. U will wind up like Buddy, if you don't watch out. U will suffer like you made others suffer. Bad, bad girls get hurt. Badly hurt, bad girls. Badly, badly punished.

"I think it's time for the police," Alex said.

"No police," Wendy said firmly. "Ninety-nine point nine per cent of these threats are empty air."

"I wouldn't want to be in the tiny percentage of dead people who ignored them," Alex replied.

"No police," Wendy repeated. She glanced at Chase, who shrugged.

"Let's just forget the whole thing," Wendy said. "Maybe I shouldn't have told you."

"Maybe not," Alex said, knowing the texting ugliness would haunt her. She resolved, however, to put it aside. She was leaving Hollywood the next evening in any case.

Chapter Eighteen

EARLY THE NEXT morning, Alex's cell rang. It was Felicity Strauss, Buddy's widow. "We need to talk."

Alex sighed. "Not a police matter, I hope."

"You certainly must understand the value of keeping things from the authorities. I happen to know about you and your previous adventures."

"If you're trying to persuade me to meet with you, badgering won't work."

"Meet with you? Are you in L.A.? Of course, I should have known. They must be reshooting the film. Can you come this afternoon?"

"I have a flight at eight," Alex said.

"Then you can be here at two."

"I..." Alex began.

"Here are the directions," Felicity said.

FELICITY LIVED IN the hills above West Hollywood, behind closed gates. There were no dogs in the vast front yard. Felicity let her into the house. There were no dogs, no cats, no canaries, not even a goldfish.

"I expected a menagerie," Alex said.

Felicity laughed. "I detest animals on the estate. My parents were horrified by the thought of pets. I grew up without even an ant farm or a turtle. Look, one might advocate homeless shelters. That doesn't mean letting homeless people live in one's house, does it?"

Alex nodded neutrally. In her former married life living in a suburban mansion , she'd known a lot of women like Felicity who supported worthwhile causes whose clients they'd never imagine letting into their homes. To be perfectly honest, how many victims of tragedy had she entertained in her mansion when she had one? She glanced around. The interior of the house was as antiseptic as an *Architectural Digest* feature. It wasn't an environment conducive to animals, or children for that matter. She was shown to an uncomfortable chair, facing Felicity, who did not offer refreshments.

"I'll get to the point," Felicity said. "I've been receiving troubling emails. This isn't new, believe me. For years I've gotten hate mail in many forms, from right wing groups who think I'm a radical activist attempting to wipe out all use of animal products. Buddy was getting his own version of threats. Then he was murdered by that stalker." Felicity's voice trembled dutifully. "Buddy was trying so hard."

Alex waited, aware of a submerged undercurrent of coolness in Felicity's voice. Pristine and hard-edged, like her décor. The trembling fear floated over the top, oil on water.

"He took a great liking to you," Felicity said. "I was *almost* jealous." She paused.

Alex waited. She didn't want to be playing a second-guessing game.

The necessity of hospitality seemed to strike Felicity suddenly. "Would you like a refreshment?"

Alex shook her head.

Felicity sighed. "Buddy was flawed. Everyone is flawed. He had past addictions. I *know* he hadn't really given them up. He was haunted, by his behavior and by someone or some people. When the stalker was murdered, I knew it wouldn't be over. Are you sure you wouldn't like a glass of wine or a coffee?"

"I'd like to know what you want of me," Alex said.

"I wanted to hire you, but my investigations showed you don't need the money. I don't want the police. I don't want any professional investigators. Lately, they tend to sell their stories to the tabloids. I need to know who is sending these messages. I won't offer to pay you. I will instead ask you please to help me." Like an icicle dripping in the sun, Felicity's demeanor melted. It struck Alex that Felicity really had cared for Buddy.

Alex sighed. "I can take a few days to nose around."

"Thank you."

"What can you tell me?"

Felicity sighed. "Buddy had a laptop computer. He was very protective of it. He wouldn't let me have access to it, not that I demanded that. It's missing. It was stolen in Sonoma during the location shoot. He was absolutely freaked out. I'm sure the police don't know this. I'm not sure who else did. I believe if you find it, you'll find out who's behind the harassment. Or at least Buddy's secret life."

"Do you have any intuitions?" Alex asked.

"Unfortunately, yes. Something to do with sex. Maybe male porn, maybe other variations of kinky deeds. I don't care. We were learning to accept each other's flaws. What more can you expect in a relationship? I'm sure you want the same."

The last thing Alex wanted was to ponder her requirements in a relationship. She stood. "I'll be in touch." She had the distinct feeling that Felicity was holding something back. "Anything else you want to tell me?"

Felicity squirmed. "No."

She was lying. It didn't matter. By now Alex wanted to know Buddy's secret.

WENDY AND CHASE were in the living room when she returned at 5 p.m. "Don't you have a flight?" Wendy asked.

"I cancelled it. I'm going to stick around a few days." Alex hesitated. "I can book a hotel room, starting tonight."

"No way," Wendy said. "We were just getting used to having you around." She smiled. "Let me guess. You're nosing around on issues concerning Buddy."

"Felicity Strauss asked me to help her."

Wendy and Chase exchanged looks. Wendy cleared her throat. "When I first came to Hollywood, I was a total hick from North Dakota. As I told you, I grew up on a cattle ranch. Beef cattle. My father was a good rancher but a bad businessman. It was tough, Alex. We kids got hard as nails, inside and out. When I came out here, I thought I could handle anything. I needed money. I acquired some bad habits. An acquaintance got me a job at a high-end escort service. I didn't do the escort stuff. I helped coordinate it. I knew everything. Every famous guy, all his weird requests. Some of them were really off-the-wall. Know where I'm headed?"

"Buddy was one of the clients," Alex said.

"I told you she was a whiz," Wendy said to Chase.

Chase nodded, fidgeting. "Tell her."

"I had a different last name when I grew up. I kept the name Wendy, but changed the last name when I started acting. I don't want my past exposed, if it can be helped. Not so much the sex part, although that's bad enough. I don't want my former addictions dug into. It's not good for my new business or my new life. If this is nothing, then I don't want the police involved. It's probably someone who knows how Buddy and I were connected. They're still attached for some reason."

"But how will you know if it's harmless?" Alex persisted.

"Isn't that what you're staying for? To find out? You could make a career of interfering with police matters," Wendy said. "You solved two impossible cases."

"I almost got killed doing it," Alex said.

"This time, you're just proving this is nonsense," Wendy said. "I think everyone, including Felicity, would agree that if it's more than ugly cyber-stalking, that we'll go to the police. I'd start with the Sloans. I have a hunch."

"So do I," Alex said.

Chapter Nineteen

LATE THE NEXT morning, Alex drove up the driveway to the Sloan estate. Ken and Shirley popped open the door as soon as she climbed from the car.

"Thanks for letting me come on such short notice," she said.

Ken slipped his arm around Shirley's waist. "Shirley had a dream two nights ago. You flew into our house dressed as Wonder Woman and collared us with your Lasso of Truth. We were forced to give up our secrets. How's that for a cosmic hint to see you?"

"Where's Marlon?" she asked.

"He's planting his snow peas." Ken laughed at Alex's puzzled look. "Marlon is going back to the land. He's turning our back lawn into an urban organic farm, starting with peas and kohlrabi."

"It's good for him," Shirley added. "His personality is meek. He's not cut out for the film industry."

Alex followed the Sloans across their manicured front lawn, around the side of the large Tudor house and into the backyard, which was the size of a city park. Next to the Olympic-size swimming pool stood a Tudor-style pool house.

"Marlon lives in the pool house," Shirley pointed out. "He came back after college."

"He took a class on agrarian anthropology in his senior year," Ken added. "He's been mumbling about sustainable agriculture ever since. The fight with Jerome sent him over the edge. He started all this yesterday. He already had the plans drawn up."

On the other side of the pool area, they spotted Marlon, wearing faded overalls and a tattered checkered shirt, digging beds in a large area cleared of expensive turf. He looked up, threw down his spade and removed his dirt-caked gloves.

As he approached, he appeared to be a different boy. Gone was his twitchy anticipation of disaster and shame. He looked like a simple pea farmer immersed in the natural order of bearing produce.

"Howdy," Marlon said with a vague Amish lilt. "Been expectin' ya."

Alex's intrinsic cynicism flashed. Marlon was a movie kid. He'd be good at impersonating idealistic simpletons as interpreted by Hollywood elitists. She refrained from rolling her eyes or any other gestures of contempt.

Marlon may have been sophomoric, but he wasn't stupid. He

dropped the hayseed accent. "Let's go up to the big house," he said. "They have better food and drink than I do."

THE SLOANS PROVIDED Alex with dark, rich shade-grown coffee infused with chicory and freshly baked beignets dusted with powdered sugar. Their cook was from New Orleans.

"We have a show for you," Ken said.

They sat together in an entertainment room complete with a theatre-size screen and elaborate projection equipment. The Sloans knew how to stage a confession, Hollywood style.

"Don't I get to ask the questions?" Alex asked. "I thought this was my interrogation."

"There'll be a question and answer period at the end." Ken pressed a key on his computer. A photo appeared on the screen. A young Buddy Brubech and Ken Sloan tossing basketballs into a hoop. "We both sucked at basketball. Men aren't supposed to admit that. There are a lot of things we don't admit."

He clicked to the next photo. He and Buddy were dressed to the hilt, in black tuxedos, against a background of chandeliers and gaming tables. Ken cleared his throat and turned to Marlon. "Son, this is where we start getting real."

Marlon emitted an anxious gurgle reminiscent of his former, less pastoral self. "I'm ready."

"I met Buddy in the late sixties. He was managing a restaurant at the Sands in Las Vegas. Buddy was from a small town in Indiana. He had a gift for being nice. He went to Purdue to become a dentist like his stepfather. Had a revelation and changed to hotel and restaurant management. His specialty was congeniality anyway."

Alex remembered Buddy's congeniality. In the old photos, he exuded that same charisma.

Ken clicked to another photo. He and Buddy wore flight suits of what appeared to be aluminum foil. They stood in frozen anticipation on the set of a sci-fi movie. "Blunt truth, okay? In Vegas, we had a fling. Look, I did it a few times in high school with some guys. I never thought of myself as queer. I always thought I'd get married, have a kid or two." He glanced at Shirley, who'd been quiet for the first part of the show.

"Show her the next one," she said calmly.

Ken, Shirley and Buddy sported western outfits, each with a shotgun cradled in their arms. "I grew up in a snobby Manhattan theatre family. I came out to Hollywood from New York in a burst of rebellion," Shirley said. "I met the boys on this, my first movie. I stole Ken from Buddy." She smiled. "We were cocky. Defiant of convention, yet attached to conventionality. Buddy wasn't going to wind up in a honeymoon cottage as Ken's bride. We all became friends. The agreement was no more hanky-panky among the men." Her smile faded.

Abruptly, Ken shut down the slide show. "I'm sorry, hon," he said.

"Dad?" Marlon said.

Ken stared at his wife. Shirley shook her head sadly.

"The escort service," Alex piped up. The Sloans looked at her with reprimand, as though she had violated a spoiler alert.

"A few years ago," Ken said, "Buddy and I got turned on to a discrete business that offered fantasy experiences. The office manager, a gal named Wendy, promised us complete confidentiality. You know, men aren't very smart, especially when it comes to guilty pleasures. Secrecy for all time? Nonsense. I don't know if we cared. Or cared enough. We did it anyway."

Shirley shivered. "All of this would just be creepy gossip if it wasn't for Buddy's murder. We were so relieved when the stalker was caught. I hate to admit it, but I was even relieved when the stalker was poisoned. Better to let it all rest without digging into any of this. Of course, we realized that, until the body was found, there'd still be some nosing around. But, hopefully, they'd find the corpse without time for too much probing into the past, which wouldn't have been relevant anyway." She stabbed the air with a finger in Alex's direction. "So, why are you here?"

"Why did you prepare this elaborate show?" Alex countered.

"I think we all agree that we don't want to involve the authorities," Ken said. "You know we didn't have anything to do with this. To be frank, the show was to get you on our side."

She smiled grimly at their response. She wasn't sure about the Sloans' motivations. However, it was clear that an awful lot of people didn't want the authorities to butt in just yet.

Ken turned the projector back on. Buddy had his arms around a striking Nordic-looking woman with a brilliant smile and haunted eyes. She could have been Felicity Strauss's sister. Alex sighed. Maybe the woman *was* Felicity's sister.

"Helena Jordan," Ken said. "A mediocre actress who latched onto Buddy."

Another photo switch, this time showing Buddy with an equally ravishing Latin-looking actress. "Buddy dumped Helena for Consuela Martinez. She was something else, a real dynamo. Talented, too."

"What happened to them?" Alex asked.

"Helena disappeared. We assumed she went back to wherever she came from. Consuela fell off a horse and broke her back. She recuperated, returned to acting, but I don't think her heart was in it. By this time, Buddy was Dr. Moody and in another world, success-wise. We felt sorry for Consuela, but knew she'd be okay. Consuela and Buddy remained friends, after a short and passionate break-up." Ken shut off the projector.

"Consuela is Salome D'Amico's aunt, to complicate the scenario. Freddy D'Amico is her brother-in-law, Maria—Freddy's wife—is her sister. Buddy became a part of the D'Amico family. He craved that."

"A lot of secrets," Alex commented.

"Let me put it this way, no one had much interest in digging up the past concerning Buddy," Ken said. "You're a better alternative to the police. If you can find some link that steers the focus away from us, we'd be very grateful."

"What about Marlon?" Alex asked.

Ken started to speak, but Marlon interrupted him. "I had sex with Buddy," he announced.

Alex was struck with some inescapable Puritan feeling of damnation. She felt reluctantly shocked. Not that she had room to judge, but isn't that what made Puritanism so feeble? It reeked with self-congratulatory hypocrisy.

"We didn't know until yesterday about Marlon and Buddy," Shirley said. "We realize we should have told Marlon about our past with Buddy."

"It was one time," Marlon said, "At my instigation. I pestered him."

A light flashed in Alex's brain. "Did Jerome know?"

Marlon's face grew a deep shade of crimson. "He caught us behind a prop wall on the set." Tears formed in Marlon's eyes. "Jerome's got a thing about homos and won't admit it. He started acting like I had a disease."

Ken held out his arms in a wide gesture. "And so, we have the Sloan saga. That's it for tonight."

"What about the question and answer period?" Alex asked.

Ken shook his head. "This was far more draining than I anticipated. Besides, you have plenty of grist for your mill. Go. Harass the other subjects in this wonderful mess."

Exactly what she intended to do.

Chapter Twenty

SALOME PICKED ALEX up in a pearl white Cadillac Escalade. "I'm sorry about the gauche vehicle," she said. "It was a gift from my parents." Norman yapped from a crate lashed into the back. "I'm dropping Norman off at his psychic counselor," she said. "We can go somewhere and talk during his session."

Alex tried to remain neutral in expression. "Psychic counselor?"

"He's been traumatized ever since we returned from Sonoma. He's wetting inside the house. He nipped at his favorite groomer last week. His new therapist is the best pet psychic in Southern California. She has a hit show on The Animal Channel."

The pet psychic lived in a slightly seedy neighborhood west of Fairfax.

"They call this 'Beverly Hills Annex.' It's a way to link your funky area with the fancy one next door. Everything's about image around here," Salome informed her. The pet psychic's house was small, older white stucco with a pretty yard on a quiet street tucked away from the commerce.

Salome pulled Norman from his crate. Alex had to sympathize with the terrier. He looked at her with limpid eyes and whimpered with anthropomorphic post-traumatic stress. Salome stroked his head. "It's okay, Norman. Meredith will help you."

Alex expected the counselor to be a blowsy middle-aged woman draped in scarves. Contrary to the stereotype, Meredith Parker was a pleasant looking woman around Alex's age, certainly no more than forty, with intelligent eyes and an open smile. She looked like a person you'd want to be *your* psychic therapist. She reached for Norman, who wagged his tail halfheartedly.

"He feels a little better today," Meredith said.

They stood for a moment while Meredith and Norman communed. "He's glad to be back. This will be a good session."

Salome looked relieved as they headed to an espresso place called Heavy Buzz on West Third. Once they were settled with their drinks, she wasted no time. "What's going on?"

"That's what a few of us would like to know."

Salome nodded wisely. "Without the police."

Two bald teenagers dressed like Franciscan monks settled in the booth next to them. Salome glanced over without much curiosity, then frowned. "Jerome told me about Marlon having sex with Buddy." She smiled grimly. "Maybe the Sloans hired the stalker to kill Buddy."

Alex held up a hand. "Let's not jump the gun. You said Buddy was like a part of the family. The Sloans told me he was in a relationship with your Aunt Consuela."

Salome shrugged. "It was over before I was born."

"Tell me about your aunt."

"She's my mother's older sister by two years. She was born in Puerto Rico and my mother was born in Brooklyn. Aunt Consuela became a sexy Latin actress. My mother wanted to be waspy American. Her name was Maria, but she changed it to Mary. She went to Barnard and dated gentile law students." Salome grinned. "Then Aunt Consuela introduced Daddy to my mother. She fell madly in love, even though he was a beginning movie director from a loud Italian family in the Bronx. They got married. Daddy got really, really famous. My family history, condensed version."

"Aunt Consuela?" Alex asked. "She had a horse accident, eventually stopped acting. Where is she now?"

Salome squinted at her. "My parents think the horse accident affected her brain. She bought a house in the hills above Malibu and became a recluse."

"Did Buddy keep in touch with her?"

"They stayed friends. He used to go up and see her."

"Do you have a match?" one of the young monks asked. He was holding a cigarello.

"No," Salome answered. "Besides, no smoking in here. And, should monks be smoking anyway?"

The friar shrugged. "In our church we can. We make our own rules."

The other friar placed his palms together in a gesture of prayer and bowed to them. "But we respect the café rules. Bless you."

Salome grinned at Alex. "In Hollywood, the churches make their own rules."

"Everybody makes their own rules, it seems," Alex commented.

Salome sighed. "That's what I know."

Alex cleared her throat. "Was it possible that Jerome was jealous of Buddy?"

Salome reddened. "You don't think Jerome and Marlon were having sex, do you? That's impossible, because Jerome, well, he could be better in his attitude towards gays." Salome jumped up. "Norman's appointment is over. We better get back."

Once on the road, Salome gripped the wheel too tightly. She almost hit a bicyclist who veered into their lane. "I thought we were friends."

"Salome, I was just trying to cover all the bases."

Salome stared out the front windshield. "Don't try and question Jerome. He'll make trouble for you, even if he doesn't mean it."

NORMAN WAS WAITING in Meredith's arms. He yelped at them, wagging his tail with almost his usual enthusiasm. Meredith smiled radiantly. "Norman had an emotional breakthrough." She handed him to Salome. Meredith's expression grew serious. "Norman was very upset, he felt powerfully betrayed by someone. That person, I couldn't tell if it was male or female, was not who he thought he or she was."

Norman barked attentively. Alex shivered.

Meredith said to Alex, "I told him you were going to help. I know you'll find the answer."

Alex had a mother who was an iconic advice columnist. She'd come to accept that. Why not embrace psychic pet counseling? "Tell him I'll find out the bad things," she said.

"You tell him," Meredith said. She, Norman and Salome waited expectantly.

Alex shrugged and turned to Norman. "I'll find the bad person."

Norman bared his teeth and growled.

"He never does that," Salome said.

"He's giving me incentive," Alex said. "He's telling me to have courage."

"How do you know that?" Meredith asked, then burst out laughing. "What a silly question. Of course he communed with you. I'm glad you're in the spirit of all this."

"HOW DID YOU convince Consuela to see you?" Chase asked.

"Salome," Alex replied. "Don't know what she said, but it worked."

They were just exiting Malibu and beginning to climb the hills above the ocean town. In no time, the roads narrowed and traffic signs disappeared behind overgrowth. The higher they climbed, the more edgy Alex grew. Descending cars nearly forced them over the embankments. She could practically feel the tires of their vehicle slipping.

Chase had insisted on accompanying Alex. The previous night, Alex had filled Chase and Wendy in on her progress, including Norman's revelations. Chase mentioned that she once had a girlfriend who lived in the Malibu hills and insisted on guiding

Alex through the mountainous maze.

"I hate this," Chase burst out. A muddy Dodge Ram pick-up towing a boat rumbled past, nearly sideswiping them, although Chase had pulled as far to the side of the road as possible without toppling over the inadequate guard rail and plummeting them down a cliff. "My ex-girlfriend calls this paradise. To me, it's a cataclysm waiting to happen. If there's a fire or an earthquake, who gets out? Mudslides, heart attacks. I think people who live up here are crazy."

Alex had to agree. It was certainly heavenly and incredibly rural, considering how close they were to sprawling urbanity. But the hills were forbidding. The foliage looked like kindling for a huge inescapable bonfire. Clearly, at least to her, the mountain dwellers were taunting Mother Nature.

It took them almost an hour to find Consuela's rugged driveway. When they pulled up to the house, three Doberman pinchers raced to the car with their teeth bared. A woman came out of the house. She waved a cane. The dogs slinked back and sat in a row. Alex and Chase stepped from the car. If anything, Consuela's glare was more threatening than the watchdogs. She was a medium height beauty with finely wrinkled olive skin and startling salt-and-pepper hair curling down to her shoulders.

Consuela led them into the house, trailed by the Dobermans. She and Chase were shown to a battered leather sectional. The dogs settled onto three dog beds, facing them. She and Chase accepted an offer of coffee. While Consuela was away, the dogs stared at them.

"I have to go to the bathroom," Alex said.

"I don't know about you, but I'm not moving until Consuela gets back," Chase replied.

"I see your point," Alex said. Now would have been a good time for the pet psychic.

Consuela returned with three mugs, cream and sugar. "I wouldn't have talked to you, but Salome assures me if it isn't you two, it will be someone worse and she's probably right." She sighed. "I cried for days. Buddy didn't deserve to die." She pointed to a dish on the coffee table that separated them. "If you give the girls a biscuit, they'll love you forever."

Alex reached into the cut glass bowl and retrieved three people-shaped biscuits.

The dogs trotted over and sat at her feet. Each one took a biscuit politely, swallowed the morsels barely chewing and looked at her expectantly.

"Enough," Consuela said.

The dogs trotted back to their beds and resumed staring.

Consuela peered intently at them. "My girls would tear you apart, if they thought I was threatened by you. Fighting is in their nature. It is my belief that even the most domesticated of creatures have an instinctual dark side. Including the human animal."

"I don't mean to be rude," Alex said. "But can we get back to Buddy?"

Consuela snorted. "Honey, wake up. I was on the subject." She sipped her coffee thoughtfully. "Buddy was a complex man who preferred to appear simple and good-hearted. He had a dark side." For the first time, she looked stricken.

"Tell us about him," Chase said.

"We met at Penny Studios. Freddy D'Amico, my sister's husband-to-be, was a young and ambitious kid willing, like the rest of us, to work for almost nothing. He hired me to work on a dreadful creature movie he was directing. The Sloans were already together and Buddy was with another actress, Helena Jordan. I stole Buddy from Helena. I was more talented and vivacious than she was. Her greatest talent was getting men to sleep with her. That's easy." Consuela laughed. "Not very feminist of me to say. In Puerto Rico, women got what they wanted. They had ways of doing it. I kept up my ties with Puerto Rico. There's something comforting, ladies, about the old ways. Who wants to be a crane operator or blown to bits on a battlefield?"

"Where is Helena now?" Alex asked, but she was distracted. Her bladder was bursting. She waved a hand. "I need to use your bathroom."

A shadow crossed Consuela's face. "Go down the hall. Third door on the right. Be quick, I don't like snooping."

Alex raced down the hall, hoping to move quickly enough to manage a little snooping before her presence was missed too much. But she was thrown off by the Dobermans, who followed at her heels and waited for her, then followed her back.

As soon as Alex returned, Chase stood. "My turn."

This time, however, Chase was gone for quite a few minutes. Consuela looked at her watch and frowned. "I have an appointment in Santa Monica."

Chase returned with the Dobermans, who surrounded Chase protectively and wagged their stubby tails.

"They like you," Consuela said. "You should feel honored. It usually takes them awhile to warm up to people. They would eat someone's arm if he was trying to harm you, now that you're a part of their pack."

Chase shivered and sat down. "I was thinking about Helena. She had deep reasons to hate you and perhaps Buddy, too. Where is she now?"

Consuela shrugged. "She was crazy and weak. She disappeared. Who knows?"

"Who *would* know?" Chase asked.

"Ask Penny."

"Penny?"

"Heywood Penny. Penny Studios." She looked at her watch again. "You must go."

THE RIDE DOWN the roller-coaster hills felt as precarious as the drive up. When they reached Santa Monica, Chase shook her stiff hands and groaned. "Detective work is exhausting. I could use a glass of wine in a place overlooking the ocean. How about you?"

Alex hesitated. Chase spoke before she could answer.

"It's okay, Alex. Friends, remember? Wendy is fine with all of this."

Alex sighed. "Then a glass of wine sounds fabulous."

At the Oceanside Café in Venice, they sat on the patio. Gulls squawked at them, inching closer, until the waiter waved them away. Alex shuddered. "I know some birds are highly intelligent. I feel like I should like them. All I can think of is Hitchcock and *The Birds*."

Chase grinned. "My favorite Hitchcock movie. We'll make a movie fanatic out of you yet." She took a sip of her wine. "Too bad you can't stay longer. Wendy and I really would love to introduce you to our friends and our world."

"Yes, well, I do have to get back." Alex felt a stab of her usual ambivalence. What exactly was she going back to? Good time to change the subject. "Consuela?"

"I managed to open a couple of doors as I rushed to the bathroom." Chase placed her hand on Alex's. Alex reacted with a little shiver, which she sincerely hoped Chase didn't notice. Chase seemed intent on her point. "Did you notice that there were pictures missing in the living room and hallway? I saw that on a detective show. Clean areas on the wall where pictures prevented dirt and grime."

"What kind of amateur investigator do you think I am? I was going to bring it up."

"She took them down, knowing we were coming."

"And the closed rooms?"

"One was a spare bedroom, nothing interesting. The other was a small office, also with pictures removed. A piece of furniture covered in a sheet. Didn't have time to look under the cover, darn it." She looked at her watch. "We should get back. Next step will be talking to Heywood Penny."

"Will he talk to us?"

"To you, this time. I have a major meeting."

"I'll miss you."

Chase smiled. "I know. We make good partners. I'll pull some strings. Penny started out as a messenger boy at Lumina when my grandfather Poppa Weiss was still the chief. He's in my network."

Chapter Twenty-One

HEYWARD PENNY WAS surprisingly accommodating about seeing Alex on short notice. He summoned her to his estate in Beverly Hills, a fortress built by a silent film star, later occupied by an Amway tycoon who committed suicide, and now the cult icon. Buzzed through the automatic gates, Alex encountered a van and a crew hoisting video gear. An efficient-looking middle-aged woman led her through the maze of activity without explanation.

The kitchen was restaurant size. Penny loomed over a pile of chopped vegetables, wearing an apron that featured a guillotine of some sort. He was beanstalk tall and looked like a cross between a Harvard economics professor and Boris Karloff.

"Welcome, Ms. Pope," he said, wiping his hands on a towel. "We were just finishing a shoot for my latest infomercial." He pointed to a device on the counter that, like the apron image, appeared to be a miniature guillotine. "A best-selling item from Heyward Penny's Lethal Kitchen Companions collection."

"Call me Alex," she said.

"Most people call me Penny," he replied. "Do you cook?"

"Not so much," Alex admitted. Alex hadn't cooked much during her marriage or before. She *had* done some prep work in a resort kitchen when she came up to the Russian River after Stacy's death. That had led to an unfortunate series of events best left in the past. "I adore good food, though."

"All the better." He gestured at her. "Come here."

Alex approached warily. Penny pointed a stalk of celery at her. It shouldn't have seemed menacing, but Penny had a possessed air. He thrust the stalk into her hand and pointed to the guillotine. When she hesitated, he retrieved the celery and poked it beneath the gleaming blade and chop, chop, chopped, giggling eerily. The stalk quickly transformed into perfect razor thin half circles.

"Could you do this with a knife?" Penny challenged.

"Absolutely not," Alex answered truthfully.

Penny seized an impressively large, phallic-looking carrot, jabbing it at her. "Emasculate it!" he cried, then cackled gleefully.

Alex was getting into the spirit of things. She grabbed the thick tubular vegetable and tried to thrust it into the chopper. The middle-aged escort, who had been frowning up to now, burst out laughing. Penny couldn't help smirking.

"That's backwards," he said. He regained his composure and

demonstrated the proper insertion. "Do you want flawless slivers or expressive chunks?"

Alex shrugged. "Chunks."

Penny gestured again. This time, Alex got the carrot properly situated into a victim position in the guillotine. With remarkable ease, the blade sank effortlessly through its tough membranes. Nice little gizmo, she had to admit. Then she shivered, remembering her purpose. She imagined Jeffrey, her gallows-humor cousin, snickering at the irony.

Penny looked at her in a way that suggested he was also attuned to the situation. "I'm a very rich man," he said. "I sell an outrageous number of these, along with an assortment of attachments. The device chops, dices, slivers and slices. It also accesses a primal darkness of the soul that my pictures once did." Penny giggled with stagy showmanship. "It didn't *have* to look like a guillotine. My next product is a battery-cooled food storage unit that looks like a casket and promises nearly eternal freshness. Are you hungry? I hope you're not a vegetarian."

"I could use a bite to eat." Alex bared her teeth with vampire glee.

"I like you, young lady." Penny pointed to a stockpot that looked like witch's cauldron. "Beef barley soup. Guess the secret ingredient."

"Ox blood."

Penny laughed. "I don't like you. I love you. Close. Beef marrow." He removed his apron. "Lunch will be served in the Heyward Penny Archival Library." He led Alex out of the kitchen and down a hallway lined with early medieval art, mostly humans in the throes of religious ecstasy or despair. They entered the library, a shrine to all things Heyward Penny. The walls were plastered with movie posters and signed photos.

Penny was not spectacularly modest. The soup *was*, however, spectacularly delicious. While she ate it, Penny set up a slide show. "I gave Buddy his start," he said, as he selected photos on his laptop and arranged them for screening from a connected projector. "I was aware of the sexual complications. I had no interest in my actors' private lives, as long as they worked hard for almost non-existent wages."

"Did the Sloans warn you about me?"

"They are loyal to the man who gave them their start." Penny turned on the projector. Alex giggled.

"*The Creature From The Sewers Below*," Penny announced fondly. "I made that potboiler in five days on a subway station set from another film. We used the set for one movie in the daytime and again at night for the other. We used tight shots and claustrophobic angles, since we weren't using real trains. The point of view of the night movie was partly from the creature, told retrospectively. Really, I predated many of the latest so-called film innovations in point-of-view shooting and non-linear plotting. Although my contributions have been recognized in Europe for many years, I am only lately being given the master status I deserve in this country."

"Is that Buddy?" Alex asked. On the screen, Ken and Shirley Sloan backed away from a slimy beast with one huge eye in the middle of its forehead.

"He was a good sport on that one," Penny said. "We invented a paste, beautifully cheap to make, but very difficult to remove. But I know you're not here to discuss technicalities of film-making." He clicked to the next slide. Buddy, in cowboy gear, clutched Consuela, who was clothed in patches of clothing, revealing a lot of bare skin.

"He was bewitched by her," Penny said. "I thought she was less spell-binding, but I appreciated her work-ethic and natural talent. I'm sure you know this by now, but Consuela fell off a horse and was never really the same afterwards." Penny reviewed the jpeg images on his computer screen, lips pursed. "But we're getting ahead of ourselves." He selected a file and projected the image.

This time, Buddy embraced Helena Jordan. Both wore space suits. "This was a satirical sci-fi number that made fun of itself, *Destruction from Another Galaxy.* I believe I was the first to use meta-commentary in conventional entertainment modalities, aside perhaps from some of the earliest silent directors who literally invented the art form. I brought the most modern literary theory into drive-ins across the nation." Penny clicked on the photo until the blonde actress's face filled the screen. Her deep-set eyes were innocent, but provocative. Her demeanor suggested she could be wearing the ridiculous space suit or anything, and still be engaging. Yet there was fragility as well in her expression.

"Helena Jordan," Penny said. "I rescued her from a dubious modeling agency that specialized in exploiting girls who were drama stand-outs or prom queens in their small-town high schools and came here to be stars. Helena, I must be frank, was not the most talented actress I ever hired. And, sadly, behind the alluring, sensual farmer's daughter persona was a very broken little girl."

Penny stared at the face on the screen. "I would have married her and taken care of her for the rest of her life. She fell for Buddy and made a mission of seducing him. Their relationship was, to my mind, based on flattery of Buddy's ego. He didn't love her. Consequently, I wasn't surprised when he left her for Consuela."

Penny sighed. "Helena needed devotion. She chose men who

wouldn't supply it, resulting in a toxic clinginess and paranoid jealousy. Buddy, like many of those men, dumped her. Helena did not have resilience in the face of rejection. This spelled doom for her as an actress, as well. If she couldn't get her directors to fall in love with her, she couldn't prevent their criticisms of her acting skills or lack thereof."

Penny flicked off the projector. "Interestingly, she was from your neck of the woods."

Alex sat up, heart quickening. "Sonoma County?"

Penny went over to a desk and opened a drawer. He glanced at her. "If you don't mind an old man's compliments, you also have a compelling allure. Work hard and you'll be magnificent."

"Wonder Woman," Alex said. "I could be Wonder Woman."

"Excuse me?"

"Never mind," she replied.

Penny grinned. "Oh, yes. The comic book character. Something like that, but better. It may take awhile." He reached in the drawer and pulled out a yellowed newspaper clipping. "I retrieved this for you from a private cache of nostalgia. Helena gave it to me." Penny handed the clipping to Alex. The caption of the short article read: *Santa Rosa Junior College actress wins Dramatics Award.*

It was Helena at roughly twenty or so. But her name was not Helena Jordan. It was Myrtle Wolinski, raised on a chicken ranch outside of Cotati and a former Rancho Cotati High School actress whose teenage adulation had carried over to the theatre department of the local community college.

"My next step is a Hollywood career," the vivacious young woman said with complete assurance. We have no doubt, if her local success is any indication, that Myrtle Wolinski is a name we'll be seeing soon in theatres around the nation.

"I suggested Helena Jordan," Penny said. "My mother's name was Helena. I forget where the Jordan came from." He squinted at her. "You don't think she was involved in Buddy's death, do you?"

Alex shrugged. "Probably not. But this is hardly a meaningless coincidence."

"She was a bit unbalanced, as I said." Penny wiped his brow, looking sadly philosophical. "I suppose it's best to get to the bottom of this with the least fuss possible. Is that it for questions, my dear?"

"One more. How do you prepare the beef marrow?"

Penny smiled appreciatively. "You are a charmer. I sell a gadget that looks like a small hatchet on steroids and is guaranteed to sever bones, should you ever get into small-scale butchering."

THAT EVENING, ALEX was alone in the kitchen at Chase and Wendy's place. Chase and Wendy came in with startled looks on their faces. "What on earth?" Chase exclaimed.

"I'm preparing beef barley soup," Alex announced. "Heyward Penny's special recipe."

"What are those macabre implements?"

"The deadly bone cruncher and torture-chamber pressure cooker reduced my stock preparation to a mere hour. Notice the perfectly guillotined vegetables. Watch." Alex situated a thick beef shank on a wooden block. She raised the enhanced hatchet and, with a gleeful giggle, whacked it in half. "I bought three sets of everything. One for you, one for me, and one for my parents, who have discovered cooking at home. Joelle made the seven-grain bread. By hand, although I offered to get her a Lady Frankenstein bread machine."

Joelle rolled her eyes. "It looks like the haunts of a serial killer in here." She glanced at Wendy. "You put in a long day. Can you eat?"

Wendy wheeled over to the counter and inspected the dinner. "I wouldn't miss this for the world."

When they'd settled into the dining room, Alex filled them in on Penny's revelations, interrupted by their occasional bursts of appreciation over her soup. She was inordinately pleased, although cooking was not something for which she'd ever felt compelled to earn praise.

"Myrtle Wolinski, budding actress from a chicken ranch outside of Cotati. Sounds like a movie plot," Wendy commented. "Even the name change to generic gentile. Do you think she had anything to do with Buddy's death?"

"Penny asked me the same thing," Alex said. "Maybe, maybe not. She was in Sonoma County when he was murdered. I'm going to track her down."

"Atta girl," Wendy said. "I guess that means you're leaving us?"

"It's time," Alex said.

"*She made me do it*," Chase cried dramatically. "*She made me do it*. I was thinking of Chip Welch's arraignment. That was his rant. There might be a connection."

"Brilliant," Alex said. "We need to find Helena. I mean, I need to find her."

"You both do," Wendy said. "You're a team. Chase will go up with you."

"I can't go," Chase said.

"Of course you can. Weren't you sending borderline coke addict Rafe Gillis up to scout that location for the *Lady Dracula* pilot? You can go with him. The studio trusts your judgment unconditionally, they'll be thrilled."

"I was considering going anyway," Chase said reflectively.

Alex cleared a lump from her throat. "You are a great help." She turned to Wendy. "Are you sure it's okay?"

Wendy gave her an inscrutable look. "Why wouldn't it be?"

Alex shrugged, feeling her face grow flush.

"Don't answer," Wendy said, grinning. "I want her to go. Trust me."

Chapter Twenty-Two

ALEX FLEW BACK the next day. When she got home, she found Paula and Rickie Coleman on the patio. Both the sisters and Henry were lounging in the weak warmth of the late fall sun. Henry looked very well nourished.

"How was your trip?" Paula asked.

"Very good," Alex replied.

"The reshooting went well?"

"Great."

Paula sat up. "I'll bet you were checking out dirt on Buddy and his cronies. Find anything?"

The Coleman sisters waited expectantly. When Alex, who was feeling weary from both the plane and the general investigative excitement, didn't immediately reply, Rickie spoke up with an air of forced casualness. "Solve any mysteries?"

"Not really," Alex replied.

"Dig up any good clues?" Rickie persisted. "Paula and I are your rabid fans. Don't disappoint us. Give us a hint. You must have found something."

Alex was well aware of Paula's connections with law enforcement. She was certain the current inquisitiveness was not based on idle gossip-loving curiosity. Rickie could easily be in the mix, too, helping the authorities. "Not much," Alex said. "Look, I really appreciate your care of Henry and my place. But I'm very tired. We can visit in a few days."

"Henry is a wonderful cat," Rickie said, rising. "I did a free grooming and nail trim."

Henry did look stunning. Alex held up her cell phone. "You guys all look great. Let me get a picture of the three of you." Before the three could move, Alex snapped a shot with her camera function. She studied the display. "Perfect. I can add it to my embarrassingly long series of Henry photos."

When the sisters left, Alex fell into bed and slept nine hours. This time, when she came out onto the patio, Wheatie and Kallinda were sipping tea in the crisp morning air. "We got back two days ago," Kallinda said. "That Paula woman, she and her sister spent a lot of time on the patio."

Alex heard a note of disapproval in Kallinda's voice. She was surprised. Both Wheatie and Kallinda were usually so mellow. "Were they doing anything bad?" Alex asked.

"No," Wheatie said. "They were nice to us and very sweet to Henry." He glanced at Kallinda, who shrugged.

"Tell me," Alex said.

"She, Paula, the older one who stayed here. She snuck some man into your place in the middle of the night. Don't get me wrong, we're not prudes. Not by a long shot. We thought it was an intruder. I shone a flashlight on him. I grew up in this town. I know him. It's the Chief Corrections Officer for the county jail, John Strong. My mother is his wife's second cousin. This is a small community. What does Paula think, sleeping with her boss, a married man? I don't care on a philosophical level. It's just stupid, though, on the human plane."

"Oh, boy," Alex said. She was thinking about the charity event she'd attended with John Strong, his sister Erica and Paula. What was up? If Paula and John Strong were having a secret affair, had they used her and Erica as beards? That was not only ugly, but stupid. In this small community, everyone had too much to lose to be pulling those kind of shenanigans. Not that it ever stopped anyone when it came to sex.

Speaking of sex, Alex picked up her phone and selected Pete Szabo's number from her contact list. She sighed, knowing she'd be taking advantage of her friend's enduring crush on her. What else could she do? Pete was a cop. Or, a deputy sheriff, anyway. Pete had resources.

"Pete?"

"Alex, what do you want me to dig up now?"

"Is that how you greet a friend?"

"When it's Alexis Pope and there's a murder in the county. I can't tell you anything regarding police business, you know that."

"You can help me find someone. Should be on public record."

"Then you do it."

"Pete, I'm in a hurry. This is your job, you can do it fast. Please."

Pete emitted a sigh loud enough to be heard over the phone. "Who is it?"

"Her name is Myrtle Wolinski."

There was a short silence. Pete cleared his throat. "Why do you want to talk to her?"

"Why did the police want to talk to her?"

"I can't tell you."

"Pete, I can't tell you either. At least for a little while."

"I'm not feeling good about this."

"We're on the same team, Pete. We want to find the truth. Where is she?"

"I know where she is." Pete sighed again. "They won't let you see her."

"Don't worry about it." She grabbed a pen, as Pete reluctantly gave her the address.

CHASE ARRIVED EARLY the next evening in a rented car. "I really could have gotten a hotel," she said, but continued to pull her luggage from the trunk.

"No way," Alex said. "Your home is my home. Isn't that our tradition now?" She hesitated. "You'll sleep on the couch. It's relatively comfortable since I bought a memory foam pad."

Chase grinned. "I'm looking forward to a home-cooked meal prepared with the Penny torture tools. No bed-and-breakfast can offer that." She bent down and stroked Henry, who was rubbing on her leg. "Not to mention Henry. No, the couch is worth all that. And I get your company to boot."

"A dubious plus," Alex said.

"Oxymoron!" Chase said with delight. "Oxymorons are clichés on steroids."

"I'm hopelessly optimistic about your arrival to help with this investigation. And that's coming from an enthusiastic cynic." Alex sighed. "I don't know. Clichés are easier."

Chase looked steadily at her. "I'll play whatever game you like. We can go back to clichés."

"No," Alex said. "The best game we can play together is the Amateur Female Sleuth game."

"Fine by me."

By this time, Wheatie and Kallinda had wandered out into the dusk from the main house. They stared at the luggage with widened eyes.

"She's just visiting to scout a location," Alex said, feeling a burning need to explain. "We're friends now."

The couple shrugged in unison. "It's cool," Wheatie said, but once again his look hinted at his archaic, well-preserved small-town boy ethics. Alex felt inordinately defensive. The last thing she would ever be was a home-wrecker, for God's sake, especially wrecking the home of her supportive new friends.

It was hard, nevertheless, to shake Wheatie's disapproving scowl from her mind later that evening as she and Chase shared a take-out organic mushroom pizza with whole-wheat crust from a wood fire oven place in Graton and pale ales from a local brew pub. Chase picked up the battered remote control for Alex's small screen television. "This is an antique."

Alex shrugged. "Until the last few years, I didn't watch much television. Then I started getting into trouble. Now I watch myself on CNN."

"Welcome to my world," Chase said. "Mind if I put on *TMZ?*"

"That's the worst tabloid trash, you said so yourself."

Chase laughed. "Everyone in the entertainment industry says that, then we all watch it."

Alex grimaced. "Welcome to my world. I've lived a hypocritical life. But I'm trying to reform."

"You're too hard on yourself. Eat your pizza."

Alex picked up another slice. "I like hanging out with you. You're as screwed up as I am."

"I'm not a model of emotional perfection," Chase admitted, grinning. "But I put up a good front, wouldn't you agree?"

"An excellent appearance of psychological togetherness," Alex said. "I try to do the same, but I don't have your skill set."

"It takes practice. I started early. Another beer?"

"No thanks, I'm getting full." Alex picked up the remote and flipped to a cable channel. Her stomach lurched. A *Lena: Amazon Queen* rerun appeared on the screen. Wendy Swann as Lena executed a feisty twirl, waving a dagger in each hand. She was confident and beautiful.

I'm still Wendy, only with MS.

Alex glanced over at Chase. Chase's hands were trembling and her face had grown pale. Alex waved the remote control. "I'll shut this off."

"Give me that," Chase said, grabbing the remote. "Your television is crap. This remote stinks." She stood up and threw the remote across the room, hitting a glass vase on a table. It toppled to the floor and shattered. Chase's expression was a contorted mess of anger and grief. "I'll pay for the vase."

"Don't bother. I got it at a flea market for fifty cents."

Chase inspected the remote. "I don't think I broke it. If I did, I'll buy you a new television with a good remote."

"You don't have to buy me anything. I have all the money I need. I don't want a new television," Alex said. She patted the couch. "Come sit down and finish your dinner. Without watching the boob tube."

"I'm not hungry anymore." Chase slumped back onto the couch. "I'm exhausted. I've been playing the good caretaker without complaining for a long time." She sighed. "I think I need to sleep."

"I have sheets right over there and a pillow."

"I'll check into Marlowe Manor tomorrow."

Alex's heart thumped. "You don't have to do that."

"Why would you want me here? I've been a selfish, destructive bitch."

"I don't see you that way." Alex's tone sounded like a muffled roar in her own ears.

"How do you see me?" Chase asked. She looked lost. She looked deflated and in vast need of a hug.

Alex hesitated. She was aware of how vulnerable Chase was being and how unusual that probably was. She inched a little closer. "I see you..." She stroked Chase's cheek. "Wendy's lucky to have you."

Chase jumped up from the couch, looking flustered. "Where's your broom?" she asked. "I'll sweep up the broken glass. I made a mess and I can mend it."

"I wish it was that easy," Alex replied. "Let me make your bed."

"I'll do it. I make my bed, then I have to lay in it." Chase smiled wearily. "Good-night, Sherlock."

Alex returned the weary smile. "Good-night, Holmes."

Chapter Twenty-Three

THE NEXT MORNING, Alex and Chase drove down Petaluma Boulevard to track Helena Jordan/Myrtle Wolinski and her secrets. Just north of town, Alex pointed to a restaurant. On its roof, an enormous smiling egg in a tuxedo perched on a fake brick wall. "That's Humpty Dumpty Diner, a greasy spoon run by an old gay man named Derek. Jeffrey and Max love it. Not only does it have the best heart-attack brunch in Sonoma County, it *is* Sonoma County in a nutshell. Or, eggshell, I should say. Where else would you find farmers, bankers, leather boys on their way to Guerneville, lesbian anarchists and Republicans?"

"After church, my parents and I went to brunch at Perkins," Chase said. "There weren't any leather boys or lesbian anarchists. Actually, my father and I went to church. My mother met us at the restaurant. She made a policy of boycotting organized religion."

"My parents wouldn't set foot in a church or a synagogue either," Alex said.

"Religion has its place. You were married. In a church?"

Alex grimaced. "With mixed feelings."

"Wendy and I discussed marriage, but we're waiting for it to be truly legal in California." Chase's voice broke. "She's probably going to die before we can do it."

"Die?" Alex reached over and patted Chase's clenched fist. "I thought she was okay for now."

Chase shivered. "I get scared." She pointed out the window. "Subject change. Trendy but cute little village."

Petaluma was Sonoma County's most southern town bordering Marin County. It had transformed from egg capital of the nation to a yuppie stronghold rivaling its Marin bourgeois neighbor. Antique stores and coffee houses mingled with a few holdout establishments selling pharmaceuticals, jewelry or chicken wings.

At D Street, Alex turned right. They glanced out the windows at the stately mansions on genteel lawns lining the wide, tree-shaded street. "Very pastoral," Chase commented.

"This is where the doctors, judges and rich farmers lived." Alex veered onto Ninth Street. They crossed B and C Streets. She nodded at the sign in front of a large institutional-looking building that had clearly been renovated to look less austere. "Spirit Foundation."

Chase frowned. "I don't like convalescent centers."

"It's very New Age," Alex replied.

"Wendy did time in a place called Courage House after a bad spill onto concrete, just before she went into the wheelchair. Upbeat joint with a world-class program for athletes with disabilities. I did not feel upbeat there. I felt angry, out of control and guilty. I don't like feeling angry or out of control, as you may have observed. And I really don't like guilt."

"That's what makes you so good at what you do," Alex said.

Chase stared at the stained glass windows and multi-denominational statuary scattered amidst the organic landscaping. "It's still a nursing home."

An earth-mother nurse with a shaggy grey-streaked seventies haircut met them at the reception desk. She wore a tie-dye nursing smock over blue scrub pants. Her name tag read Gracie. Alex took a deep breath and tried to let the babbling of the water chimes trickle over her. "We're here to see Myrtle Wolinski."

Gracie frowned. "The police have already been here. Are you relatives?"

"No. This is Chase Stuyvesant. She's a Hollywood producer. Lumina Studios is thinking of making a documentary, a tribute to Myrtle and her life. We'd love to talk to her. We'll keep it as brief as possible." She glanced at Chase, who was struggling to not look sideswiped by Alex's improvisation.

"A tribute?" Gracie hesitated. "She's been through some tough times. She deserves some good attention for a change. She was a great actress at one time."

Alex kept her expression neutral. "Myrtle told you that?"

"She doesn't like to be called Myrtle. It makes her very disruptive. She likes Helena."

"Helena told you she was a great actress?"

Gracie nodded. "She told me she was one of the best. She opens up with me." Her expression darkened. "She was already in and out of confusion, poor thing. Now she's only occasionally lucid. I'll be honest with you. I do not like and have never liked proselytizing Christian fundamentalists and their condemnations. I do my best to be accepting of all of humanity, however, in order not to repeat their blind hatred."

"What does this have to do with Helena?"

Gracie shook her head sadly. "Helena is suffering. I can't revile her way of seeking salvation. She almost didn't survive the suicide attempt that brought her to us. Now this thing with her son. I almost wish no one had told her."

"Her son?" Alex asked.

Gracie looked at them with astonishment. "You'd have to live in a cave to not know about Chip killing Buddy Brubech. Then getting poisoned himself."

"Wait," Alex said. "Chip Welch is Helena's son?"

Gracie shook her head sympathetically. "It's a terrible business." A sly look crossed her face. "Buddy Brubech deserved what he got. Destroying Helena's career. Other bad things." She stopped abruptly. "No more, I shouldn't have said what I did." Her shoulders stiffened. "I'll let you see her. I will have to be present at all times. If Helena gets upset, you'll have to leave. Wait here."

When Gracie disappeared down a hallway, Alex turned to Chase. From the look on Chase's face, Alex assumed they were both thinking the same thing. *She made me do it.* Alex felt a quickening of excitement, but Chase frowned.

"Alex, we can't lie to this woman about some kind of tribute."

"How many life stories get researched for projects that never get made?"

"Sorry, that doesn't cut it. There is no project and there never will be."

"You'd make a lousy homicide detective. You're too principled."

Chase lifted an eyebrow speculatively. "I'm not invincible to corruption. You're going to have to be more inventive, however."

"Helena is delusional anyway. She hungers to tell her story. The attention is her life blood."

"Good," Chase murmured. "Very good. I'm getting corrupted."

"I'm right," Alex said. "You know I am."

Alex was more right than she'd imagined. When they entered the room, they found Helena Jordan, nee Myrtle Wolinski, propped up in her bed, fully made up. Her unlined face was powdered to a glistening semblance of youth. She was, they knew from their research, sixty-four. Helena directed a delighted smile at them that transformed her pretty face into an ageless beam of seduction. The room smelled of incense masking urine. Someone in the next room was screaming. However, lying in her bed in a hospital gown, Helena looked like a fifties star in a tearjerker in which the actress could be dying without a hair out of place. On her nightstand, pictures in gold frames threatened to crowd out a water glass and a box of tissues. The pictures were an even mix of Jesus portraits and actresses in religious movies. On the walls, a collection of crosses on chains hung from hooks.

"Perfect," Chase whispered.

Gracie waved them in. "I told Helena you were with Lumina Studios."

Helena's radiant smile became a frown. "Women," she spat out. She laughed bitterly at their expressions. "In my day, producers were mostly men with big egos. I don't know if women have it in them to be great producers and directors."

She waved them closer. "Are you lesbians?" She laughed at their startled looks. "Don't be shocked. We had them in my day, too. They like to act as strong as the men. Of course, homosexuals are damned to hell. I hope you're not lesbians. If you are, I'll pray for you. Repent before you burn in eternal damnation."

"Your tribute could be like Joan of Arc," Chase suggested.

Helena pointed an accusing finger. "Shame on you, trying to dupe a sick woman. You're not here to make a tribute to me. Did that bitch atheist veterinarian, Buddy's little trophy wife, send you to spy on me?"

"No," Alex answered. "We're looking for the truth."

"The truth?" Helena laughed. "The truth is that Our Lord Jesus works in mysterious ways." A look of pain crossed her face. "My poor son. He fell in with Satan's female accomplice. She taught him to play evil games based on devil pagan rituals. Chip was already doomed. He was going to hell for playing Satan's games. He was under the power of a witch who entranced him. She made him do it."

"Who?" Alex asked.

Like the third lid of a cat, a veil formed over Helena's eyes. Her lips trembled and a small stream of saliva dribbled from her mouth. Her head began to jerk.

"Out," cried Gracie. "She's having a seizure."

Chase was right. Despite the inspirational posters and towering tropical plants, Spirit House was an unsettling place. Lavender couldn't hide the odor of human frailty. Alex shivered, as they stood outside Helena's door. Two young doctors and a younger medical intern raced in. No one questioned their presence, so they waited until Gracie came out.

"She's all right," Gracie said. She glanced around. "I'm off in fifteen minutes. Meet me at Humpty Dumpty's."

Chapter Twenty-Four

THE HOSTESS AT Humpty Dumpty's looked like a transvestite, but was gay owner Derek's mother, a hulking ancient Germanic giantess with a square jaw and a five o'clock shadow. A short, plump waitress in a muumuu led them to a booth in the steamy, crowded dining room. When Gracie arrived, the waitress pulled out a stack of grandchildren pictures and spread them like a deck of cards on the tabletop. "My daughter is on her fourth marriage," she said, sighing. She glanced at Gracie. "How's your Barbara doing?"

"Don't ask," Gracie replied. "The last boyfriend got arrested for dope." They both sighed deeply.

After the waitress had brought them coffee, Gracie pointed to a gathering of Sonoma County sheriffs occupying several tables on the other end of the diner. "I already told them everything I know. Nothing is getting done. They're overworked. You two seem on the ball."

Gracie shrugged. "It's a free country. I can say anything I want. I spent my youth at anti-war rallies. The FBI tapped my phone. I'm not going to change now." She grinned at them. "Maybe you'll want to research me for a movie. I met Patty Hearst." She leaned across the tabletop. "Chip used to come alone to visit his mother. Then a young woman started coming along. She never went up to the room to see Helena. She sat in the waiting room. When Chip came back down, she took his shoulder and marched him away. It was a little creepy, like she was his guard."

"Do you know who she was?" Alex asked.

"They never told me her name."

"What did she look like?"

"She was a pretty little thing. Pixie haircut, dark hair. Chip was not a bad-looking boy, but he was odd. I remember wondering what was up with that girl. Unless she just liked having him so spellbound by her."

"You have no idea who she was?" Chase persisted.

"No," Gracie said.

"Who would know?"

Gracie shrugged. "Chip worked at a video store in Santa Rosa. They might know." She wrote down the name of the store. "My daughter's boyfriend, the one in jail for dope, was a cult movie nut. He knew Chip through the store."

She leaned in closer. "Helena is not a bad person. She's a religious fanatic, but she was broken-down by wanting too much from men. What's the difference? Now Jesus is her boyfriend-savior. I'd like to see her at peace. I can't do this with my own family. Maybe I can help her. Go to the video store."

CRAZY HEARTS VIDEO was located on the shabbier south end of Mendocino Avenue in Santa Rosa, just before the entrance to Highway 12, bookended by a palm reader's den and a tattoo shop. As they passed the den, the palm reader waved to them. She was seated behind plate glass at a golden silk-covered table.

"She wants us to come in," Chase said.

"Of course she does," Alex replied. "She wants to rip us off."

"Where's your spirit of adventure?"

"I thought you were the practical one," Alex said. The palm reader was waving with determination. Chase opened the door to the den, grinned at Alex, and stepped in. Alex sighed and followed.

"I saw your future needs," the palm reader said. She was a jaundiced woman of an indeterminate age and ethnicity wearing gypsy knock-off wraps that could have been bought at Target. "My name is Reeta."

"How much?" Alex said.

"Do you have a coupon? I had an ad in the FrugalWise flyer."

"We weren't coming here," Alex said. "Why would we have a coupon?"

"Doesn't matter. I'll give you the discount."

"We don't want a discount."

Chase took out her wallet and handed Reeta a twenty. "Enough?"

Reeta shrugged and tucked the bill into a fold in her sarong or whatever it was. "I feel you're playing with fire, the two of you. I saw you as witches before a flaming bonfire."

Alex shivered. "I hate predictions. Especially from store-front psychics."

"Let me see your palms."

Chase marched up to Reeta with her palm extended. Alex took a backwards step. "Alex," Chase said.

Alex minced forward with a clenched fist. Reeta gently unfurled it. "Aah. The two of you are blessed in your relationship. You'll enjoy many years together as a loving, committed couple."

"You see?" Alex said, pulling away. She wagged an accusing finger at Reeta. "We're not even together. We're friends."

"Be careful. Don't go down in flames," Reeta said.

"What does that mean?" Chase asked.

Reeta shrugged. "That's the twenty dollar reading."

Chase started to pull out her wallet again, but Alex slipped her arm around Chase's waist and pulled her from the den. "I suppose you want a tattoo next?" she said, gesturing at the tattoo shop.

"I have one."

Alex blinked in surprise. "Not you."

"You really need to get to know me better."

"Where is it?"

"Out of sight."

"What is it?"

Chase shrugged. "It's something I don't share with anyone except my nearest and dearest."

Alex's curiosity index was surging. "How do I join the club?"

"You probably don't want to. Too many complications."

Alex still had her arm around Chase's middle. Good lord, they could be a couple, the way that they were bantering. To top it off, Chase didn't seem to be struggling much against Alex's stronghold. Simultaneously, they stepped away from one another. Chase led them into the video store.

"That lady next door is a rip-off artist," the guy at the counter called to them. "But she hits home runs sometimes."

"You were watching us?" Alex asked.

"Slow day," he replied.

"You see?" Alex said to Chase. "I said the woman was a fake."

"Now you really sound like a wife," Chase replied. "I-told-you-so behavior."

"That's mean," Alex said.

Chase reddened. "You're right. Why do I get nasty when I'm offended?"

"Ladies, can I help you?" the bored guy at the counter said. "The gay and lesbian section is on that wall over there."

"Are we giving off some kind of vibe?" Alex asked. "Bitchy dyke couple?"

"Doesn't matter," Chase said, approaching the counter. "I understand Chip Welch used to work here."

The counter guy, whose name tag read Mitchell, frowned at them. "Are you kidding? Between the cops and the media, we've had our fifteen minutes of glorious fame. Poof. Now it's gone. Sorry about Chip. He was okay. Just got promoted to assistant manager. That guy knew more about movies and games than an encyclopedia. He was, like, a genius. Didn't have much of a personality, though."

"We're looking for his girlfriend," Alex said.

Mitchell snorted. "He was a total dork. I never heard about any girlfriend."

"Are you sure?" Alex persisted.

"Hey, Ben!" Mitchell called. He shrugged. "I didn't know the guy very well, but he and Ben were buddies."

A bulky young man with linebacker shoulders and soft facial features who had been casually restocking shelves looked up at them.

"Did Chip have a girlfriend?" Mitchell called to Ben.

Ben shrugged. "Not that I know."

"See?" Mitchell said.

Ben gestured to Alex and Chase. "Come take a look."

They followed Ben to a section labeled Cult Classics. Displayed prominently was an altar worshipping Helena Jordan movies. "Chip's mom was mad at him. She thought he was going to hell for playing computer games invented by the devil. He still loved her. He stocked every horrible movie she made. I don't care what crime he did. Chip was a great guy. He must have just blown a fuse."

"You were friends?" Alex asked.

Before Ben could reply, a prim-looking man wearing an ugly corporate tie emerged from a back room. Both Ben and Mitchell straightened up like toy soldiers. He glanced at Alex and Chase. "Good morning, ladies. A national chain bought the store. I'm the new corporate manager, Charlie Fox. Pardon the mess. We're making some big changes." He looked at his employees with oily, transparently phony advocacy. "Can you boys handle this?"

"We're on it," Ben said.

"All systems go," Mitchell added.

Charlie Fox retreated to his office. Ben pulled a card from a shirt pocket and handed it to Alex. "He'll be out reforming us again any minute. This is my other business number. I repair computers in my home." He looked meaningfully at her. "Come see me." He cleared his throat. "In the meantime, can I rent you a few videos? Make my boss happy."

"No problem," Chase replied. ""My accomplice could use a better education in American film classics."

"Cool," Ben said. "Let me rustle up some of my favorites. DVD or VHS?"

"VHS," Chase replied. "Alex is low tech. We need to rent one of your VHS players, too.

Ben sighed. "Lousy picture quality."

"Terrible," Chase agreed.

"Enough," Alex cried. "I feel like a criminal."

"Not a crime, maybe just a sin," Ben said, grinning. "I'll be right back."

He returned with two videos. "*Casablanca* and *Brokeback Mountain*. One is a classic and the other is the best gay love story ever. Maybe one of the best love stories ever, gay or not."

THAT EVENING, ALEX and Chase were seated on the couch with multiple cartons of take-out Chinese food spread on the coffee table. "*Casablanca* or *Brokeback Mountain*?" Chase asked.

"You choose. I picked the dinner," Alex replied.

Chase studied the VHS cases. "Ben has good taste. Let's watch *Casablanca*. One of my favorites."

Alex jumped up. "Let me get some wine." She returned with a bottle of red, displaying the label. "Erica Strong sent me a mixed case of her best varietals. I think she has a crush on me."

"Can't blame her," Chase said, smiling.

Alex reddened.

Chase cleared her throat. "I'm sorry about last night. I'll go to a hotel after we watch the movie."

"I told you, you don't have to go. Drink the wine with me."

Chase opened the bottle and poured. She sipped at the cabernet. "Erica Strong is a genius. Maybe you should get together with her. What a connection."

"How mercenary."

"It's the Hollywood in me." Chase picked up the remote. "Forget it. Watch Humphrey Bogart sacrifice himself for Ingrid Bergman."

They ate with chopsticks and drank the exquisite wine. As *Casablanca* unfolded, Alex laughed to herself about Ben's choice. An impossible love triangle. Despite or perhaps because of the ironies, when Bogart touched Bergman's face at the end, Alex felt a tear running down her cheek.

Here's looking at you, kid.

She glanced over at Chase. Her friend was crying, too.

Chapter Twenty-Five

WHEN THEY ARRIVED at Ben's place in Southland the next morning, he unlocked a steel-grid front door barrier that could have held back an army of barbarians. The windows on the cottage were barred. "It's not a real safe neighborhood," he commented. "Hope you didn't leave anything in your car." From somewhere in the house, a baby wailed.

Alex wondered how Ben's repair business could survive in this little urban war zone. Ben grinned at her. "I deliver and pick-up from my customers. My wife and I are saving to buy a condo. She just got a nursing gig at Saint Joseph's Trauma Center. Meantime, we trade off watching the baby."

An exhausted-looking woman with mussed-up hair came into the living room, carrying the wailing infant. She was a foot shorter than Ben and half his body weight.

"This is my wife, Lisa," Ben said. "And my energetic daughter, Vivien."

Vivien let out a few more high-pitched shrieks, then fell instantly asleep. The quiet was startling. Alex glanced around. The house was furnished with cheap but pleasant discount furniture and a wild scattering of infant toys. Altogether, the atmosphere was typical young parent organized chaos.

"Pretty normal, huh?" Lisa asked. She smiled at their guilty-looking faces. "It's okay. A lot of people think gamers are weird."

"Watch and learn," Ben said. He directed them to a couch facing a large monitor. Lisa placed Vivien in a bassinet and joined them. Both parents sat side-by-side, clutching keyboards.

"My user name is also my character's name and it's unique," Ben explained. "I'm Seth Rockbreaker, a 42nd level dwarven warrior." Ben pressed a few keys. A hugely muscled, armor-clad animated man brandishing a gleaming sword raced into the courtyard of a menacing fortress. "I'm what's called a melee fighter. I'm cunning and adept at martial arts and hand weapons."

"I'm Ravi Lightheart, 42nd level white witch," Lisa said. "Seth was almost killed in the last encounter, but I saved him. I'm in the cleric class. I specialize in healing and defensive magic." An animated woman in flowing white robes gestured on the screen. She had large boobs and tiny feet. It was not the time, however, to question dubious gender stereotypes aloud.

"Why do you play the games?" Chase asked. "Why not just

rent a movie? I'm being honest. I've always wondered."

"Because it's not passive," Ben said.

Good point, Alex, worshipper of all things Wonder Woman, thought. She was the last person to criticize fantasy heroics.

"Did Chip play with you?" Chase asked.

"No, he was into *Metropolis*. It's more of a superhero thing, in present time. We never played it. But I'm sure Chip most definitely rocked." Ben went over to a bookcase. He picked up a photo and brought it back to them. A motley assortment of young people crowded into the shot. Alex recognized slightly younger versions of Ben, Lisa and Chip.

"This was our group," Ben said. "A few of us, like me and Lisa, never played any games in high school. Some of the others did, but Chip was the master. He got us all into it. Ever heard of *Dungeons and Dragons*?"

"It's a board game," Chase said. "Geeks played it in high school and college." Chase reddened. "I'm sorry. You know what I mean."

"It's not a board game, but never mind." Ben grinned. "Hooray for geeks." He stroked Vivien's head. "My daughter can become a dweeb with a nose ring. She can become a cheerleader. I'll love her for whatever she is. But I'll be really proud if she's a nerdy computer genius."

"Chip was the best player in the entire county," Lisa said. "He learned *Dungeons and Dragons* when he was a kid. He became our DM or Dungeon Master, that's the one who creates the stories, the settings, who referees. Our group was solid because of him."

"Besides his mother, did Chip talk about his family?"

"He had a grandmother he was real close to. She helped raise him, since his mom was kind of nutty. Also, there was this stepfather. Chip was cool about everything, at least on the surface. But if he ever got going on the stepfather, he got weird, choked-up. Say, I'd think about talking to that guy. He's a big used car dealer. Wally Welch Auto Empire. Does these whacko commercials on the boob tube. You watch those, I'll bet you think he's got some ugly secrets." Ben shrugged. "That's what I know about his past. As for college, I graduated in computer technology, Lisa did nursing. I don't even remember what Chip majored in. He wasn't that into it."

"You stayed friends with your group after college," Alex prompted.

Ben frowned. "I worked for Alliant Technologies for a while after graduation, but I quit. I'm not a corporate man. Most of our former college buddies, they're just hanging around, playing games or building computers or doing music. They survive on minimum wages jobs that are hard to get fired from. Hey, that's my

generation, you know?" He reached over and patted Lisa's knee.
"Times have changed. Now the woman can provide the health
insurance. I'm okay with that."

"Speaking of which," Chase said, "we were trying to track
down Chip's girlfriend."

"Told you at the store," Ben said. "Don't think he had one."

"I told you he did," Lisa piped up. "He had one. I could tell."
She smiled at Chase and Alex. "About a year or so ago, Chip was
different. You know how a person looks when they're in love? Chip
had that dreamy face. He had this constant expression of wanting
to brag, but feeling like he had to keep a secret."

"Is it possible that it was an online romance?" Chase asked.

Ben grinned at her. "You are smart lady. Good detective. We
wondered the same thing. Chip could have had anybody online.
But, let's face it. It's not the same as a warm body. Here's a clue for
you. We didn't tell the cops because they didn't ask. This is better,
anyway. Two cool lady sleuths tracking down the truth." Ben
glanced at Lisa for approval. She nodded her agreement.

"Just about the same time that Chip went all goo-goo, this
pretty chick started coming into the store and flirting with him.
Chip got all puffed up with hope and hormones. Then she stopped
coming and he didn't act very upset. Well, was it because he was
hiding his disappointment? Or was he doing something with the
pretty lady? At the time, we thought he was covering up his
feelings. Now, we wonder. What if he was seeing her in secret?"

"Why would he do that?" Alex asked.

Ben shrugged. "Maybe she was married. Love is strange.
Maybe he embarrassed her. He looked like a sixteen-year-old
poster boy for a teeny-bopper website."

"Can you describe her?" Alex asked.

"Little. About Lisa's size. Dark hair, cut short."

"A million women," Chase said. "Anything that made her
special?"

Ben grinned. "Tight jeans and a nice butt."

Lisa poked him without much rancor. "Get past the
testosterone and think."

"Animal t-shirts," Ben said. "Tight ones." Lisa started to poke
him again, but he waved her off. "Save this animal, save that one.
We have a pets-allowed policy, or at least we did before the
corporate take-over. She brought dogs on a leash. Either she had a
lot of dogs or she was some kind of pet sitter or something."

A bell went off in Alex's head. She reached for her cell phone
and activated the saved picture function. "Take a look at this."

Ben's face lit up. "That's her. The littler one."

Alex held the screen out for Chase to see. The photo was of

Paula, Rickie and Henry, taken on the patio at Sandy's place.

THEY HAD LUNCH at a hole-in-wall burrito place on E street, near Santa Rosa Plaza. Chase studied the photo Alex had shown Ben. "So, Rickie Coleman was Chip's girlfriend. Where do we go from here?"

Alex took a bite from her *carnitas* burrito, chewed slowly, then swallowed. "Maybe Rickie made him do it. Maybe Helena is lying and she made him do it. I think we need to talk to Wally Welch. Problem is, getting him to talk to us." She grinned, taking in Chase's expression. "I know. You'll do it. You have your ways."

Chase smiled back. "Let me think about. Where there's a will, there's a way."

"Cliché," Alex cried.

FOR THE REST of the day, they went their separate ways. Chase reminded Alex that she'd actually come up, in part, to do some work for Lumina Studios. She planned on a scouting trip with Rafe Gillis to a dense and foggy forest location in Occidental that would serve as a substitute for Transylvania. Alex decided to make a short pilgrimage to Namaste Fitness, Sebastopol's premiere health and fitness facility.

"At last," Jerry, Namaste's bald and muscular owner, cried. "Girl, we need you. I have somebody teaching kickboxing, but it isn't the same. Everyone misses you."

"Nice to be wanted," Alex replied. She glanced around.

"Sandy isn't here," Jerry said. "She and Mary are on another anniversary vacation. I can't keep track. They celebrate each month." He slapped her bicep. "I'm losing money. I love you anyway. But please let me put you back on the class schedule."

Alex hesitated. "Jerry, I need a change. We all have to move on."

Jerry sighed. "Change is good." He settled a beefy hand on her shoulder. "Think about it before you leave us." He squeezed her upper deltoid. "New job or new honey?"

Alex blushed. "Neither."

Jerry cocked his head. "Gotcha. You don't have to tell me."

When she left the fitness center, Alex headed straight for the meditation garden on the other side of the parking lot. She hid behind a towering redwood tree, seated on a stone bench. The spot reminded her a little of the herb garden she'd spent quiet time in at her former mansion. After her husband's death, after terrible months of self-imposed isolation, she'd gone out one day and puked into the lemon thyme, then encountered a neighbor who'd triggered her move to Sonoma County and her new life. Today, her stomach felt queasy again. She felt on the edge of an important change. This time the instigator was Chase.

THAT EVENING, ALEX and Chase brought home sushi from a place Jeffrey had recommended, and studied Wally Welch commercials. Decked in a jeweled crown, "King Wally" was a self-mocking monarch bestowing impossible deals on luxurious vehicles and credit to everyone. His ads were outrageous, fun and intentionally cheesy. Wally Welch was a human cliché.

Chapter Twenty-Six

WALLY WELCH PRESIDED over a mansion in the Sonoma Mountain hills above Bennett Valley Road in Santa Rosa. Like Heyward Penny in L.A., he was surprisingly accommodating about meeting with Alex and Chase on short notice. The hilltop castle boasted a five-car garage and a high-end Ford parked in each bay. Wally answered the door, wearing his crown. He laughed at their expressions and wagged a finger at them. "You came here in a *Toyota?*"

"It's a rental," Chase explained.

"Demand a Lincoln next time," he said. "Come in."

The palace was half home and half auto museum. In the middle of the opulent living room, a mint-condition Model T perched on a platform, cordoned off by golden ropes. Vintage auto ads enlarged to mural size plastered the soaring walls. Wally pointed to a massive sculpture composed of engine parts. Alex's eyes widened.

"Isn't that an amazing coincidence?" Wally announced. "I did some research on you ladies last night, just as you did on me, no doubt. Ms. Pope, that piece of your father's is worth a fleet of Continentals. I bought that sculpture twenty years ago, before Arthur Pope became so famous. I love his early stuff. Too bad he gave up on the auto themes." He pointed to a huge movie poster. "And you, Ms. Stuyvesant. Your great-grandfather, Poppa Weiss, one of the last great Hollywood tycoons, produced a film masterpiece about Henry Ford." He laughed, clearly enjoying his situation. "Now, what can I do for you?"

They sat on a sectional couch composed of seats restructured from limousine parts. A horn tooted loudly and a miniature version of the Model T rolled into the room, driven by a boy around ten years old. The boy climbed out of the car and carefully carried over a tray containing a King Wally carafe, King Wally cream and sugar containers, and three King Wally mugs.

"This is my stepson. His real name is Ralph, but we call him Ranger."

Ranger poured their coffee with a concentrated frown. He had slicked back hair and wore a pressed white shirt under a black apron.

"Good boy," Wally said. He glanced at them with mocking silent acknowledgment. Of course, in their homework, Alex and Chase would know that Ranger was the son from a previous marriage of Wally's fourth wife, a woman about Alex's age.

Before they could begin their questions, Wally's expression darkened. He removed the crown. He was shiny bald and resembled a paunchy Yul Brynner, capturing the actor's sexiness in *The King and I*. No mystery that Helena Jordan had married him. He had the big ego she was apparently attracted to.

"Ugly business," he said, shaking his head with detached regret. "Chip, my first stepson." Wally's eyes grew teary. On some level, he was hard not to like. He had the air of a man who understood he was partially a joke.

Was he acting? Alex wasn't sure. She glanced at Chase, who gave her a minute shrug.

Wally, clearly, didn't miss a thing. "I'm being *honest*. I'm sure you've done things you pray you could eliminate." Since there was no other answer than 'yes,' he continued. "Helena, Myrtle Wolinski, was a bad choice in my life at a time when I was struggling with addictions to alcohol, prescription pain killers and macho bullshit. Helena came to the house to do my second wife's hair and we met." He smiled ruefully. "An affair. Divorce. Ugly publicity in this community. You know the story. Helena and Chip became my new family."

A loud horn from a huge clock shaped like a cherry red Bonneville bellowed the hour. Wally grinned at their startled jumps. "Helena hated that clock. She was very noise-sensitive. In fact, she was very sensitive all around. So was Chip, for that matter. They were quite a pair, two little frightened mice."

Wally made an aborted sucker punch at himself, stopping short of his jaw. "Jerk. Shut up. Be nice." He arranged his lips into a tight smile.

"When Helena and I married, Chip was nine. They were living in a rental unit near downtown, off Seventh Street, behind the beauty parlor where she worked. Helena wanted to keep working. I didn't like it. The only brave thing she ever did in our relationship was stick to her guns about it. She had to live with me bullying her about working. I told you, I wasn't a good man. I grew up with a father who pushed me to be a man. I thought I turned out all right. What a laugh. I turned out like him. A control freak afraid of his women victims. And of children, including Chip, who *was* kind of a pansy freak."

"More coffee?" Ranger asked. He had a distinct lisp and no apparent reaction to Wally's confession.

Wally reached over and stroked his stepson's head. "Now I understand that my tormenting Chip made him more of a pansy freak. Poor kid. I'll tell you. Ranger likes to cook. He pretends he's the butler. I give him love, no matter what I think."

Ranger climbed back into his car and motored from the room.

Wally leaped up and put his crown back on. "I *like* gays. Are you girls gay?" He held up his hand, before they could speak. "Never mind. Chip wasn't even gay, anyway." He stalked the room, looking as if he might break out in a tragic heartfelt Broadway musical number. Wally found the photo he was looking for and brought it to them.

In the photo, Wally and Chip stood on a dock. Chip held up a large dead fish. He looked like he was about to puke. Wally jabbed the photo. "See? The kid was such a wuss. I can't imagine him chopping off someone's head. Gotta be someone else involved." He sat down, removed the crown, dabbed at his eyes.

Alex thought it might be a good time to insert a question into the silence. "What happened with Chip? With the three of you?"

"You've heard of shotgun weddings? I had a shotgun divorce." He stood again, located another picture, brought it over to them. "This is Helena's mother, Esther, in front of the fully loaded Ford 250 with four-wheel drive I gave her. Truck was so big we had to adapt the sucker so the little witch could drive it."

The little witch was the woman with the cockatiel who'd been with Rickie Coleman at the vet the day she and Chase had taken Henry for his foxtail removal. If it was a coincidence, it was a very meaningful one. *Synchronicity*, Alex's mother called it. The meaningful coincidences that proved that all the universe was connected under the surface.

Wally picked up his narrative. "When Chip was fourteen, he got nabbed for supposedly diddling around with two little sisters, aged five and seven, who lived in the little rental unit behind the beauty parlor where Helena and Chip used to live before our marriage. Seems like he used to go back there when his mother was working, baby-sit for them. Got caught undressing them. He *insisted* he was just putting them in fairy tale costumes he made up, but the little girls' mother went hysterical and called the police, seeing her kids in undies, with Chip bending over them." Wally shook his head. "He did have the costumes and the little girls sided with him. He got carted off to jail anyway. To make a long story short, I contacted a buddy in the court system and Chip got his hand slapped. But I really got on his case after that, jerk that I was."

Wally rubbed his eyes, as though to erase an ugly image. "He talked back to me. I belted him. His mother came after me and I slapped her. They pranced off to grandma's house. I sobered up and went over there the next day to apologize." Wally slapped his thigh in a gesture of appreciation. "The old dame came out of the house with a shotgun and chased me off the property. They never came back. See? Shotgun divorce."

"Can you tell us about Buddy Brubech? Did Helena ever talk about him?"

"Talk?" Wally snorted. "She was obsessed. Pictures, mementos. After the first few days of our relationship, she didn't mention him. I was too jealous. I know she always had that love-hate fixation, not surprised she infected Chip with it. Still, like I said, the kid was weird, but he wasn't an ax murderer. Not enough guts for that." Wally glanced at his car watch. "Gotta get to the lot. We have a special no-interest lease going this month."

Alex took out her cell phone and held it out to him. "Do these two look familiar?"

"You kidding?" Wally exclaimed, staring at the photo. "That's Paula Coleman, the best female athlete to ever come out of this county and her animal nut sister. Don't know why Paula came back here for some low-level corrections job. Could at least have become a sports announcer making big pay on ESPN." He shrugged. "This is off the record, girls. It might be said that at a drunken party a number of years ago, a married asshole might have hinted to another married asshole, me, that he was humping one of his school athletes, with some obvious hints to make it clear it was Paula." He jabbed his finger at the image of Rickie Coleman. "The other one is just a tree-hugger and animal freak. We have a lot of those in this county."

"Did you know Rickie Coleman and your former mother-in-law were friends?"

Wally shrugged. "Big deal. Esther was into animals, too."

"What if I told you that Rickie Coleman and Chip had taken up with each other?"

"Too much," Wally said, grinning. "You girls are good. This is a small county still, especially among the old-timers. You dig deep enough, you'll find secret connections like the sewer lines threading the Paris underground." He stood, took a handful of Wally coupons from the coffee table and handed them to Alex and Chase. "Fill these out and you may win an Escalade. The stub gets you a free bratwurst and a Coke at my dealership."

Chapter Twenty-Seven

AS THEY DROVE up Esther Wolinski's driveway, she came out of the house and aimed a shotgun at them.

"I told you we should have called first," Chase said.

"I told *you* her number was unlisted."

"Get out," Esther said. She squinted at them. "You're the one with the cat that had the foxtail. How is he?" She still hadn't lowered the gun.

"Fine," Alex said. She climbed from the car with her hands in the air.

Esther laughed. "Put your hands down. You and the other one, come inside."

"Thank you, Granny," Chase said. Alex had already filled her in about Granny's anti-ageism preferences.

Granny laughed. "Always makes me sound like something from a fairy tale. That's funny." Alex, who made a practice of studying people's movements, watched as Granny led them to the house. She moved like a graceful younger woman.

Esther's ranch had a slightly deserted feel. Behind the main house, a row of chicken barns lay collapsed into weathered ruin, walls leaning precariously. One small coop remained sturdy. A flock of clucking chickens strutted in and out an open hatch, scratching the dirt, pecking at bugs. Weeds and discarded farm parts spread in all directions, leading eventually to a surrounding enclosure of thick shrubby trees scattered among towering eucalyptus. Altogether, it looked like Granny had quite a spread, maybe five acres of seclusion. With the recent real estate bust, it probably wasn't worth the zillion dollars of a few years before, but it was still prime property.

"Who's that? Knock, knock. Come in." Three cockatiels sat in a row, scrutinizing them as they entered the weather-beaten house. Aside from a mild odor of bird poop, the living room was cozy and inviting. Granny removed a sheet from a couch and gestured for them to sit. "I don't drink coffee. I will prepare a protein shake with raw egg." She disappeared without waiting for a response.

"Birds. Birds. Birds," a cockatiel said.

"We can see that," Chase said to the cockatiels. The room was filled with bird imagery, on the walls, on every available surface. Songbirds, ostriches, parrots, exotic chickens, ducks and geese. Granny returned with three tall glasses filled with thick yellowish potentially salmonella-infused liquid.

"Drink," Granny said.

For the sake of the investigation, Alex took a slug. It was good, in a strange way. She poked Chase. "It tastes better than the green stuff you made me swallow."

Chase took a tentative sip. "Not bad."

Granny smiled with approval. "Eggs go in and out of style, but they'll never go away. But you didn't invade me for an egg commercial. You came about my Helena and Chip."

"Chip! Chip!" The cockatiels appeared agitated.

"I told you. Chip went away. To a good place." Granny, too, looked upset. "My birds loved Chip. They know he met a bad end." Granny squinted at them. "You talked to my daughter already. Did you get to the lousy ex-husband yet? Probably. He'll take any attention he can get."

From the room next door, a short, elaborate bird song rang out. "That's my email alert," Granny explained. "I have high-speed internet." She gestured around the living room. "Chip understood my world. Chip loved the chickens and the cockatiels. More important, he understood why I loved my birds, something I'm afraid my daughter, his mother, never did." She pointed a finger at them. "Of course you Googled me."

Alex shrugged. "Newspaper articles. You had a spot on a documentary about the Jewish chicken farmers in Sonoma County. We didn't have time to watch it. We know you came from Warsaw, your parents were sent to the camps, you got sent to the countryside and were hidden on a farm with sympathetic gentiles, then left Poland for Marin County, adopted by a surgeon and his wife."

Granny smiled in wonderment. "The world is changing. So much you find out in so little time on computers. But you don't always find out the nuances, do you? On the farm, I learned to love and respect animals, even if you slaughter them. Do you understand?" Granny's voice shook. "Do you understand how horrendous it is that humans slaughter other humans and innocent animals because of hatred and greed?"

They did understand. There was no need to respond.

"I was a very bright girl," Granny continued. "Very good at math. I went to San Francisco State University for engineering, met Saul Wolinski and fell in love. We thought we would be engineers. When his parents died, he inherited the chicken ranch and we took it over." Granny sighed. "It was an active community, these Jews who came to Sonoma County in the early times, some of them religious and some of them atheist political activists. Two camps. A thriving small world in a bigger American world where we didn't have to fear persecution. At least not mass extinction."

Granny sighed. "I loved my chickens. I cared for them when they were sick. I had Helena help me, of course. When she and Chip came to live here, after the divorce from that auto empire fool, I had Chip help me. At least *he* learned to love birds."

"Chip," one of the cockatiels said. "Chip."

Granny winced. "I feel so bad for my girls."

"Helena didn't love birds?" Alex asked.

"Feh!" Granny cried. "Her name is Myrtle. But she insists on Helena." At Granny's agitated reaction, the cockatiels raised their wings and beat the air. "She won't answer to anything but Helena," Granny said. "She was always like that. Making up who she was."

Chase nodded sympathetically. "But she loved you and Chip."

"Helena loved Helena. Helena loved people who indulged her fantasies. I admit I was a little harsh with her. The poor thing was a dreamy weakling, encouraged by a dreamy father. When he died, Helena was only six. I was forced to run everything myself. I *loved* this ranch and my animals. I loved Helena, too. I only wanted her to be more prepared for the ugliness in the world. She *did* have a winning side, like a beam of light bewitching people, especially men. A schoolteacher hooked her up with a child-modeling agency. She hated the farm. We needed the money. That was the beginning of her career." Granny shook her head. "She didn't have the strength to be a success. I knew that."

Alex knew it was time to bring up the delicate subject they'd come for. "What about her relationship with Buddy Brubech? We promise to be discrete."

"Silly girl," Granny said. "Would I have let you on this property, unauthorized in your meddling, if I didn't want to talk? I don't trust the authorities. They often collaborate in schemes, if you know what I mean. Helena was obsessed with Buddy Brubech. But I don't think he made her crazy. She was a porcelain doll waiting to break."

"And Chip?" Alex prompted.

Granny sighed. "Chip was a chip off his mother's block. I tried to make him stronger, like I did his mother. I'm sorry for what happened, but he was impaired." She shrunk in her chair. "I'm getting tired. I need you to leave."

"One more question." Alex didn't think Granny looked in the least bit tired.

Granny's eyes narrowed. "Yes?"

"Did you know your friend Rickie Coleman and Chip were involved?"

"Not possible," Granny said firmly.

"We have evidence."

"Such smart girls," Granny said. "Such intelligent, determined girls." She stood. "I hope you don't get yourself in trouble. Good-bye."

"Bye-bye!" a cockatiel cried.

"Take care," the second cockatiel cried.

"Have a nice life," the third one cried.

Chapter Twenty-Eight

AS THEY WERE driving along Stony Point Road back to Sebastopol, Alex's cell rang. It was about 4 p.m.

"It's Gracie, the nurse from Spirit Foundation. Can you meet me at Humpty Dumpty?"

Alex glanced at Chase. "Gracie has something."

"We're becoming a repository for everyone's secrets."

"What a wonderful thing," Alex said, grinning.

Gracie was already in a front booth when they arrived. "I like you girls," she said. "But I'm afraid. There's some dirty laundry." She glanced over at the sheriffs having their coffee klatch on the other side of the room. "The authorities in this county are mostly good eggs. I don't want a few bad apples to spoil the bunch."

Alex did not look over at Chase. She didn't want to distract Gracie with any reactions to her multiple clichés.

"My daughter's low-life boyfriend was just released from jail. Ordinarily, I wouldn't pay attention to a word he says. He's a liar and a cheat, besides being a thief. But he's a movie fanatic and he's always loved Helena Welch. He hears a lot and he listens, unlike some of the other blockheads in the county jails. He knew Chip and liked him, too."

The waitress came over and refilled their cups, lingering as though she'd love to get in on the conversation. Gracie waited, tight-lipped, until the waitress gave up.

"The loser, as I call him, told my daughter, who told me, that Chip's poisoning was something that, if the reason got out, would be very detrimental to some high mucky-mucks."

"How did he find that out?" Alex asked.

"He had a cellmate who knew something," Gracie said. "As I understand it, bragging is a common activity in jail. The cellmate bragged about something to my daughter's boyfriend. It involved Chip Welch." Gracie pulled out a card. "I'm a link in a mystery, isn't that cool?"

Alex glanced at the card and showed it to Chase.

"It's the cellmate," Gracie said. "His name is Eddie Price. He was conveniently granted early release. Get in touch with him. He might be persuaded to brag to two lovely women like you."

"But this is a business card for Erica Strong Vineyards," Alex said.

"That's where he works. My son doesn't know his home phone."

"Eddie works for *Erica Strong*?" Alex asked.

Gracie looked puzzled.

"Never mind," Alex said, standing. "Thanks, Gracie. You've been a great help."

By the time they got back to the Knight hacienda, it was nearly 6 p.m. Henry meowed with poignant misery at their extended absence and his near starvation. Alex fed him his organic kibble, then pulled out a bottle of wine from the Erica Strong gift collection and filled a couple of bowls with pretzels and baked chips.

They traipsed out to the patio, bundled in sweatshirts. The air smelled of wood smoke. Dried leaves blew across the flagstone pavers. Birds chirped from the trees. For the first time in her life, Alex wondered what kind of birds they were. Now she had birds on the brain. Nevertheless, the evening was lovely and it was nice to be settled with Chase and Henry. She realized with a start that she felt a feeling of home. She realized with a jolt that the feeling was something she wasn't sure she'd really ever felt fully in her life ever before. The insight was as deeply disturbing as it was pleasurable.

"I could get used to this," Chase said, breaking into her reverie.

Alex stood, speaking as she walked away. "I could get used to you being here, too." She walked quickly out of speaking range before Chase could reply. She returned with her laptop. "I'm Googling Eddie Price."

"Enlighten me about our lead suspect," Chase said.

"Eddie Price has a long arrest record, all involving theft or burglary or fraud. Comes from a prominent local family. A black sheep. His brothers and sisters are all upstanding members of the community." Alex sighed. "Whatever upstanding means anymore. This investigation is beginning to look like something from a soap opera."

Chase smiled. "It's human nature."

"Isn't that depressing to you?"

"At the risk of sounding as pompous as Jerome, that's what makes life what it is. Real life is terrible and marvelous. If you expect it to be just one or the other, you're bound to be cynical. Being optimistic is a challenge to accept evil as the counterpoint to good."

Alex sighed. "Okay, okay." She held out her phone. "Here's a challenge. Get Eddie Price to talk to us."

Chase stood. "Challenge accepted." She went into Alex's place and returned in ten minutes, looking like the Cheshire cat. "All taken care of. Tomorrow afternoon."

"You're something else."

"Thank you."

Alex sighed. "What's up for tonight?"

"There's a glee club performance at the high school. If we hop in the car, we can make it and grab a bite to eat after."

"Glee club?"

"I love stuff like that. I told you, I was a totally straight–arrow in my youth." Chase hesitated. "Is something wrong?"

Alex winced. "I had some ugly dealings with the local high school a few months back. Remember, I told you. I got myself into trouble."

Chase shrugged. "Doesn't matter. You have to live in this town. Embrace it. Go back to the scene of the crime and be strong."

"You're right." Alex sighed. "Promise me that we *don't* make fun of glee club when we get back, no matter how much they suck."

Chase looked startled. "Why would we do that?"

"My husband and I used to go to nerdy obligatory events and then ridicule it all afterwards. I'm not proud of my duplicity."

"I appreciate your disclosure," Chase said. "I don't care what you did in your past. I evaluate you on how I perceive you now. However, we can agree to avoid making fun of *anyone*. I don't believe in it."

Alex smiled at Chase. "That's what I like about you." Her smile faded. "What about talking behind someone's back?"

"I apologized," Chase burst out. "Alex, let go."

Alex shrugged. "What's so good about letting go?"

Chase grinned. "It's cathartic."

Alex shivered. "One of my mother's favorite terms."

"Oh, no," Chase cried with exaggerated horror. "Let's not get into a discussion on mothers. The road to hell, cliché intended." She reached for the video case on the coffee table. "Forget the glee club. Let's watch *Brokeback Mountain*. By the way, it wasn't lost on me that our friend Ben picked out two quintessential tales of impossible three-way love triangles."

Alex ignored the remark about the love triangles. "You talked to Eddie Price. Will he see us?"

Chase smiled triumphantly. "Told you I'd do it."

"I love you," Alex said impulsively. "You're great."

Chase's smile froze on her face. "Don't say that."

Alex felt queasy. "I meant as a friend."

"Can we just stop talking?" Chase said. "Let's watch some television and be quiet."

If possible, *Brokeback Mountain* was more a gut-wrenching tear-jerker than *Casablanca*. Alex and Chase sobbed uncontrollably by the final moments.

"Catharsis is exhausting," Chase choked out.

"No kidding," Alex replied, throat raw.

"Alex?"

"Yes?"

"I don't feel transformed."

"Neither do I," Alex said. "Let's get some sleep. Maybe finding some answers to our mystery will help."

THE NEXT MORNING, Alex woke early from a nightmare in which she had given birth to a baby and then somehow lost it. She was searching futilely for the lost child when she heard a soft "Knock, knock." She sat bolt upright, clutching her covers. In her anxious state, she'd forgotten she had a houseguest.

"Did I startle you?" Chase asked. "You mentioned wanting to get up early." She was standing at the edge of Alex's sleeping nook, with a tray, which held two coffees and a plate of toast. She grinned. "Like Ranger. I'm playing butler." She hesitated.

Alex patted the edge of her sleeping platform. "Breakfast pajama party." At Chase's conflicted expression, she threw off the covers and got up from the mattress. "Let's go sit upright."

"Good idea," Chase said with obvious relief.

Chapter Twenty-Nine

THAT AFTERNOON, AFTER a nice lunch in a little bistro in Graton, Alex and Chase drove down the lane that led to Erica Strong's vineyard. "Lovely place," Chase commented. They arrived at the main building of the winery. Erica Strong marched out. Chase whistled under her breath. "She really is a hot number."

"You're not kidding," Alex said. "You should see her t-shirt collection."

As they climbed from the car, Erica crossed her arms over her chest in a defensive posture. Unlike the last visit on the evening of the charity event, Erica did not look welcoming. "I would have preferred if you hadn't involved me and my workplace in your shenanigans."

Erica turned to Chase, looking angry and protective. "Eddie Price is a deluded misfit from a nice family. Pretending you're going to do a story on him, that's harsh. What are you up to?" Erica turned to Alex. Her look was more complex, both apprehensive and appreciative. "The only good thing about all this is seeing you again. What's up, Wonder Woman?"

Alex shrugged. "Ridding the world of evil. You know."

Erica laughed. "Then I can't turn you away, can I? Eddie is in the barreling room."

EDDIE PRICE WAS a skinny, gawky man with wispy facial hair. His face was etched with permanent neediness. He wore baggy coveralls and was swabbing the slick cement floor. The barreling room was cool and smelled of fermentation. He set his mop down and wiped his hands on a cloth. He glanced at Erica, who gestured kindly at him. "Take a break, Eddie. You three can use the small conference room on the west end."

Eddie bowed to Erica and stared at Chase and Alex, looking as expectant as a beauty pageant hopeful. "I have so much I want to tell the world. Can't believe someone from Hollywood wants to feature me."

It seemed like everyone on the planet would tear their guts out for their fifteen minutes of fame. Alex felt mildly guilty, until she reminded herself that she really was trying to rid the world of evil, on some level anyway.

Eddie Price appeared to think of himself as a polished

operator. He didn't make eye contact, generating familiarity by thrusting his slight frame forward and speaking from the side of his mouth, like Groucho Marx without Groucho's intelligence or humor.

"I understand you were a model prisoner," Alex began.

"A trustee," Eddie said. "I was given responsibilities, no problem. I know my stuff. I pretty much ran the kitchen by my last *incarceration*." Eddie took a moment to savor his use of a big word.

"You ran the kitchen when Chip Welch was poisoned?" Chase asked.

Eddie frowned. "I thought you were here to tell my life story."

Chase made as though she was holding up a camera and aimed it at Eddie. "You're a quick study, Eddie. Today's movies have to be relevant to today. Look, we know you have some *very interesting* insights into the prison system. That's a subject that would be interesting to the public. Let me tell you, if we get that story, then we can practically guarantee you a role as a consulting producer. It pays well and could lead to other things."

Eddie looked conflicted, but intrigued. "It could lead to me getting in big trouble, that's what it could lead to."

Chase sighed. "Eddie. You already told someone."

A small bead of sweat had formed on Eddie's temple. "Just some druggie kid. I guess I was bragging." He squinted, looking over their heads.

"It's a great story, Eddie," Chase prompted.

"Yeah," he said. "The Death of Eddie Price."

"Let me start the story," Chase said. "Someone told you Chip Welch deserved to be gotten rid of."

Eddie shrugged. "Cop snitches are gotten rid of, that's who are gotten rid of. But Al Pacino didn't die in *Serpico*. The druggie kid told me to rent that movie when I got out. He was a real movie nut. *Serpico* was good." He frowned. "I may be a thief, but I hate anyone who hurts little children." He shuddered. "We get some real monsters, raping little kids. Chip Welch was the worst. That's what we found out in the jail. That he raped some little girls when he was fourteen. He deserved what he got. He would have got worse, but he was in solitary. No one could get to him."

"Except through his food."

Eddie smiled slyly. "Yeah." He adopted a mask of innocence. "Not that I know anything about that."

"Eddie, just tell a story. Let's say a guy wanted to get rid of some scumbag. They could slip something in his food pretty easy. It wouldn't be really hard to get hold of the poison either, would it?"

"Not if you were *capable*," Eddie replied.

Chase sat in deep thought for several minutes. Alex was appreciating the tactic, though not sure where Chase was going with it. She was sure, however, at how clever she thought Chase was. Good God. She realized she was actually getting a crush on Chase. She shook away the thought. Now was possibly the worst time for that kind of revelation.

"In *Serpico*, Pacino informs on bad cops and lives to tell the story. Did you know the real Serpico was a consultant on that movie?" Chase asked.

Alex thought she remembered reading that the real Serpico had fled to Switzerland to avoid being killed. Another topic left unspoken.

"No kidding," Eddie said.

"His name was on the credits and he got a pretty good sum of money."

"No kidding," Eddie repeated.

"You know Paula Coleman," Chase said.

Eddie nodded, eyes flickering.

"How about her boss, John Strong, Erica's brother, the one who got you the job here? You knew him, too."

"Everybody knew both of them." Eddie sounded petulant. "They liked me. Made me a trustee."

"Could that be because you did them favors?" Chase asked.

Eddie threw up his hands in frustration. "All right. I might have done some favors for them."

"You knew they were love-birds," Chase said. "Did you catch them at it? Is that how you knew?"

Eddie's mouth fell open.

"Eddie, you're a smart guy who gets things done. Tell me," Chase persisted.

Eddie's eyes bulged from the effort to decide whether to brag or not. Ego won. "Caught them screwing in a broom closet," he said.

"You helped them get rid of Chip."

"I don't know," Eddie replied warily.

"It doesn't matter," Chase said kindly. "Chip was a real sleaze, like you said. Deserved to die, anyway. Here's what I don't understand. Why would Paula and John want him dead?"

"I wondered the same thing," Eddie said. He realized suddenly the implications of what he said and looked like he might start to cry. He stood up abruptly. "I'm going to get in trouble. Oh boy. That's it. I'm not talking to you anymore. I don't want to be a consultant." With that, he fled out the door of the conference room.

Alex's heart was thumping. "That was incredible. How did you put all that together?"

"It's the kind of thing I lay awake at night and think about," Chase said.

"I have nightmares in the middle of the night," Alex admitted.

"That's what I used to have. Now I do this instead. You should try it."

"Maybe you can give me lessons."

Chase's eyes widened. "Are you flirting with me?"

Alex jumped up. "Of course not."

Before Chase could challenge the obvious lie, Alex noticed Erica Strong looming in the doorway. Alex wondered if Erica had overheard the last of the conversation.

"Am I interrupting something?" Erica asked, her tone suggesting she had been listening.

"Nothing," Alex said, blushing.

"Do you have a minute?" Chase asked. "We have a few questions."

Erica took the chair formerly occupied by Eddie Price. "Did you bamboozle poor Eddie into confessing to crimes he's probably too dumb to commit?"

"I think you underestimate Eddie," Chase said. "Or how creative people can become in the jail system."

Erica glared at Chase. "Oh? I wasn't aware of your authority on jail systems. Or human nature. Or my lack of such insights, for that matter."

Chase glared back. "I also have some thoughts on family bonds and the sacrifices we'll make for our relatives. Such as giving jobs to losers who do your relatives favors."

Erica stood up. "This is not business for two amateurs. This is a police matter."

"Exactly." Chase smiled. "Have you ever seen *Serpico*?"

"I have."

"Then you know police protect their own."

Erica suddenly looked defeated. She directed her next remark at Alex. "We sometimes hurt the ones we love. You probably know that as well as anyone."

Alex shuddered.

"That wasn't a very nice thing to say," Chase interjected, glancing protectively at Alex.

"This isn't a nice state of affairs," Erica replied. "I was just discussing why people do things they may regret for the sake of love. I'm sure you can think of a few of these kinds of circumstances yourself."

"None of which is relevant to the present state of affairs," Chase said stiffly. "Alex doesn't need to be harassed about her past."

Her investigative partner was losing her cool and messing up a potential revelation, although Alex appreciated Chase coming to her defense. She needed Chase's skills more than she needed a lady knight in shining armor. "I know this is hard for you," she said to Erica. "I could see last time we were together how much you love your brother."

Erica swallowed a lump in her throat. "John was my idol. He still is, in many ways. That's why this pulls me apart. What is it with *men*? My brother may have been weak, taking up with that woman, but I blame her. Not very feminist. I don't care. There's always been rumors about her taking up with older married men. I blame Paula Coleman for getting my brother in trouble."

"A lot of trouble," Chase said. "Like poisoning."

"You'll see. It was Paula. Not my brother. He's just a wife-cheater." Erica slumped in her chair. "My mother has a weak heart. If this gets out, it will kill her."

"If?" Chase said.

Erica stood up. "I so wish you'd left all this alone."

"It would probably only have been a matter of time," Alex said.

"True." Erica smiled at Alex. "I don't blame you. You have your reasons for 'fighting evil.' In fact, I admire you." She glanced challengingly at Chase, then turned back to Alex. "When this is all over and your friend goes back to Hollywood, perhaps you and I can start all over. Two wounded soldiers in the battle of love."

AS THEY WERE driving back down the lane, Chase grinned at Alex. "That was some melodramatic cliché, that last remark from Ms. Strong. *Two wounded soldiers in the battle of love.*"

"I thought it was meant sincerely," Alex replied.

"You don't *like* her, do you?" Chase said.

"Why?"

Chase shrugged. "I'm your friend. I wouldn't want you to be hurt by getting involved with someone that could bring you trouble."

Alex shrugged. "Is there anyone who doesn't bring a person trouble?"

"Some people are more trouble than others. I don't like Erica Strong, even with her t-shirts and vests."

"Don't worry," Alex said. "I'm not in a rush to get involved with anyone as of today. I'm feeling overwhelmed with what people do in the name of love."

Chapter Thirty

PAULA COLEMAN WAS waiting for them on Alex's patio. "Have you considered locking your entry gate? Anyone could drive up here day or night."

"Pete says the same thing," Alex replied. "It's the tradition to keep it open. Sebastopol was always a safe place."

Paula shrugged. "Nowhere is safe anymore."

"Apparently not," Chase replied. "What brings you here?"

Paula looked back and forth between Alex and Chase. "Are you two shacking up now?"

"Chase is just visiting," Alex replied.

"I see," Paula said with a sly smile.

"Don't read into this," Chase said. "You hardly have room to talk."

Paula's expression lost all semblance of nonchalance. "Why did you start meddling? You're going to get good people hurt."

"People have already been hurt," Alex said. "Murdered."

"They weren't good people." Paula wrung her hands obsessively, like Lady Macbeth. "I so wish you'd left this alone. Justice was done."

"Paula, you should know this better than most. That's for the law to decide," Chase said.

"I know better than most that it's not that simple when it comes to the law," Paula said.

From around the front of the house, Wheatie appeared, holding his flute. "Everything okay?" He grinned self-mockingly. "If you need man-power."

"Everything's fine," Alex said. "The last thing we need is man-power." All told, Wheatie was probably the wussiest person on the patio. She glanced at the other women. "Maybe we should go inside."

They trooped into Alex's unit, with Wheatie watching suspiciously. "Shout if you need me," he called after them. "I mean it."

Inside Alex's little place, Paula magnified. The top of her head was only a foot below the plastered ceiling. Although she hunched over, self-conscious of how much space she was taking up, her bulk was impossible to ignore. She glanced around for a substantial seat and then lowered herself onto the lumpy but sturdy couch. Almost immediately she started to sneeze, a series of painful snorts in rapid succession. "Allergies," she choked out.

As if on cue, there was a burst of impatient meows from outside the front door. Alex got up and allowed Henry entry. He paraded in, meowing his pleasure that his company had arrived, for Henry believed that everyone came to Alex's place to visit him. Paula rubbed her eyes and sniffled, looking miserable.

"I can lock him outside," Alex said. She and Chase took seats in the two lumpy armchairs facing the lumpy couch.

"Don't bother," Paula said. "Rickie told me the dander is everywhere regardless if the cat is inside or not. Dander causes the allergic reaction."

"How did you ever stand house-sitting for me?" Alex asked. "Why?"

Paula shrugged. "I have medication if I need it. I forgot it today. Alex, don't be dumb. I needed to watch you. To see what you were doing, snooping around. Dealing with the allergies was a small price to pay." She sneezed violently.

"We can go back outside," Alex offered. Paula looked so miserable that for a moment Alex almost forgot the nature of the encounter.

"I want this over with, right now." As if she was reaching for a tissue from her sport duffle, Paula bent down. She pulled out a revolver.

"Are you sure you wouldn't like some coffee instead?" Alex asked.

"That's not funny," Paula said. She aimed the gun in Alex's direction. "Do you have espresso? You seem like the type. Caffeine helps my allergies."

Alex stood slowly, heart pounding. At least they wouldn't be murdered before a round of espressos. "I can make steamed milk for cappuccinos," she offered.

"I'm lactose intolerant," Paula said wistfully.

"We have soy milk," Alex replied. "Chase likes it."

"I *don't* like it. It's good for me," Chase said.

Paula grinned. "Are you sure you're not fooling around? You sound like a couple."

"Actually, I'm in a committed relationship," Chase said. "I don't cheat."

The ironies of the conversation on spousal cheating were not lost on three smart women. "Soy latte?" Alex asked, leaving the undercurrents submerged.

"That would be lovely." Paula sneezed again and almost dropped her gun. Alex contemplated a difficult defense move, but waved away the thought. Her chances of succeeding were slim and she didn't want Chase hurt in the rescue attempt. Maybe there was still time to work out another solution. In the meantime, coffee sounded fabulous.

As she filled the espresso machine, she marveled at how powerful immediate gratifications could be. She had always wondered how death row inmates could eat elaborate last meals before their executions. Now it suddenly made more sense.

Alex brought a tray with three cappuccino cups to the coffee table. Paula sighed and set her gun down. With lightning speed, Alex grabbed the gun and pointed it at Paula. Paula laughed. "It's not loaded. It's a stupid, broken reject anyway."

"Are you crazy?" Chase cried out.

"I might be going crazy. I've tried to protect people all my life. I didn't load the gun. I was afraid to. I'm being backed into a corner." Paula took a big sip of her cappuccino. "I never drank coffee until I went to Europe to play ball. Now I love it, the stronger the better."

The bizarreness of the situation was getting to Alex. "How about a biscotti? I have imported macadamia nut biscotti dipped in Belgian chocolate." She grinned. "Confess and you get two."

"Coercion," Paula said. She drained her cup. "Did you know I was a superstar in Europe? I got recognized on the streets in Madrid and Rome. I was always on television, I almost got a perfume contract with Armani." She frowned. "Not only was I good, but I was a team player and I never tried to hurt anyone on the court, not in a vicious way." She gestured to Alex. "Sit down and have your coffee. I'm not going to kill you. At least I don't think so. I'll earn the biscotti." Henry came over to her and rubbed her leg. Paula reached down and stroked his slick coat. "Hi, fur ball."

Henry purred. Paula's hands were very large, which made for very sensuous stroking. "Some men don't like big women," Paula said. "And a surprising bunch of them do. Especially more mature ones." Henry flopped over and let Paula rub his belly. She glanced at Alex. "I wish you'd put that gun down. It's disconcerting having you point it at me, even if it isn't loaded."

Alex stood and took the gun with her to the kitchen area. She got out a nice earthenware platter and placed eight biscotti and two cat treats on it, then set the plate on the coffee table. Alex shrugged. "Cookies make the world a better place."

Paula grabbed a cookie and a cat treat, took a big bite of the cookie and fed the treat to Henry. "I know what you like," she said to the cat. She smiled at Alex and Chase, but her eyes were serious. "I know what men like, too. I learned early."

"How early?" Alex asked.

"Too early," Paula said, not making eye contact. She ate

another biscotti, chewing thoughtfully. "It messes a kid up. It's not right."

"It went on all your life," Alex said sympathetically. "You never escaped."

"You've been snooping, so you know that I was already involved with some of my coaches. It got serious when I was twelve. I was always a star player and a favorite of everybody. My coach at that time told me he loved me. What did I learn? How to please everyone. How to never disappoint anyone. On the nights after we lost games, I cried myself to sleep. The only one who knew was my little sister Rickie, since we shared a room. Rickie was my little doll. She loved me no matter what. Do you have any more espresso?"

Alex fired up the machine and delivered another round. Her hands were shaking, as much from the caffeine overload as the situation. Paula, on the other hand, appeared weirdly content.

"Of all my closeted affairs, John Strong is the best. Was the best. He broke it off, due to this recent bad business. Too bad. I'll really miss him. He's a fabulous man and a great lover." Her shoulders drooped. "None of this can come out. The disgrace will be tragic."

"It's too late," Alex said. "Eddie Price is bragging."

Paula slapped the couch angrily. This set off a series of sneezes, as the dander flew. After she could breathe again, Paula glared at them. "Eddie Price is a complete loser and a compulsive liar. Whatever he told you, forget it. He'd snitch on his grandmother if he could get something from it."

"Eddie was freed from jail quite conveniently," Alex said.

Paula shrugged. "Eddie *may* have done us a few favors. But do you think we'd be so stupid as to have him poison Chip Welch? Look, in the jail system, guys who molest kids are dead meat. It was probably only a matter of time before Chip was taken out, once it got around that he raped little girls."

"Chip wasn't charged with rape when he was fourteen," Alex said. "Only misdemeanor charges."

"You see?" Paula said. "That's the ugliness you should be investigating. How scum with rich stepfathers get off the hook for rape."

A pounding on the door interrupted them. Before anyone could react, Rickie Coleman burst in.

"What are you doing here?" Paula cried.

"What are *you* doing here?" Rickie shot back. "I *knew* you'd do this." She turned to Alex. "Why couldn't you leave well enough alone?"

"It doesn't matter," Paula said. "The whole thing is unraveling.

Sit down. Have some coffee. We're doomed. Enjoy the moment."

"Like a cappuccino?" Alex asked.

"They're really good," Paula said.

"I can't believe you're all sitting around drinking coffee." Rickie collapsed onto the couch next to her sister. "Do you have soy milk?" she asked. "I've tried so hard to give up caffeine and refined sugar."

"Have a biscotti. Imported macadamia nut with Belgian chocolate," Paula suggested.

"Stop! You are a compulsive enabler." Rickie grabbed a cookie and took a bite. "A temptress."

"Look who's talking," Paula replied with a tone of desperate irony.

Rickie threw the remainder of the biscotti across the room. "Paula, what did you say to them?"

Paula glared. "I told them about John and me. I told them Eddie Price misinterpreted our helpful gestures. I suggested Eddie may have tried to gain some cred with the jail population by offing Chip because of Chip's twisted behavior."

Rickie started to speak, but Paula waved her hand. "Don't get involved. You had nothing to do with this."

Rickie threw up her hands. "Chip was *not* a child rapist. He was a dreamer who liked dress-up."

Chase had been quiet for awhile. Now, she spoke up. "You were involved with Chip."

"That had nothing to do with anything," Paula said insistently. "This was all my fault."

"No way," Rickie said just as insistently. "I'm not letting you take the blame. You're not going to jail."

"Rickie!" Paula cried. "There's *no jail*. No one committed a crime. Not us. You just happened to be dating a loser. I just happened to be dating a married man. We made mistakes, but we didn't commit any crimes. Did we?"

Rickie blinked rapidly. Alex knew what it was like to wander around in a state of waking nightmare. She'd been like that for six months after Stacy's death. She recognized the look on Rickie's face. Rickie was self-flagellating due to incriminatory secrets.

"No crimes," Rickie said, but she didn't look very convincing.

"I wonder," Chase said. "If it's ever justified to hurt, even kill, people who are evil and going to get away with unspeakable acts."

Paula and Rickie stared at her.

"What do you think, Rickie?" Chase asked.

"Don't answer her," Paula said to her sister.

"You played *Metropolis* with Chip."

Rickie nodded.

"You were very good."

Rickie shrugged. "Chip was very good. The best. I was okay. Not too bad."

"You and Chip played computer games where bad people had to be killed. Rickie, what if those games weren't enough?" Chase persisted.

"Don't answer," Paula said.

Rickie tightened her lips. She looked like Eddie Price, torn between the release of confession and the obvious consequences of spilling the beans.

"What if vigilantes in real life took care of evil that would be gotten away with otherwise?" Chase asked.

Rickie looked tortured. "Some people could get away with anything."

Paula jumped up. Her bulk and anger filled the room. "Quiet, Rickie. Don't let them bully you. Let's go." She held out her hand and Rickie took it, rising from the couch.

Paula turned to Alex and Chase. "You're not going to leave it alone, are you? People could get hurt. More people, I mean."

Paula's tight features and wretched tone made Alex very nervous. "Even if we did, the police are investigating," she said.

Paula shrugged. "Harroway and Green are good detectives. But you two have a way of ferreting out secrets. Have it your way. But don't say I didn't warn you."

"Is that a threat?" Chase demanded.

"Of course not," Paula snapped. She bent down and took the last two biscotti. "For the road."

"Tell me what really happened and I'll buy you a truckload," Alex said, only half-joking.

Paula chose to laugh. "Bribing an officer of the law. That's a serious crime."

AFTER THE COLEMAN sisters took off, Chase turned to Alex. "I don't know about you, but I have some serious sugar and caffeine tremors going on."

"Same here," Alex replied. "Plus butterflies in the stomach from what may be going on."

"Should we call the police?"

"I think we should call Tiger Claw Restaurant and make reservations."

"You're right." Chase grinned. "Police can wait until tomorrow. Sushi calls its seductive song."

When they returned home from the Japanese place, they stood under the starry sky, more at peace with the world in general after a transcendent meal. "According to Paula, all of this is a series of unfortunate coincidences, at least as far as she and Rickie are concerned," Chase said.

"I want to believe them, but we know the truth." Alex sighed. "I don't know about you, but I'm beat."

"Let's go to bed." Chase laughed, looking embarrassed. "You know what I mean."

Alex smiled coyly. "Not really. Want to elaborate?"

Chase's expression grew serious. "We can't do this."

Alex glanced out into the darkness. "Where's Henry? I wish I didn't worry so much about him. I can't make him an indoor cat, although I know he'd be safer."

Chase shrugged. "I guess none of us wants to be an indoor cat." She grimaced at the tacky metaphor. "Henry's fine. Up communing with the barn cats."

They went inside. Alex poured each of them a glass of Erica Strong wine and they settled next to each other on the couch.

"Tell me about Henry," Chase said. "You mentioned you adopted him under adverse circumstances."

Alex hesitated, took a sip of wine, then spoke. "Do you remember the extra on the set who played a deputy sheriff?"

"The gorgeous one with the Slavic features. Wasn't he really a Sonoma County sheriff's deputy?"

"Yes. Pete Szabo. He and his twin sister Mary are my good friends. Pete killed Henry's owner."

"Oh, no."

"The guy was a meth addict. It was a justified act. But Pete fell apart for awhile. He got someone to get Henry from the pound. He gave Henry to me. That's the story of Henry."

"Ugly beginning, happy ending."

Alex sighed. "I wish I could say the same for our current adventure. I'm not feeling hopeful."

Chase drained her glass. "Don't jump the gun. I say we go to bed and take up the trail in the morning."

Alex shivered.

"What's wrong?" Chase asked.

"Your cliché reminded me of Reeta the psychic. *Don't go down in flames.* I wonder if she meant you and I are jumping from the frying pan into the fire." Alex stood. "You're right. Let's go to bed." She paused. "Separate beds."

"Of course," Chase said stiffly. "I would never suggest otherwise."

Chapter Thirty-One

ALEX TOSSED AND turned. After what seemed like an eternity, she fell into a troubled sleep, dreaming of flames. A pair of hands grabbed her. A siren wailed. She fought the tight grip pulling at her.

"It's me," Chase said, "It's okay. It's me." She was kneeling beside Alex, trying to pull her from the sleeping alcove.

Alex, dazed, pressed against Chase. Outside the nearest open window, flames crackled in yellow and orange. Chase tightened her hold. "I heard something being thrown," she said. An acrid smell of smoke drifted into the room. They got to their feet and raced out through the patio doors. The arbor attached to the granny unit was engulfed in flames. The fire crept towards the house. Wheatie and Kallinda were valiantly trying to douse the blaze with garden hoses. A sheriff's car screeched up the driveway. Pete Szabo rushed out with the little fire extinguisher from his cab and began releasing ineffective bursts of retardant spray on the growing inferno. "Are you all right?" he called to them.

"Fine," Alex called back.

Thankfully, the fire trucks arrived just as it looked like the flames might reach the house walls. The firefighters hooked up. An explosion of water hit the arbor. In the meantime, Pete came rushing up to Chase and Alex, looking upset and frightened. "Are you sure you're okay?"

"Okay," Alex said. "Not hurt."

"The paramedics will check you out," Pete said, his voice shaking. "What happened?"

"I don't know," Alex replied.

"I heard a crash," Chase said. "It sounded like breaking glass."

"We came home late," Kallinda interjected shakily. "The patio arbor was burning, starting to advance on the house."

"Did you see anyone?" Pete asked.

"We saw a car taking off down the driveway, then racing down Patterson Road," Wheatie said. "Driving crazy."

"Whose car?" Pete asked.

"Paula Coleman," Kallinda said. "She stayed here before, so we know her Buick."

"What's going on here?" Pete groaned. "Alex, have you been messing around in police business again?"

A smoky-smelling woman in bulky firefighter's gear

approached them. "Someone threw a Molotov cocktail at the house. It fell short and ignited the arbor. But the fire was on its way to the house pretty fast."

Alex surveyed the mess. The arbor was a charred skeleton. The meditation garden was a soggy, trampled ruin. In a small miracle, the Buddha had survived. He was covered in wet soot, but still upright. Alex jumped. "Where's Henry? Where's my cat?"

Just then, another firefighter came down the driveway. He was carrying a cat cage, with Henry yowling inside. The firefighter handed the carrier to Alex. "Found him inside the barn up there locked in this cat carrier. Any reason for the cat confined like that in the barn?"

"I didn't do it," Alex said.

"Someone who didn't want Henry in the house while it was burning," Chase said.

"Okay, my friends," Pete said grimly. "Time for a nice heart-to-heart about this nasty incident. If you're really not hurt, I want you to get some rest and then come down to the station tomorrow. This seems extremely suspicious." All of a sudden his expression turned doleful. "Were you two in there together? Of course you were."

"She's a friend staying on the couch," Alex explained, a little miffed that she felt obligated. She loved Pete in many ways, but she was not responsible for his crush on her. Pete, realizing his inappropriate tone, frowned and turned away, adopting a more professional demeanor.

"I still want you to get looked over by the paramedics," he said.

They were really okay, at least physically. After the authorities had left and Wheatie and Kallinda had returned to the main house, Alex and Chase went into her unit. Alex was still shaking, however.

"I can't believe Paula did this," she said.

"She said it herself," Chase replied. "She's feeling backed into a corner. It's going to get worse, that's my prediction. Eddie Price will *not* keep his mouth shut. I'm sure of it."

Alex shuddered. "You know, I like her. Even after she pointed a gun at me."

"The gun wasn't loaded. Wait 'til next time. And something isn't right with that sister of hers either." Chase hesitated. "Are you okay to go to sleep?"

Alex shrugged. "I don't think so. I'm kind of afraid. I hate to admit it."

"I'll stay in your bed with you," Chase said. She smiled. "Platonic."

Alex had been hoping Chase would offer. "Platonic," she

echoed. She went over to Henry's cat carrier and released him. "Henry will join us. He'll chaperone."

Despite her words, Alex had to admit a slight thrill when Chase crawled in beside her. They both settled down, avoiding body contact, but the vibes were just as strong without actual flesh-to-flesh contact.

"Deputy Pete is in love with you," Chase commented.

"He is," Alex said. "I think he understands, though, that he doesn't stand a chance."

Chase grinned unsurely. "Because he's a man."

Alex laughed. "There's that. I think. Even more so, he's too nice. Too safe."

"What are you looking for, Alex?"

"Trouble," Alex said and sighed. She was acutely aware of how much she liked lying in bed with Chase. Now that was a good case of trouble, wasn't it? "Show me the tattoo," she said.

"What?"

"You said you had one. That you'd show it to me."

Chase laughed. "A promise is a promise." She pulled back the cover and exposed her right thigh, just below the hipbone. Etched on her soft, smooth skin was the image of *Lena: Amazon Queen*. "I promised Wendy she'd always be with me."

Alex gulped. Oh, no. Wasn't that something? It looked like Wendy Swann as Lena had joined them in their little nest. A complicated threesome. Alex rolled over on her side, facing the wall away from Chase.

"Did I upset you?" Chase asked.

"No," Alex lied. "Let's get some sleep."

IN THE MORNING, around 9 a.m., they went down to the station. Pete informed them that Harroway and Green wanted to see them. When they got to the questioning room, the homicide detectives gave Alex a reprimanding look. They glanced at Pete. "Is Alex on a tear again?"

"Looks like," Pete replied.

Clarissa Harroway inspected Alex and Chase with a wicked grin. "You two spent the night together? Aren't you Wendy Swann's partner?"

"As I've said before," Alex replied stiffly, "you have no room to judge."

"It was an official and legitimate question," Clarissa said, but she was clearly enjoying the gossipy implications of the situation. Green, as usual, looked completely indifferent. Human nature, including sexual escapades, never fazed him.

In the brightly lit room, Alex and Chase filled in the detectives regarding their escapades. Alex explained how Eddie Price had most likely poisoned Chip Welch as a favor to Paula Coleman.

Clarissa sighed. "Ugly business. One incident and the media blows it all up and all of a sudden all of Sonoma County law enforcement is corrupt and morally degenerate. Let me get this straight. Eddie Price, who we all know is a braggart, got early release for knocking off Chip Welch. Assuming Eddie isn't lying and assuming Captain Strong and Paula were really going at it, what's the point? Chip confessed."

"Confessions," Green said sadly. "You know how they fare in a court of law. Right now, we are combing the county for the rest of Buddy Brubech's body. For substantial evidence. The case is far from over."

"All previously understood," Clarissa said. "But why kill Chip?" She leaned towards Alex and Chase. "Why do I have the feeling that you two dug up some relevant information which until now you didn't bring to us?"

Alex grinned. "Because you're so intuitive?"

"Just get on with it," Clarissa said.

"Rickie Coleman, Paula's sister, was dating Chip Welch," Alex said.

"How do you like that?" Green said appreciatively. "The plot thickens."

Green was a nice man. Alex did not react to the cliché. "It's possible that Rickie was involved in the murder."

"This is going to be good," Clarissa said. "I just know it."

"Rickie and Chip were heavily involved in internet computer games. The kind where you're superheroes defending others. Chip's mother was involved with Buddy in the past and he dumped her. What if Chip decided to get revenge? What if the game became real?"

Green frowned. "I'm not averse to considering weird killings. I've seen a lot of them. But I'm not sure that's enough motivation to kill anyone."

Alex and Chase glanced at one another. "You explain," Alex said to Chase.

"I love it," Clarissa said. "Sherlock Holmes and Watson, amateur female division."

"Buddy had a nasty history of sexual escapades dating back for some time. When we talked to Rickie, she alluded to punishing people who exploited others. To eliminating evil people. In L.A. recently, Alex witnessed an incident involving a radical anti-porn activist. We're wondering if Rickie was a radical feminist in disguise. She and Chip got carried away, bringing their game into the real world. Buddy Brubech was a symbol of two-faced evil and he was going to get away with it."

"Far-fetched," Clarissa said, but she looked intrigued and so did Green.

"Like the seventies," Chase said. "Guerilla acts of vengeance."

"Not impossible," Green said. "I still want that body."

"Paula was Rickie's protector, her big sister. Chip didn't mention Rickie in his confession. But he was loony. He probably would have babbled their secret eventually, implicating Rickie in the murder. Suppose Paula arranged for him to be murdered. She floated the rumor that he was a molester."

"We all know about that," Clarissa said. "Molesters don't survive in prison."

"Then she got Eddie Price involved to seal the deal," Chase concluded.

"Interesting," Green said.

A sad-faced Sebastopol police sergeant interrupted them. "Bad news."

Green stood and went out with the sergeant. He returned looking uncharacteristically upset, leaned over and whispered something to Clarissa, whose jaw dropped.

"Very bad news," Clarissa said, her voice shaking. She shook her head, looking extremely upset.

Alex had a distinct idea what was coming next.

"Paula and Rickie were found at Paula's place," Clarissa said. "It looks like murder-suicide. It appears, from first analysis, Paula shot Rickie, then herself. Happened sometime between when Paula left your place and about an hour ago, when they were found."

It looked like Paula had been backed into the corner a step too far.

THAT AFTERNOON, CHASE left for the airport. They parted under the charred patio arbor. The house was relatively unscathed. Smelly but livable, with no interior damage. Alex took comfort in the fact that the gardens were trampled, but Buddha had survived. His calm face looked over the mess with appropriate acceptance.

"Back to normal life," Alex said with a false heartiness.

"I'll miss you," Chase replied.

"Same here."

After a brief hesitation, they embraced. Alex had to stop herself from clinging. She pulled away. She couldn't fight the feeling that her home was breaking apart. It was a stupid, wishful thinking bit of nonsense, better stuffed into the dark shadows of her unconscious along with the other silly bits of nonsense that were best left suppressed.

"We'll keep in touch, of course," Chase said.

"Of course."

"Alex, if you ever need us."

Alex was very conscious of the term 'us.' She reached down and picked up Henry, who was rubbing shamelessly on Chase's leg. "I expect an invitation to the premiere of the movie."

Chase smiled. "That was never a question." She saluted, climbed into the Toyota and rumbled down the driveway. Alex was standing in the same place when Wheatie and Kallinda came out. They were carrying a set of folding chairs and their instruments. "Out of the wreckage, a phoenix rises," Wheatie said. He glanced down the driveway, then looked at Alex sympathetically.

"Don't say one word, "Alex said. "Just play."

THE NEXT DAY, Alex got a call from Felicity Strauss, Buddy's widow. "All of this is terrible," Felicity said.

"Tragic," Alex replied. "Buddy was involved with them somehow."

Felicity sighed. "The police will keep investigating, but I'm done. Thank you for looking around for me. I don't need you anymore. It's over, as far as I'm concerned. I can't live every day waiting for a resolution that may never come."

Alex understood. Felicity was slipping into deep denial. Fine. Time to put the whole Buddy Brubech thing to bed.

Chapter Thirty-Two

FOR ONE ENTIRE week, Alex heard nothing from Chase. Was she surprised? She shouldn't have been. Chase needed to get on with her busy life. Alex, on the other hand, needed to get a life. Her heart leapt when the phone call came from L.A.

"Alex?" Chase said.

I thought you'd never call. Alex cleared the lump from her throat. "Hi," she said casually.

"I've been meaning to get in touch with you," Chase said.

"It's only been a week. I'm sure you're really busy."

"We're fast-tracking *On A Silver Platter*. Terrible as it sounds, we need to take advantage of all this Chip Welch publicity. We want you to help us with the trailer. We've choreographed a great fighting dance. Could you come down for a day of filming?"

"When?"

"We need you on Tuesday. Can you fly out ASAP?"

Alex had already mentally cleared her schedule and was internally packing her bags. "I'll see if I can arrange it."

"Thank you. Thank you. Thank you."

"One thank you is enough."

A hesitation on the line, then Chase spoke. "I miss you."

"Uh huh," Alex said. "How's Wendy?"

"She can't wait to see you again."

Alex snapped her phone shut and went out to the patio to survey the repair work. Sandy Knight had decided to take advantage of the misfortune to revitalize the patio and gardens. As Wheatie and Kallinda had prophesized, the new landscaping was a phoenix rising from the ashes. Beautiful broad paving stones, an elaborate arbor constructed of ecological bamboo and a new set of multi-denominational prophets carved from marble or shaped from clay.

Since the murder-suicide of the Coleman sisters, the media was in a euphoric frenzy. To his credit, John Strong had come clean about his affair with Paula. He was insisting, however, that the poisoning of Chip Welch was Paula's doing, a huge step further than he had ever intended their antics to progress. Eddie Price was backing John up. Of course, all of that was very convenient, since Paula was dead.

Something wasn't right. Alex knew it. The police knew it, too. Yet they'd made it perfectly clear that Alex's meddling was to stop.

Most frustrating to all involved was the fact that Buddy's body still could not be found. Alex had promised to keep out of the whole thing. Still, she was tempted to meddle. Going to Hollywood was just what she needed. She had only one difficult call to make.

"I have to cancel the date we made."

Erica Strong sighed. "Let me guess. You're going to L.A."

"It's about the movie. I'm doing the trailer. I'm sorry." Alex had relented to Erica's appeal for a fresh start.

Why did she feel guilty? She was beginning to understand becoming a spinster. Relationships, to reverse the cliché, seemed to always be saying you were sorry.

"How's Chase? I'll bet she misses you," Erica said.

"She's back home, settled back in her world, with her girlfriend," Alex replied huffily.

Erica laughed. "Good for her. Alex, one thing you should know. I will never limit your world, whatever becomes of us. Go to L.A. and have a blast. Call me when you get back and we'll reschedule."

"Thank you." Alex disconnected and immediately booked her flight.

ON SUNDAY AFTERNOON, Alex was mildly disappointed to be picked up at the airport by Taffy, who informed her that Chase and Wendy were blitzed by compulsory obligations. On the other hand, Taffy was thrilled to see Alex again. On the trip from LAX to Santa Monica, she informed Alex about the LGBT projects in the works for the coming year in Hollywood. "It's driving the bible bangers crazy!" she said.

"I don't know," Alex replied. "I worry about the backlash. Look at the horrible gay bashings and gay kids committing suicide."

Taffy nodded thoughtfully. "It's not right. It's awful. But, listen, Alex. This is like Pandora's box. The lid flew open about us and it can't be closed. Sexuality and gender issues will never be the same again."

Alex sighed. "I hope you're right."

Taffy laughed. "If you can't trust a dyke chauffer with a Ph.D. for philosophic profundity, who can you trust?"

DINNER WAS SERVED at 8 p.m., once Chase and Wendy had rushed in. Both women looked tired, but Wendy brightened up when she greeted Alex. "I forgot how cute you are. Good thing I'm so committed. I have something for you." She held out a wrapped package. When Alex hesitated, she grinned. "Open it."

"Good lord." Alex held up the buttery soft red leather camisole.

"Is it too fem for you?" Wendy asked.

"I don't know if I can do it justice."

"Try it on," Wendy suggested with a lecherous tone. She turned to Chase, who had been quiet since they'd arrived in the dining room. "This was an impulse. What do you think? Isn't it perfect for her?"

"It's great," Chase said, but her tone was unenthusiastic.

"Are you okay, honey?" Wendy asked with concern.

"Overworked and stressed," Chase replied. "I'm okay. Really."

Alex jumped up, holding the package. "Be right back. Modeling session." She ran out to the closest bathroom.

When she returned, Wendy, Taffy and Joelle burst into catcalls and applause.

"Phenomenal," Wendy burst out.

"Is it too revealing?" Alex asked.

"Are you kidding?" Joelle said.

"You really ought to come down here and get into performing," Taffy added.

Chase stood up abruptly. "Sorry to be a party-pooper, but I have to go to bed. I have a headache." She turned to Alex. "Filming is on Tuesday. I'll have a short choreographed script to you tomorrow morning and rehearsal is in the afternoon."

When she'd left, Joelle served dessert. She and Taffy departed, leaving Alex and Wendy alone in the room.

"Chase has been a little moody," Wendy said.

Alex finished her parfait and sighed. "Delicious."

"Chase really likes you."

Alex attempted to look indifferent. "I like you both."

Wendy grinned wickedly. "As a unit?"

Alex blushed. "As a couple. As individuals in a couple relationship. You know." She stopped garbling and stood.

Wendy rolled over and took Alex's hand. "It's fine, Alex."

"Okay," she replied to Wendy's remark.

The word was the tip of an iceberg.

Chapter Thirty-Three

MONDAY MORNING, ALEX woke up in a panic, forgetting where she was. The pleasant chirping of the southern California birds and the sunlight streaming through the open curtains reminded her of the day's plan. She had an internal boxing match going on between her opposing emotions. One punch of exhilaration followed by a counter punch of conscience. One minute she wanted to throw her arms around Chase and the next she wanted to flee from the temptation.

The choreography notes had been slipped under her door. She studied them for a few minutes, then realized how hungry she was. In the dining room, neither Wendy nor Chase looked like they'd slept any better than Alex. "We need to talk," Wendy said solemnly.

Before Alex could reply, Wendy's phone chimed the arrival of a text message. Wendy read it and glanced up, frowning. "You're not going to believe this."

Alex's heart began to race.

"The text messages are back. They started in the middle of the night. We almost weren't going to tell you, now here's another."

Alex took the cell phone.

Oh so bad. U girls don't learn. One potato, two potato, three potato, four.

Four rotten potatoes, buried in the compost. Do you want to be the next? Five potato, six potato, seven potato. Don't you know how to give up? Figure it out instead of sticking your noses where they don't belong.

"One potato, two potato, three potato," Chase said. "Four."

"Chip, Buddy, Paula and Rickie," Alex said. "Do Rickie and Paula count?"

"Of course they do. Five, six, seven," Wendy said. "Me, and you two. Amazing. There's someone else involved."

"Someone new or someone who's been there all along," Chase said.

"I'm betting someone who's been there all along," Alex said. "Trouble is, with Buddy's past, it could be any number of people."

"Is it time to go to the police?" Wendy asked.

Chase and Alex glanced at one another. With that glance, Alex understood they were a team.

"I'd like to poke around just a little more," Alex said.

"I think we can come up with a few more clues," Chase added.

"Then the police. I promise." She looked pleadingly at Wendy.

Alex expected Wendy to argue. Surprisingly, Wendy relented almost too easily.

"Be careful." Wendy sighed. "Ridiculous warning. Just don't get bumped off. I don't want to be alone."

LATER IN THE morning, Alex threw on some shorts and a muscle shirt and went out onto the sunny veranda. She flicked on her iPod and flowed happily through a series of graceful but menacing moves. It felt wonderful. She was reminded of the daily *katas* she'd performed every morning in her old kung fu days. In that spirit, she finished with a prayer bow. A glimmer of hope sparked in her. Maybe she was starting to emerge from her doldrums.

She came out of the prayer to find Wendy staring at her through the glass of the veranda doors. Alex removed her ear buds and shut off her iPod as she went back inside.

"That was awesome," Wendy said.

"It took a lot of training," Alex replied. "It's the only thing I stuck with long enough to get good at."

"You're hard on yourself. You strike me as being good at a lot of things."

Alex shrugged. "Getting into trouble."

Wendy grinned. "Call it taking risks. Come inside and have breakfast with me."

Alex smiled back. "You too."

"Me what?"

"Taking risks," Alex replied. "You're very brave."

"Don't," Wendy said, her tone now dour. "I hate when people act like handicapped people are special for just trying to live like everyone else. It's so fucking condescending."

"I hate when handicapped people assume they're being condescended to when a person is just giving them a compliment. I meant about your new business venture and your dedication to your relationship with Chase. You're a very cool person."

"Okay," Wendy said. "Love fest is over. Let's eat."

IN THE EARLY afternoon, Taffy drove Alex to a dance studio on Santa Monica Boulevard. Chase was conferring with a familiar-looking woman in a multi-pocketed vest. Chase caught sight of Alex. A delighted expression appeared on her face. Alex felt a responsive shiver.

"You remember Jill?" Chase asked.

"The woman who thought I was a mistake from out of town," Alex said.

Jill reddened. "You did an excellent job," she said gruffly.

"Jerome and Salome are in Kenya protesting elephant slaughter," Chase said. "You're featured in the trailer with your veil on, so there's no problem. Jill is very capable and experienced. She's a wiz with trailers."

"I worked out a nice number based on your suggestions," Alex said.

"Bring it on," Chase replied.

"I will. I most definitely will." Alex floated to the dressing room and climbed into her outfit. She had a full heart. Nothing could squeeze it up. Not the ridiculous storyline of the movie or the absurdities of her present life. She felt as close as she ever had to an empty mind. *This is joy*, she thought. *Grab it while you can.*

She returned to find Chase and Jill watching her expectantly.

Watch this, girls.

Alex twirled with controlled abandon, a dervish both lethal and transcendent. She channeled her anger and her love, her hopes and her fears, her mourning for the past and her desires for the future. When she finished, there was dead silence. Alex sucked in a breath, preparing for Jerome Lasky-like criticism.

"Very nice," Jill said.

"No kidding," Chase added. "Can you repeat that tomorrow?"

"I hope so."

Alex smiled at the worried reactions of the other two women. "I might make it better."

BY NOW, ALEX was getting used to the dynamics of on-location sets. Tuesday morning, she arrived to find the crew setting up in an alley just south of Melrose Avenue. A crowd of curious tourists watched from behind a barrier. It was nearly impossible to suppress a feeling of self-importance as Taffy led her though the maze. Jill was waiting for her.

"I don't remember any alleys in the movie," Alex said.

Jill shrugged. "Since when are we worrying about consistency with this piece of work?"

Alex laughed. "Silly of me."

"Chase is at an emergency studio meeting."

Alex felt a surge of disappointment. "They seem to have a lot of those."

"She'll be here as soon as she can. Go get dressed and made-up. We'll get started as soon as you're ready."

Alex was relieved to find Chase on set when she arrived back in full costume. If anything, she felt even more alive and excited than she had at the rehearsal. She wasn't sure what she was channeling, but it didn't matter.

As expected, there were delays. The sun and clouds would not cooperate, leading to tantrums from the director of photography and the lighting crew. A nearby construction project had to be begged into silence. Two incensed homeless men had to be bribed from their encampments of sleeping bags and a shopping cart.

In the first take, a cameraperson slipped on a piece of rotting garbage in the smelly but picturesque narrow back alley. More problems on two more takes. It didn't matter. Alex was in a zone. On the fourth take, she was as fresh as the first, if not more so. Aware of Chase's scrutiny, she twirled and leaped through her self-choreographed *kata*.

"Cut," Jill said. She gave a high-five sign to Alex. "Great. Perfect. Let's wrap it."

Like coming down suddenly from a powerful drug, Alex wilted. Much to her own consternation, she sank to the gritty cracked asphalt. Chase rushed up and bent down to her. "Are you okay?"

"This is stupid," Alex said, between anxiety hiccups.

"Totally natural," Chase said. "Let me help you."

Alex allowed Chase to guide her into standing. Chase hugged her. "You were fantastic."

Alex shivered. She pressed into Chase. "I don't want it to be over."

"Neither do I," Chase said.

Alex pulled away. "I meant the dance."

Chase frowned. "I know what you meant."

"Am I interrupting something?" Jill asked.

"Not at all." Chase cleared her throat. "I think we need a decompressing celebration. I know a very hot new restaurant that I can pull some strings for reservations tonight."

"Sounds good to me," Jill said. She and Chase turned to Alex expectantly.

Alex felt drained. The last thing she wanted to do was go to a hot spot. She didn't, however, want to be perceived as a spoilsport. "Celebration it is," she said.

Chase walked her to the car. "Jill is great, isn't she?"

Alex shrugged. "Nice woman."

Chase gave her a prompting look. "She's talented and attractive and unattached."

Alex stopped abruptly and faced Chase. "Are you matchmaking?"

"What if I was?"

"I don't need your help in that respect," Alex replied. "She's not my type."

"What is your type?"

Alex tapped Chase lightly on the collarbone. "Someone like you."

Chase backed away. "Don't say that."

Alex frowned. "I was being theoretical."

"I was being *practical*. Don't you want to find someone nice?"

"On my own time and with my own timing."

"You two okay?" Taffy called to them from the nearby waiting car. Alex walked away from Chase with a wave of a hand. "I like Jill. Nice woman. Okay."

THE BAD MAMA on Sunset Boulevard was so happening that it took connections like Chase's to be allowed entry at all, much less lacking reservations made far in advance. But the whole thing was really a game, Chase explained on the trip to the festivities. It wasn't like The Bad Mama didn't have the space available on any given night. The impossibility farce was the key to its popularity.

That the restaurant-night club was winning its snobby maneuver was evident as Chase and Alex arrived. Outside the entry guarded by burly bouncers, paparazzi crowded the sidewalks, jostling among the peons for vantage points as a stream of the entitled hustled along a carpet patterned like Dorothy's yellow brick road.

A simultaneous cry rose up. "It that for us?" Alex asked.

"Fat chance," Chase replied. "Look."

A black limo had just rolled up in the valet parking line. The chauffer released Jill, their director, and a gorgeous woman in a skimpy sequined outfit. "Wow," Alex said. "That's Dagny Dexter with Jill. So much for setting me up on a blind date."

Chase laughed. "Dagny is Jill's *stepsister*. Oh boy, everyone's going to go bananas now. What a publicity coup. Wait, we'll all walk up together."

As the foursome traversed the yellow brick road, fans screamed and cameras flashed. Once inside, they were led to a VIP table as heads turned even among privileged insiders. Dagny Dexter was on parole for shoplifting and had just released a movie about a modern-day Cinderella. She was the hottest ticket in town for the moment.

They screamed their dinner orders to a waiter wearing orange spandex. A bottle of expensive champagne mysteriously appeared unordered. It was uncorked by a tall sommelier in yellow spandex.

The food was horrible. The deafening music negated

conversation. The persistent strobe lights were so psychedelic it was a miracle no one developed a migraine or had a seizure. By 11 p.m., things appeared to be just getting going. Blessedly, they called it a night.

They parted with Jill and Dagny on the yellow brick carpet. Jill was professional and polite. In fact, she seemed rather cool, giving Alex a distant thank you before disappearing.

As she and Chase drove home, Alex laughed. "I don't think she liked me. Not in the woo-woo sense, anyway. Blind date meltdown."

Chase frowned. "You gave her not one iota of encouragement. She asked you to dance and you refused."

"I would have refused Ginger Rogers. I have dance exhaustion."

"You didn't talk to her."

"I didn't talk to you. Or her famous stepsister. I could hardly hear the waiter about the dinner specials. If you wanted to set me up with someone, why choose a place where we couldn't have a conversation?"

"You have a point," Chase admitted. "Next time..." She stopped. "I guess there won't be a next time. Your flight is tomorrow."

WENDY WAS WAITING up for them. She slumped in her wheelchair, hands trembling. "So, was it great?"

"You need your sleep, honey," Chase said.

"I couldn't. How was it?"

"I liked the last hot spot better. They all stink, really, unless you're twenty-something." Chase went over and stroked Wendy's head.

Wendy sighed. "I miss a lot of things. The torturous nightclub scene is not one of them." She glanced at Alex. "You?"

"Not so fun," Alex admitted.

"I think it's my genetics," Chase said. "The genes for public spectacles inherited as the great-grandchild of a Hollywood mogul."

"I think Alex and I can forgive you," Wendy said. "Just don't start genetically expressing the Poppa Weiss traits for smoking cigars or dog track betting." She picked up a remote control. "Get a load of this. I taped it for you."

Wendy flicked on the 55-inch plasma flat screen. The obsequious hosts of a vastly popular entertainment gossip show appeared with their smirks. Wendy fast-forwarded to a wild scene. It was The Bad Mama. Who should be traipsing along but Chase,

Alex, Jill and the reason for the hoopla, Dagny Dexter? Wendy grinned at Alex. "You're officially tabloid fodder." Her grin faded. "What's wrong?"

"I've been in the tabloids. Sorry, this just brings up bad memories." Alex shrugged and turned to leave. "No matter. I need to get some sleep. We have a big day tomorrow."

Before Alex could reply, her cell phone rang. "Well, this should be interesting."

"Tell," Wendy said.

"Felicity Strauss." Alex answered the phone. "Hello." She listened, nodding gravely. Finally, she disconnected. "You're not going to believe this."

Chapter Thirty-Four

ON THE SECOND visit, Alex noticed that Felicity Strauss's home was not as pristine as before and neither was Felicity. She had dark circles under her eyes and a rash on her neck. The coffee table was littered with dirty glasses, piles of mail and magazines, and, most surprisingly, an ashtray filled with butts. The air reeked of sour smoke.

As soon as she and Alex sat, Felicity lit up and inhaled deeply. "Mind?"

Without waiting for an answer, she snubbed the cigarette out. "Disgusting. No one smokes in their own homes anymore." She glanced plaintively at Alex. "It took me awhile to get to the grieving stage. It hit me like a ton of bricks. I hope you understand."

Did she understand? Alex had spent a good portion of her own spousal grieving time in her suburban mansion wearing unwashed pajamas. She *really* understood.

Felicity indicated a bottle. "Chivas Regal. Want a shot?"

"What a coincidence," Alex said. "A favorite grief medicine of mine."

Felicity poured a healthy dose of the scotch into a murky glass that Alex hoped would be disinfected by the alcohol. Felicity sipped from her own glass. She belched, then giggled. "I feel so stupid."

Alex let the warmth of the scotch run down her throat. "Let's agree we're both past being embarrassed."

Felicity stood. "Come with me."

Alex drained her glass. "I hope this isn't a trap."

Felicity giggled. "You'll see."

Like any foolish amateur sleuth, Alex followed Felicity towards potential mayhem. They climbed a set of stairs to the second floor, then took another, narrower flight to an attic floor. There were three rooms behind three closed doors. Felicity paused in front of the door open to the most isolated room. "This was his private sanctuary." She threw open the door.

Alex gasped. "Roosters?"

"Roosters," Felicity said.

The room was a shrine to the barnyard cock. The walls were lined with rooster posters, paintings and woven fabric hangings. On a display shelf, stuffed birds glared at them with menacing disapproval. Statues and little porcelain figurines covered nearly every available surface. The only thing missing was a live bird.

"The Year of the Rooster," Alex said. "He told me that was his astrological sign. He had an amulet. They found it in Chip Welch's possession when he was arrested."

"I gave him the amulet," Felicity said. "He had a thing about roosters."

"Obviously." Alex wandered the room, studying the photos, paintings, hangings, sculptures and the creepy glaring taxidermy fowl.

"I thought it was cute," Felicity said. "Odd, but endearing. In my animal-rights work, it's pretty typical for people to be smitten with creatures. Why not roosters?" She shivered.

"Something wasn't right," Alex said. "You knew he was hiding something."

"Buddy was a sweet, tortured man with an ugly past. He wasn't evil."

Wasn't that what people said about the serial killer who lived next door and helped old ladies across the street? Then their crimes were uncovered. "No," Alex said carefully.

"I *hoped* it was sex," Felicity said. "I hoped you'd find secret affairs or kinky rendezvous with prostitutes were at the bottom of this. When those two women in Sonoma did themselves in, I was *relieved*. I thought it was over."

"What happened?" Alex said.

Felicity trembled. "More emails. Text messages. Hints about the roosters. Someone is playing a terrible game."

"About roosters?"

Felicity walked over to a tufted leather chair. She slumped into it.

"You're sitting backwards," Alex said.

"I sure am." Felicity rested her arms on a set of sturdy pads protruding from the chair's backrest. "I did some research on the internet. Oh my God, this wasn't at all what I expected. Do you know what this chair is for?"

"Not the foggiest," Alex replied.

"It's an English antique chair from the late 19th century meant to be sat on backwards to observe a gambling event."

"Why backwards?" Alex asked.

"I have no idea. A man thing?" Felicity said. "But let's get to the game."

Alex sighed. "Now you're playing games with me."

"Look around the room. Get ugly."

Alex absorbed the weird feel of the room. She thought about the pathological possibilities. Roosters? Felicity was staring at her expectantly. An event with roosters? It wasn't show creatures at the county fair, that's for sure. Before she could ponder further, Felicity spewed her frustration and disgust.

"*Cock-fighting*. Breeding roosters big and strong so they can peck and claw one another to death. I married a man infatuated with one of the most repulsive animal cruelty practices on the planet. Can you even imagine the irony? How did he think he'd keep it a secret? Maybe he didn't. He was so haunted. Someone out there is still driven to torture me. They're playing a game with me, like Buddy gambled on cock-fights."

Alex shivered. "The game is too dangerous now. I think it's time for the police."

"No. There is still a very small chance this can be kept secret."

"Almost zero," Alex said. "And you're putting yourself in danger."

"I don't care. I want your help one last time."

"I don't want to be responsible for another death," Alex said.

"You can't keep out of this. I know you. And you have access to the person who can help us get to the bottom of this."

"You're right. I'll get in touch with her."

"HOW DID YOU convince her to see us again?" Chase asked. They were climbing the steep road to Consuela's place.

"I warned her that Buddy's secrets could come out in the ugliest of ways. I suggested we could help prevent his image being forever remembered as an evil monster," Alex said. She gripped the edges of the car seat. "Slower, please. I'm going to puke."

"I warned you about that chocolate-covered doughnut at the café. Not before a drive into these hills."

"You sound like a wife."

"If you were my wife, I wouldn't nag. I don't believe in it." Chase veered right sharply to avoid a crater-sized pothole.

"Aaagh," Alex cried.

CONSUELA AND THE three Dobermans were waiting for them. The Dobermans raced out, wagging their stubby tails. Consuela did not appear as pleased. She led them into the living room and allowed them to give the dogs a handful of biscuits.

"Follow me," she announced. In the den, she pointed to the chair that had been hidden underneath a sheet during their last visit.

Alex sucked in a breath.

It was the twin to the antique cock-fighting chair in Buddy's rooster room. "I bought these. One for me, one for him. A romantic purchase after he took up the sport. I got him into it."

Consuela glared at them. "I grew up in a vibrant culture with traditional roles for men and women. And, in Puerto Rico, cock-fighting was a perfectly legitimate activity for the men."

"The pictures you took down?" Chase asked.

Consuela sighed. "Yes."

They followed her to a row of photos arranged on a table.

She picked up the first. "This was our first trip to Puerto Rico together." A young, gorgeous Buddy and Consuela flanked a wiry, smiling middle-aged man with crooked teeth and weathered brown skin. "Uncle Carlos. He was a respected rooster breeder, one of the most admired on the island. His cocks were the strongest, the best fighters. He was a tough man in many respects, but also kind and generous. He saw Buddy's need for a male figure. He showed him the ways of the sport. By the time Buddy and I broke up, Buddy was a part of the family, including a relationship with Carlos like father and son. My sister and her husband found out about the cock-fighting, but chose to ignore it."

"Freddy and Mary D'Amico," Chase said. "Who else knew about the cock-fighting? Salome?"

"I don't think any of the children knew," Consuela said. She picked up another photo. Buddy was in a row with the D'Amico family, all of the group intertwined. "Salome and her brothers were a different generation. They wouldn't have understood. Their Uncle Buddy could do no wrong. Buddy gave Salome her first pet dog, Janet Leigh."

"Yes, we know," Alex said. "Consuela, did Helena know?"

Consuela frowned. "Bitch. I told you she disappeared. I believe Buddy knew where she was. Because he needed to send her checks."

"Helena was *blackmailing* Buddy?" Alex asked.

"He hinted. I knew."

"Not about sex. About cock-fighting."

"His biggest secret." Consuela shrugged. "He insisted he'd given it up. That's what he told my sister and her husband. In recent years, he stopped going to Puerto Rico. Too many chances to get caught at the fights, even if it was still legal. No more respect for privacy anywhere."

Consuela pointed to another photograph displaying a row of people in black. "Carlos died a few months before Buddy took up with that dreadful veterinarian. He was devastated. In my opinion, she was his rebound, his alternative anchor."

"She couldn't ever find out about the cock-fighting, could she?" Chase asked.

Consuela laughed bitterly. "Buddy was terrified she would. He knew, in his heart of hearts, there was always the possibility." She shook her head. "I really thought he'd given it up. Now I wonder." She glared at them. "Buddy was a troubled man, but good at heart."

"A question," Alex asked.

"Yes?" Consuela said hesitantly.

"Why sit backwards?"

Consuela smiled. "During the fights, a writing desk was set up at the back of the chair. A man could account for the proceedings on the desk while resting his arms on the yolk formed by the arms of the chair."

Alex shivered. "The birds pecking each other to bloody deaths."

Consuela shrugged. "As I mentioned last time, we are not far from the animals in our brutality. Only more advanced in how we practice our inhumanities."

"I'M FAMISHED," ALEX said as they barreled down the winding road.

"Not queasy anymore? This cock-fighting business makes *me* queasy.""

"My stomach is too empty to be queasy. I almost ate a dog biscuit."

"Wendy made me promise to come straight home after we finished," Chase replied. "She's having Joelle prepare a nice farewell dinner for the three of us."

As they reached the bottom of the hill, Alex's cell rang. "Hello, Felicity."

"I don't want to see you hurt because of Buddy."

"I appreciate that."

"Then let me warn you. I am fully committed to animal-rights. I even support what some might consider subversive demonstrations if the perpetrators are extreme in their cruelty. Throw pig blood on Hormel executives and I'm happy. However, there are groups that go beyond my approval. The most radical are fanatics in small cells, like terrorists. They don't have web sites, they don't reveal their identities. We know they exist through groups who support them and even those groups don't know who these people are. I've put out some feelers. No one will tell me anything concrete, but there are subtle hints. Alex, these people are dangerous. Drop this. I don't want your help anymore."

"I'll consider it," Alex said.

"Please do." The phone went dead.

"What was that about?" Chase asked.

"Let's wait. I want Wendy to hear this."

"Is this about her? Is she in danger?"

"Be patient," Alex said. "If you haven't put two and two together yet, then you'll need to hang on."

JOELLE OUTDID HERSELF. The farewell meal was fabulous. But the revelers were not feeling terribly exuberant.

"Someone is out there who knows where Buddy's body is. Who might have had a hand in killing him," Wendy said, once she'd been filled in. Joelle helped her to take a sip of wine. "Most remarkable thing? The hatred was about abusing animals, not sex."

"Which makes the link to you pretty weird," Alex added.

"I don't get it," Chase said.

Alex and Wendy glanced at one another.

"She's usually so quick," Wendy said fondly.

"She's outguessed *me* a few times," Alex added.

"Come *on*," Chase said. "Out with it."

"Leather," Wendy said. "I promoted the slaughter and skinning of cows raised in animal concentration camps. At least as far as animal-rights groups are concerned. Bunnies. We use bunny fur. Worse, in the minds of the animal-rights community. I don't have a problem with leather or fur. My relatives were trappers. I learned how to trap."

Chase sighed. "We sit on the hide of dead cows, wrap our feet in their skins, not to mention enjoying a good Sloppy Joe."

"Don't get me going on Sloppy Joes," Wendy said. "I grew up on them. Frankly, I have made my decisions about animal rights. I won't be bullied into dropping my fashion line. LenaWear lives on."

Chase turned to Alex. "I do think it's time to go to the authorities."

Alex took a sip of her wine and stared off into the distance. "Uh huh."

"*Alex*," Wendy said.

"Look at me," Chase said.

Alex directed her gaze in Chase's direction. She knew she might as well have been wearing her Salome veil.

"Promise me you'll go to Harroway and Green when you get back."

Alex sighed. "I promise." She knew she'd keep the promise if she made it. She just wasn't sure how immediately she'd do it after she got back home.

Chapter Thirty-Five

"WE KNEW YOU'D be back," Lisa said. Vivien gurgled happily in her arms. "Ben was on a repair job, but he just called. He's on his way." It was Friday morning, the day after Alex had arrived home.

Alex followed Lisa back to the couch. "How did you know I'd be back?"

"You seem like a type that doesn't give up." Lisa hugged Vivien to her chest and shivered. "Poor Chip. Got in over his head."

Alex suppressed a grin. Lisa didn't seem aware of her own gruesome pun. Before Alex could comment, Ben arrived, lugging a heavy sack of electronic tools. "The girl sleuth. Where's your partner?"

"She retired," Alex said.

"Not *your* style to retire. You don't give up, do you?"

"Apparently everyone thinks so."

Ben grinned. "We get it. Gamers, remember? We never give up."

"We *did* tell you everything we know," Lisa said. She fussed with Vivien's coverall, not making eye contact.

"You told me Chip and Rickie played Metropolis. It looks like they carried the game too far. It looks like there's a game that some people have carried *way* too far."

"I hate this," Lisa said. "This is exactly the kind of thing the Christian fundamentalists use against us. Even other people think we're weird, right on the edge. Most normal gamers are just like us. One or two exceptions and all of a sudden we're all obsessed monsters about to explode into violence."

"Well said," Ben added. "What do you think, Vivien?"

Vivien drooled and waved her hands, exuding unconditional love.

Ben frowned. "If someone was trying to hurt Vivien, I'd kill him if I had to. But I know the difference between games and reality. I don't know what happened with Chip. All I know is he was a good guy, overall."

"Rickie was okay, too," Alex said. "In my opinion."

"Then what?" Ben asked. "Surprise me."

"What if there was a third person?" Alex asked.

Ben's face lit up. "Bingo. Hey, you're smart. There were three people in Chip's Metropolis squad. He told us he had two trusted comrades in his game. Now we know Rickie was one of them."

"The other one?" Alex asked.

Ben shrugged. "Could be anyone. Wouldn't have to be local. Identities are secret."

"Ben, the third party is local. He or she is making threats. This isn't a game anymore."

"Obviously." Ben frowned. "Sounds like a police matter to me."

"It is." Alex paused. Ben and Lisa waited with looks of nervous apprehension. "However, it might be even better getting them involved with a blockbuster piece of information."

"I think I know where this is leading," Lisa said.

"Same here," Ben said. He smiled slyly at Alex. "Go ahead. Your move."

"I suppose it would be theoretically possible to hack into the Metropolis site and find out the third party's identity."

"Theoretically yes. Almost anything could be hacked, theoretically."

"Not legally."

"No."

"But if that information could be brought to the police as a *suggestion?*"

"If you could find a dude willing to explore this issue," Ben said carefully.

"Would you know anyone like that?" Alex asked. She made a show of glancing at Ben's bag of tools.

"I'd have to ask around."

"Would you?"

Ben scooted closer to his wife and Vivien, put his arm around Lisa's shoulder. "I'm sure this guy would want to remain anonymous."

"I promise," Alex said.

"Don't take this wrong. I'm not sure I trust you. You're a gamer, too, of a certain type."

"I can't blame you for not trusting me. But we're all on the same track. In the end, justice will be served," Alex replied.

Ben stood. "I don't like this. That's why we play fantasy games on our couch."

"But you'll 'find' the hacker?"

"I'll check around," Ben said. Vivien, with the in-the-moment consciousness of infancy, burst out in a wail of despair.

"Thank you," Alex said. "Time to go." She headed to the door. "Get back to me."

As she headed back to the car, Alex wondered if Ben would

follow through. She was pretty sure he would. It was a terrible but excellent game they were playing.

ALEX PASSED RICKIE'S grooming shop on her way to The One World Holistic Pet Care Center in the strip mall in Cotati. The grooming shop was darkened and locked. She lugged Henry, in his transporter, to the vet's office. He yowled plaintively. Alex felt mildly guilty forcing him to be an accomplice in her investigations. She pushed through the door, adopting the look of a concerned pet owner. "Henry, last minute appointment. Thanks so much for seeing us."

"We don't turn our patients away," Brittany the receptionist said. "Hello, Henry."

As Alex had hoped, the waiting room was empty. It was almost six and the office was due to close. "The doctor is seeing her last patient," Brittany said. "We'll get Henry in as soon as possible."

"No problem. We can wait." Alex peered into the transporter. "Of course, that's how it goes. He already seems better. Maybe I panicked." Henry glared at her with a guilt-tripping scowl.

"Better safe than sorry," Brittany said sympathetically.

Alex waited a brief moment. "How do you like those latest developments in the Buddy Brubech murder?" she asked.

"Oh, we're devastated," Brittany said. "Can you believe Rickie was murdered by her own sister?"

"Terrible," Alex said.

She glanced around the room at the misty-eyed animal posters. "What about that elderly lady with the cockatiels? She must be heartbroken."

"Esther is devastated," Brittany replied.

Alex sighed sympathetically. She sat in silence. The receptionist, she knew, was a chatterbox. The quiet wouldn't last long. "I don't understand why good people are victims of senseless violence," Brittany said.

"Terrible," Alex repeated, shaking her head. "Animals, too. Victims of abuse, creatures who can't defend themselves against humans."

"Monsters," Brittany said. "The abusers deserve to experience what they hand out."

"No doubt," Alex said. "Do you mind?" She pointed to Henry. "He hates the cage."

"It's fine. No one else will be coming."

Alex placed Henry on her lap. He settled down, purring. "He seems much better," Alex observed.

"Well, the doctor will check him out thoroughly."

Just then, the vet came in from the back. She took Henry, leaving Alex and the receptionist alone.

"Tell me about the radical animal-rights groups," she said bluntly.

Brittany's mouth fell open. "What do you mean?" she said, rather shakily.

"You know, the ones that are so secretive that the only ones that know their identities are members of their cells."

"I have no idea what you're talking about."

"I believe you do."

"Who are you? Why do you want to know?"

"In Sonoma County, there have been numerous 'actions' attributed to radical groups. Bunny farm liberations, defacing biotech sites that use animals for research."

"Monsters," the receptionist said. "No better than Nazis. They deserve what they got."

"I wonder if Rickie knew about them," Alex said. "She was so impassioned about animals." Alex paused. "Like you are."

Brittany stiffened. "I have no idea what you're talking about. I'm not a part of any radical group."

"But you're sympathetic."

"Of course I am."

"I wonder how Dr. Sally feels about all this," Alex said.

"She's a saint," the receptionist said.

"Who would do anything to help an injured animal? Sickened bunnies. Monkeys burned in experiments."

The sainted vet came out, holding Henry. "He's fine. A specimen of good health and obviously gets excellent, loving care."

"False alarm," Alex said.

"Better safe than sorry," the vet said kindly. "If you'll excuse me, I have to tend to some of our overnight patients."

"Leave us alone," Brittany said once the vet had disappeared. "You'll be doing more harm than good." Her girly, innocent features took on a crafty tinge. "Besides, like you say, these are groups that no one can crack. Your guess is as good as mine. Or the police. That will be forty-three dollars."

Alex handed over a credit card. "Thanks for the extra effort to help Henry."

Brittany wouldn't make eye contact. "Any time."

ON THE TRIP back to Sebastopol, Alex's cell rang. "Ben?"

"I have a name for you. The third party in the trio. The hacker gave it to me. Now will you go to the police?"

"Yes," Alex lied. She disconnected, then speed-dialed another number. "Hi."

"You have something?" Chase asked.

"I have the answer."

"You're taking it to the police."

Alex didn't answer.

"Alex."

"Of course I am."

Eventually.

Chapter Thirty-Six

GRANNY WAS WAITING for Alex in the driveway of her ranch. When Alex emerged from her car, Granny pointed her shotgun squarely at Alex's chest. Alex stood in front of the Lexus with her arms raised above her head.

"This is just a formality," Granny said. "I'm probably not going to kill you."

"You killed Buddy."

Granny lowered the shotgun. "That was an unfortunate boo-boo. Anyway, he was a weak, deceitful man. You're a snoop, but you're interesting and bright." She gestured to the house. "Inside."

The cockatiels recognized Alex.

"*How do you do?*" cried one.

"*Party time,*" cried another.

"*An eye for an eye,*" cried the third.

Granny pointed to the couch. When Alex sat, Granny indicated a heavy chain and a padlock lying on the coffee table. "Chain yourself."

"Forget it," Alex said.

Granny placed the shotgun close to Alex's forehead. "Silly girl. Chain your legs and torso tightly. You can leave your arms free. For the moment."

Alex contemplated trying to grab the gun, but the odds of success were extremely poor. On the other hand, being chained by a wacky grandmother with a gun was not exactly a walk in the park. All things considered, she decided to go with the chains. At least her head wouldn't be blown off right away.

Alex finished arranging the chains. Granny looked content. "Care for some eggnog?" she asked.

"No thank you."

Granny laughed. "I'm clearly a crackpot off the deep end. You refuse my offer?"

Alex grimaced. "If you insist."

When Granny returned, she placed a tray on the coffee table containing two glasses of murky, questionable egg product. "Wait. Forgot the shotgun." Shotgun placed on the coffee table as well, Granny looked expectant as Alex sipped.

Nutmeg assaulted Alex's taste buds. Maybe *she* was going off the deep end, too. The drink was yummy and she was alone with a killer despite multiple warnings. "Better than last time," she said.

"I like the extra nutmeg."

"I knew it was only matter of time before you showed up," Granny said. "Are you wearing a wire? Did you contact the police, like I told you *not* to?"

"No. I didn't contact them," Alex said.

Granny laughed. The cockatiels bristled. "Maybe you are foolish, like Buddy. More likely, you're addicted to vigilantism. I like you. You remind me of myself." She took a sip of her eggnog. "It's not the nutmeg. I've added a big dose of brandy for the winter months." Granny sighed. "It's ridiculous to pretend we don't know what you came for."

"I came for the last few pieces of the puzzle."

"I adore games," Granny said. "Puzzles are excellent. Tracking killers is better."

"Tell me about Buddy," Alex said.

Granny smiled slyly. "Not so fast. It's your turn to give a puzzle piece."

"Whose rules are those?"

"Mine. I have the shotgun. How did you find me out?"

"I had someone hack into your computer game, Metropolis. He or she got your identity for me. You, Rickie and Chip were a fighting group. Top-level. But that wasn't enough, was it?"

"Games are games," Granny said firmly. "Real-life injustice is another. I have seen the worst in human nature. All my relatives were murdered by Nazis. That is not a game. Exterminating innocent animals is not a game." She gestured at her cockatiels. "They're listening."

The cockatiels did appear to be watching.

"*Make my day*," one of them cried.

"I made the mistake of exposing them to Clint Eastwood movies." Granny sighed. "His conservative values, not so good. But he knew how to track down bad people. Did he ever."

"Like you tracked down Buddy."

Granny glared. "He deserted my daughter. But she was also weak, like him. And he did provide for her financially, with a little bit of encouragement."

"You were blackmailing him?"

"Call it what you like. He was compensating my daughter for her pain and contributing a portion of his wealth to atone for his two-faced life. I hated him, once Helena told me about the cock-fighting. I was silent, since he paid. Then he had the audacity to take up with Felicity Strauss, a woman with true values. Helena tried to commit suicide, wound up in a nursing home. He lied, he pretended to be a protector of animals. He was the worst kind of evil, the man who preaches one thing and does another, thinking they can get away with it. He needed to be taught a lesson. One he wouldn't forget."

"You were the leader of the animal protection cell. Rickie and Chip were following orders from you."

"I had them bring Buddy here. We wanted to teach him a lesson he wouldn't forget. I had him crouch with his head on a wooden block and held a hatchet over him. We discussed cock-fighting." Granny sighed. "Buddy had a fighting spirit, after all. He refused to apologize. He got up, started to walk away. That's when I had my unfortunate moment. I shot him."

"You killed him with the shotgun. But?" Alex asked.

"Then I chopped his head off," Granny said. "To make the point." She shrugged. "Make lemonade from lemons. Since we had the head, why not use it?"

"You had Rickie and Chip put it on the silver platter."

Granny frowned. "They weren't happy about it, believe me." She stood. "I have prepared a visual explanation." She disappeared and returned with a laptop and a set of wires.

Alex's mouth dropped open. "Buddy's missing laptop."

"*Show time,*" one of the cockatiels said.

"I'm sorry," Granny said to the birds, then turned to Alex. "They can't watch this." One by one, she took the birds to another room, while they squawked with shocked disappointment.

Granny returned and connected the laptop to her television. "Such a wonderful time, the way these things work. I'm using the TV as a monitor. I want you to see this as largely as possible."

"You're pretty good with that stuff, aren't you? You acted differently the first time we talked to you," Alex said.

"At that time, I was trying to throw you off track. Now I'm not."

Granny activated the computer. "I was always good at this kind of thing." She opened a web site. "I am using Buddy's member password to get access."

Alex gasped. On the screen, after a few clicks, a horrific fight between two mighty cocks in a dusty ring filled the room, accompanied by cries of rabid prodding by a live audience of men with faces expressing twisted pleasure.

"This is a site in Thailand," Granny said. "Now, any sick monster can watch from anywhere in the world. Including Buddy Brubech, who was sponsoring animal-rights with his precious wife." She glanced at Alex. "Are you all right?"

Alex was not all right. She was revolted and the eggnog-brandy consumption wasn't helping. "Please turn it off." She started to rise. It was silly. What was she going to do? Hop away in chains?

Granny picked up the shotgun. "Watch."

The birds pecked and clawed at one another until the ring dripped blood. In what seemed like an eternity, one of the cocks fell panting and shivering with gladiator-like valor. He tried to rise again, then fell in a twitching mass.

Alex was appropriately revolted. Before she could recover, she realized Granny wasn't done.

Granny quit the web site and moved quickly into a PowerPoint slide show. In succession, she scrolled through cattle feedlots and chicken slaughterhouses; rats electrocuted in research projects and monkeys, their stomachs bloated with noxious chemicals. Granny clicked and clicked. Starving, filthy dogs in puppy mill breeder's cages. Drowned kittens in wet rag piles. Alex grew woozy.

"Enough?" Granny asked.

Alex nodded plaintively.

"Then, I'll go check on my birds. Don't go anywhere." She picked up the shotgun and left the room. Alex was considering hopping to the door when Granny returned.

"An eye for an eye," Granny said. "I've been reconsidering. I might have to kill you. I'm feeling agitated."

"It's too late. They're going to get you," Alex said.

"True." Granny sat, sighed. "Should I kill you? I really can't decide." She squinted at Alex. "I *do* like you. Why did you come here, Alex?"

"To find the truth," Alex said.

Granny cackled. "Dig deeper, my friend. Speaking of which, Buddy's body is buried in a shallow grave in the eucalyptus thicket. Alex, this is your chance to live. Tell the truth. Why did you come here?"

Alex closed her eyes. She envisioned a cone of orange light surrounding herself. She envisioned a wise third eye in the center of her forehead. She opened her eyes. "I feel more alive when I'm in danger. I feel brave and strong."

Tears formed in Granny's eyes. "A girl to be proud of." Granny set her sights on the television. "Aaagh," she said in frustration and pulled the trigger. A mighty blast ripped through the set. From the other room, the cockatiels screamed. The distant wail of a siren grew louder, more insistent.

"I called the police just now when I left the room."

"I'm sorry, Granny."

"Don't be. You almost didn't make it. Be grateful." Granny set down the gun and shrugged. "I'm eighty-four years old. What are they going to give me? Life in prison?"

Epilogue

LUMINA STUDIOS GAVE *On A Silver Platter* the full treatment. The premiere was at the Egyptian Theatre on Hollywood Boulevard. The evening's special guest was Quentin Tarantino. Alex flew down with Erica Strong. In the past month or so, Alex had permitted the term 'girlfriend' to be said aloud. She still winced, however. Erica, bless her, accepted all of Alex's ambivalence.

As they drew up to the red carpet in a limo arranged by the studio, Erica reached over and adjusted the silk scarf hiding Alex's face. "Are you all right?"

"I said I'd do this. For the sake of the movie. For Chase and the rest."

"I didn't ask that. I asked if you were all right."

"Why do you flinch every time I mention Chase?"

Erica looked intentionally blank. "Why do you change the subject whenever I ask you how you're feeling?"

"Don't ask me." Alex squirmed. The thing she most disliked about Erica was her tender attentiveness. Also the thing she liked best. She took in a deep breath, energizing as the chauffeur threw open the door. This was her good-bye to Salome.

The crowds screamed as she flew out and thrashed her way through the best interpretation yet of Salome's dance. Alex channeled her ambivalence and doubts, her shadowy passions and her very human yearnings. She interpreted the obscure connections of love and hate, the attractions of revenge and the desire to connect. Cameras flashed, the crowds continued to roar. She went as over the top as she could manage.

Bless you, Buddy, wherever you are.

At the end of the carpet, standing as still as Lot's wife turned into a pillar of salt, Chase waited. Alex danced to within inches of Chase's chest, then collapsed in a heap at Chase's feet. A collective sigh rose up. Chase bent down to her.

"Really over-the-top," Chase whispered. "We're talking Isadora Duncan on cocaine."

"Thank you, I think."

"I love you."

"Please don't say that." Alex sprang from the carpet. "I love you, too, but it doesn't matter."

By this time, Erica Strong had caught up. She took Alex's hand and smiled at Chase. "Thank you for the invitation. We couldn't wait to be here."

Chase raised an eyebrow at the couple pronoun. "Glad you could make it."

Another wave of screaming arose. Salome and Jerome climbed out of their limo. "Let's get inside," Chase said.

Wendy was waiting for them, pushed by Taffy. Alex drew in a breath. Wendy had shriveled. Her limbs were badly twisted and she shook with sharp tremors.

"The body is poor, but the spirit is rich," Wendy said. "I just had the most incredibly condescending and insulting interview on the planet with that patronizing bitch from *Hollywood Tonight*, KiKi Bennett. If I didn't need the publicity for LenaWear, I swear I'd shoot her. Let them lock me up. What will I get? Life in prison?" She laughed at their expressions. "Of course I'm being horrible and incorrect. We'd better get in. Almost time for the show."

IT WAS BETTER than Alex ever imagined it could be.

On A Silver Platter was the next *Pulp Fiction*, only funnier, less insulting to women and more optimistic about humanity. Jerome deserved the joy of making his elders proud. The audience reacted to every skillful trick of editing, but the artsy pyrotechnics were overwhelmed by the fundamental soul of the story. Jerome had either become possessed by the ghost of Chekhov or someone had helped him shape the final cut. Alex knew the answer. She felt a surge of affection for Chase, who would deny the importance of her intervention during the edits and her creative input. If Chase were to be confronted, which Alex had no intention of doing.

The energy at the reception was electric. For added kicks, the servers were hunky men in Salome drag, while the women caterers wore butch LenaWear leather. Alex and Erica wore matching outfits for the reception, designed by the genius t-shirt lady in Sonoma. When Ken, Shirley and Marlon Sloan came up to them in the boisterous room, Alex made brief introductions.

"We followed your adventures," Shirley said. "Right up until the police rescue at that woman's ranch. I can't believe you went there alone."

"Why does the heroine ever go up the stairs in the creepy house when she knows the serial killer is in the bedroom?" Marlon asked. "I think we should make a movie from this."

"Rumors are that it's already in the works," Alex replied.

They were interrupted by the arrival of Salome and Jerome. "Just caught the end of that discussion," Jerome said. "I'm negotiating with the studio right now for *On A Silver Platter: The Real Story*."

"Then I hope you consider us for the parts of ourselves," Ken said.

Jerome laughed. "Everyone will play themselves, playing themselves."

"I'm confused," Salome confessed. She laughed, too. "See? I'm already myself, playing myself as interpreted by myself as dumb, when I'm not." She turned to Alex. "My Aunt Consuela asked about you. She liked you."

"She had a funny way of showing it," Alex said.

"She was protecting Buddy," Salome replied. "I don't think she'll be playing herself in our movie. She loved Buddy. She's the only one that knew all his secrets."

At the mention of Buddy, there was a momentary silence.

Across the room, Alex spied Felicity Strauss, who'd graciously agreed to attend. Coincidentally, Felicity was stumping the talk shows, promoting her new book, rushed to print: *My Life with Buddy Brubech*. A portion of the proceeds were going to P.E.T.A.

Shirley Sloan broke the silence. "I'll go to my grave feeling conflicted about Buddy. I should hate him for his evil side, but I knew his goodness, too. It's unsettling. In addition, I may never be able to buy a pair of leather gloves or eat a chicken leg without thinking about the implications."

There was a nod of general consensus, broken by the arrival of Chase. "Somber-looking group," she commented. "We have a hit on our hands. Critics *and* the public. Already rumors about Oscars."

"It's just a statue," Shirley said.

Everyone burst out laughing. Shirley grinned ironically. "What's so funny?"

"Funny would be Buddy getting a posthumous golden man," Ken said.

"Funny would be one of us channeling a clairvoyant speech from Buddy at the ceremony," Shirley added. She signaled one of the hunky waiters in Salome drag. "I need a drink. My funny bone needs a drink."

AT THE END of the evening, Alex took leave of Erica to go to the restroom.

"Alex? Got a minute?" Wendy asked. She approached, wheeled by Taffy.

"Anything," Alex asked, with the usual surge of guilt she felt whenever she was within Wendy's sphere.

"Come," Wendy said, indicating a deserted meeting room.

Once they were inside, Wendy asked Taffy to wait outside. Alex's pulse raced.

"I'm dying," Wendy said.

"No," Alex said.

"Why do people say that?" Wendy asked. "Yes. I'm dying."

"I meant I hoped it wasn't so."

Wendy shrugged. "People think they know what it's about, that they can prepare. Don't bother. Besides, that isn't what I came to ask. I have a request."

"I told you. Anything," Alex said.

"Take care of Chase. She loves you."

Alex reddened.

Wendy smiled. "I have no judgments. We don't need to get into any explanations. When I go, I want you to consider a relationship with her."

Before Alex could reply, Chase burst into the room.

"Good God, I was worried. Wendy, you disappeared..." Chase broke off. She stared at Alex and Wendy. "What were you two cooking up?"

"Nothing," Wendy said.

"Nothing," Alex echoed.

Chase turned and glared at Taffy, who'd also come into the room. Taffy raised both arms in surrender. "I wasn't here. I don't know."

Chase sighed. "Is it worthwhile to persist?"

"Absolutely not," Wendy replied.

Taffy started singing The Pointer Sister's famous song, *We Are Family*. All one hundred and sixty pounds discoed with light-footed abandon as she sang. She ended with a John Travolta pose.

"That was odd," Chase commented.

Taffy laughed. "Don't you see? Make the sequel to *Platter* a musical."

"Life is a cabaret," Wendy said. "I like it. I could come back as an angel, a la Tony Kushner's *Angels in America*."

"Kind of tacky," Alex commented.

"Art meets kitsch." Taffy said. "Welcome to our world."

Other Linda Morganstein titles you might also enjoy:

Ordinary Furies

Alexis Pope's life has come undone. Just when she thought she'd found guaranteed security and conventionality, her husband's death casts her into a self-imposed solitary confinement in her suburban mansion. Unsure as to whether she'll ever stop grieving, she's reluctant to accept her gay cousin Jeffrey's offer to come up to the Russian River resort where he works.

Then, a revelation in the form of a nosy fundamentalist neighbor signals enough. Little suspecting she's jumping from the frying pan into the fire, Alex plunges into the refreshingly frantic world of restaurants in the funky chic town of Guerneville, California, a gay and New-Age haven in the redwoods. But peace of mind is elusive. A series of vicious events at the resort forces Alex to revive her abandoned skills as a self-defense instructor.

In this first book of the series, Alex begins to explore her changing sexuality. Like many women, she must face her denials and repressions before coming to terms with her attraction to women. For some women, these are issues not easy to face, and this series explores both the difficulties and rewards of lesbian "late-bloomers."

ISBN: 978-1-935053-47-7

Harpies' Feast

In Dante's Hell, suicide victims are transformed into dead trees that can still feel pain. The harpies, birds with women's faces, peck at their limbs. In *Harpies' Feast*, the second in the Alexis Pope mystery series, Alex plunges into a mystery exploring teenage suicide and the pain of teen bullying.

Still grieving an unfortunate death, Alex befriends two theatre people visiting California wine country to work on a local production. Alex is drawn to the attractive lesbian playwright and grows protective of the teenage actress, the target of a group of mean local girls.

The adolescent torment leads to perplexing disasters. In the search for answers, Alex confronts the glory and sting of relationships and the boundaries of sexual orientation.

ISBN: 978-1-935053-43-9

My Life With Stella Kane

In 1948, Nina Weiss, a snobby college girl from Scarsdale, goes to Hollywood to work at her uncle's movie studio. She is assigned to help publicize a young actress named Stella Kane. Nina is immediately thrown into the maelstrom of the declining studio system and repressive fifties Hollywood. Adding to her difficulties is her growing attraction to Stella. When a gay actor at the studio is threatened by tabloid exposure, Nina invents a romance between Stella and the actor. The trio become hopelessly entangled when the invented romance succeeds beyond anyone's dreams. This is the "behind-the scenes" story of the trio's compromises and secrets that still has relevance for today.

ISBN: 978-1-935053-13-2

About the Author:

Linda Morganstein is an award-winning fiction writer who also happens to be the product of a Borscht Belt childhood in the Jewish hotels of the Catskills. In the seventies, she dropped out of Vassar College and drove a VW van to California, where she lived in Sonoma County for many years. She currently resides in the Twin Cities of Minnesota with her understanding partner.

For more information go to:
www.lindamorganstein.com

VISIT US ONLINE AT
www.regalcrest.biz

At the Regal Crest Website You'll Find

- The latest news about forthcoming titles and new releases

- Our complete backlist of romance, mystery, thriller and adventure titles

- Information about your favorite authors

- Current bestsellers

- Media tearsheets to print and take with you when you shop

Regal Crest titles are available from all progressive booksellers including numerous sources online. Our distributors are Bella Distribution and Ingram.

CPSIA information can be obtained at www.ICGtesting.com
Printed in the USA
BVOW030923190911

271406BV00002B/27/P